Hostage in Time

—

By: Linda Lauren

Copyright © 2011 Linda Lauren
All rights reserved.

ISBN: 1456541773
EAN-13: 9781456541774
Library of Congress Control Number: 2011900729

This book is dedicated to the memory of my mother, Frances.

Thank you for traveling through time with me, and for your pre-Internet research skills! You are always in my heart. I love and miss you.

Acknowledgments

No story is every told without the love and support of family and friends. I would like to take this opportunity to express my deep gratitude to everyone for Embracing The Universe with me.

A thank you goes out to my father, Jerry, for his love and confidence in my abilities, no matter what they are! Pop, I love you.

Thank you to BFF Susan Dolinko. You are my family, and I thank you for your endless patience as a reader, spiritual sister, and friend, and for those endless trips to historic sites. Feel free to put that "off duty" sign on... for now!

Thank you to Todd Evans and Jeffrey Moran, my BFFs and spiritual brothers. I am so grateful to have you on my team! I am blessed and overwhelmed by our familial connection and your rare ability to create inspiration and love.

Heavenly gratitude goes out to Major and The Collective for their guidance in the writing process. You are a very special presence in my life.

Lots of blessings came from the moral support of my dear friend Salli Stevenson. I hope Jim is looking down on us and smiling at the memories we share with "Mr. Mojo."

I want to express appreciation to Dolores Stewart Riccio for receiving and sending those "rainbows" and bestowing her loving friendship. So wonderful is our connection!

No book would be complete without my little Gidget & CosmoDoodle, my two little fury buckets of love, and their "cousins" Grace and Floyd. You are perfect pets and mascots! Thanks for keeping me in Smile Mode!

Finally, nothing I ever do is without all of you. My clients, friends, and readers I have not met yet, I am forever in your debt for picking up this book and allowing me to share my story of traveling through time.

God bless,
Linda
June, 2011

Fling me across the seas of space
and the fabric of time.
Make me nothing and from nothing
once again everything.

Rumi

CHAPTER ONE

April 16th – The Present

The sun lazily curled through the window of Amanda Lloyd's bedroom. The quartz crystals that dangled from the panes bounced reflectively in dancing prisms of color. Amanda rolled over onto her side and slowly pushed open her eyes, at once responsive to the warmth that embraced the room. With a long stretch of her arms she propped herself up against her pillows. What to do on this glorious Sunday, she thought. *What to do with the rest of my life, for that matter.* Since the layoff from the magazine, it would be back to freelance photography, which wasn't necessarily a bad thing, as her bank account was in formidable condition.

The knock at her door shattered her reverie. Knowing who was on the other side made her inwardly smile.

"Come on in, Carrie," she announced while grabbing for the pink robe she kept on the chair nearby.

"I can't believe you're still in bed," Carrie reprimanded as she deftly juggled two cups of coffee and a platter of wheat toast in one hand.

"Having a waitress for a roommate really pays off!" Amanda quickly reached for one of the cups.

"It's already nine o'clock!" Dressed in an "I Love New Jersey" T-shirt, jeans, and sneakers, her shoulder-length brown hair tied into a ponytail, Carrie Stern looked more like a teenager than a woman about to turn thirty.

"So, it's nine o'clock. Does this mean you'll turn into a pumpkin soon?"

Amanda took a bite of the toast. Though only three years younger, she often felt like Carrie's kid sister.

Carrie shook her head and sat on the edge of the bed. "My God, woman, you are so frustrating. Wasn't it you who insisted on dragging me on one of your historical day trips? This is Reenactment Day, isn't it?"

"Serenity! The Brisbane house!" Amanda dropped the half-eaten toast onto the plate and quickly washed down what she had eaten with the remainder of her coffee. "I can't believe I forgot."

"You've had a lot on your mind, Amanda, what with losing your job and all. If you don't want to go—"

"Oh, no, you don't." Amanda jumped out of bed and rushed to her closet. "Give me twenty minutes. I'll meet you downstairs."

"Can't fault me for trying," Carrie said with a smile.

With a quick turn from the closet, Amanda reached for the nearest thing she could find—a hanger—and hurled it as Carrie quickly closed the door behind her.

* * *

Relieved at having showered the night before, Amanda quickly pulled on a pair of black pants and a frilly white blouse and plopped down at her vanity table. Staring at her tired reflection, she decided she didn't like what she saw. Her normally creamy complexion appeared pale, her dark brown eyes seeming to have lost their vibrancy due to years of deadlines. Shaking her head at the image of her disheveled hair, she sprayed liquid styling mist into it and pumped up the voluminous dark curls with her fingers. Frowning at her reflection, she stuck out her tongue.

"Better do something quick," she scolded herself. "Go out like this and you'll scare the neighbors!" She applied a light mauve blush to her high cheekbones, a bit of mascara to her lashes, and finished off with a swirl of burgundy to her lips. That would just have to do. Before leaving the room, she put on a black blazer and grabbed her fedora from the bedpost to top off the outfit. Halfway down the stairs she stopped short and looked down at Carrie who stood impatiently tapping her foot at the front door.

"Aren't you forgetting something?" Carrie asked.

With the snap of her fingers, Amanda rushed back into her room, picked up the video camera, and hoisted her tapestry bag over her shoulder.

CHAPTER TWO

Carefully situating her equipment in the back of the station wagon, Amanda slipped in behind the wheel and started up the car while Carrie fidgeted with the seatbelt.

"I know it's the law, but I hate these things," she complained.

"It's only a fifteen-minute ride. We'll be there before you know it." Amanda adjusted the rearview mirror and backed out of the driveway. "Look on the bright side. It's a sunny day and we are going to one of Montclair's most celebrated historical houses."

"History was never one of my favorite subjects. It was a close second to math, and you know how much I hate math."

"Yes. Well, I think you'll enjoy Serenity."

Carrie shook her head. "The only house I like is the one we live in, and that's because we live rent free since your parents..." Realizing her mistake, Carrie turned and touched a hand to Amanda's shoulder. "I'm sorry, Amanda. I have this habit of putting my foot in my mouth."

"It's OK, Carrie. It was a long time ago." Amanda rounded the corner and continued along Franklin Avenue. "Before seatbelts were mandatory," she added tightly.

"So tell me about this Brisbane place. Why is it so special?" Carrie asked to change the subject.

Amanda smiled. "It was once the home of Jonathan Brisbane, a lawyer and close friend of Thomas Edison's. It's referred to as the Brisbane house now, but back in the nineteenth century it was affectionately known as Serenity."

"Wow!" Carrie's eyes widened in surprise at the cars parked bumper to bumper along both sides of the street. "People sure take this reenactment thing seriously, don't they?"

Amanda nodded and slowly maneuvered through the traffic before making a left turn onto a side street. "I'm afraid we'll have to park and walk a bit."

"No problem. What exactly is it they do here? What do they reenact?"

"Life in the nineteenth century," Amanda replied as she pulled into a newly vacant spot just beyond the turn. "The historical society volunteers are called docents, people who have researched the family and history of the time period. Some even pretend to be actual members of the Brisbane family, which tends to lend a sense of realism." Pocketing her keys, Amanda opened the back door and hauled out her equipment. "They tell you all about the house and the people who lived there as they take you through the tour. You get to sample what people used to eat, how they slept, and went about their days," she continued. "I thought it would be a good opportunity for me to get some footage for a magazine piece I've wanted to do about the time period."

Nodding, Carrie followed Amanda up the street and around the corner. Keeping pace with Amanda's quick steps, she nearly bumped into her when Amanda stopped short as the mansion came into view. Though she had read and heard a great deal about the rambling Brisbane mansion, she was not prepared for the awesome sight in front of her. Built of stone, brick, and wood, it was independent of any strict rules of architecture. Gabled roofs flowed with dynamic nooks and angles that scrolled throughout its chiseled balconies. The windows were soft sheets of stained glass that spoke of a quiet elegance from a long time ago.

The front of the house boasted a piazza that faced a pond that was bordered by soft, mellow willows and Japanese quince. Amanda inhaled the engaging amalgam of fragrances that seemed to be a sweet assault on the senses. Her eyes swept across the panorama of shrubs, floral arabesques, and beds of emerald velvet that colored the landscape. From previous research, she knew there was a vast herbal garden in the back of the existing thirty-five acres, as well as a greenhouse that charged the air with roses, rare mimosa, and gardenia. She again inhaled the heavenly blend and was at once mystically lightheaded. *Serenity.* The name was certainly appropriate. Gathering up the equipment that had gently dropped to her side, Amanda motioned for Carrie to follow.

"I smell food!" Carrie pursued the scent around back as Amanda paid the admission for the tour. "I'll catch up with you later," she called while hastily retreating to find the source of the delightful aroma.

Amanda laughed and shook her head. She smiled at the docent as she stepped into the hallway, her eyes reveling at the rich red mahogany that merged into the floor, walls, and ceiling.

"Have you ever been here before?" the woman asked.

"No, but I've read extensively about Serenity. I must say I didn't expect this!" she exclaimed, her hand sweeping the area where they stood.

"A lot of people have your same reaction." She handed Amanda a booklet. "Feel free to roam the first and second floors. The third floor, however, is not open to the public. The society has restorative plans that are ongoing." The woman smiled. "You may feel free to take pictures, but do not go beyond any of the roped-off areas. If you have any questions, please don't hesitate to ask. There are plenty of us here to answer them for you." She paused, adding, "We close at five o'clock."

"Thank you." Taking a seat along the sidewall of the entrance, Amanda bent down to her camera case and hauled out the video camera.

She took aim, focused on the sparkling chandelier, and zoomed in on the circular ceiling painting of the marriage of Cupid and Psyche garbed in regal splendor. She panned over to the sweeping grand staircase. A marvel of workmanship, it was carved of limestone with priceless Gobelin tapestries draped along the walls. The eye of the camera took in the floor of polished marble, the vases, and gilded baskets filled with roses of pink and dark crimson.

Halfway down the hall were immense stone fireplaces where great logs once blazed to warm the occupants. The dining room was aglow with lights that illuminated a long dinner table set with an inviting damask cloth, gold service, crystal, and china laying in wait for a long-ago dinner party.

The paneled oak and rich mahogany continued into the rooms on the second floor, and in her movement, Amanda tried not to collide with or disturb the other visitors. Stopping at the open library, she stood awestruck at the leather volumes of books that covered floor to ceiling. Several loveseats were situated cozily around the central fireplace. She sighed in envy of the simpler time when reading was a major pastime.

She continued on, held captive by the glorious world of the Brisbane family. She passed the grand ballroom, the art gallery, and the bathroom that boasted the luxury of an alabaster tub. At the end of the second-floor hallway was a well roped-off bedroom with a four-poster canopy bed with heavy dark draperies covering the windows. *Wouldn't it be wonderful,* she thought, to step onto the lovely Aubusson rug!

Though the tap on her shoulder was light, Amanda jumped, the camera nearly slipping from her shoulder as she turned.

"Sorry if I scared you, but I've been looking for you everywhere." Carrie smiled. "This is some place! Wish I could stay longer."

They moved to a bench along the wall and sat down. Amanda glanced down at her watch. "It's only twelve o'clock."

"The restaurant called me on my cell. Seems one of my comrades isn't showing up for her shift and they want me to fill in."

Amanda sighed. "OK. I guess I'll drive you over. Just give me a minute to put my gear away."

"Don't be silly. The head docent around here told me there should be a bus coming by soon. Stay and enjoy yourself."

"You sure?" Amanda didn't want to leave, but she also didn't want to feel guilty about Carrie having to take mass transit, another thing about life her roommate hated.

"No problem. I'll see you later."

Amanda removed her fedora and placed it on the bench beside her. She leveled the camera up to her shoulder and scanned around the corridor to the end of the hallway, the red light blinking repeatedly as she filmed the door. Centering the viewfinder on it, she zoomed in for a tight shot to read the sign.

Private: No Visitors Beyond This Point.

She picked up her fedora and planted it on her head. Seeing no one on the floor, she cautiously walked to the door. This is probably where the renovations are taking place, she thought. Perching the camera back onto her shoulder, she pressed the record button and opened the door.

CHAPTER THREE

A gust of wind hurled her off balance as it propelled her up the flight of stairs to the third floor. At the top, she paused to catch her breath before looking around. Lifting the camera back up, she pressed her eye to the viewfinder and closely focused in on the bronze sign on the first door to her left.
Jonathan Brisbane – Private!
So, this was where the real action in Serenity had taken place, she thought. This very room was probably where Jonathan Brisbane and Thomas Edison had formed their alliance to make history together. She hesitated only a moment, her hand on the knob. No one seemed to be on the floor. *It couldn't hurt to just take a peek.* The point of debate was swift. With a shrug, she turned the knob and stepped inside.

This room was an office. The walls were paneled in oak and a large desk was the nerve center of the room. Behind it was a credenza, and to the left, a wall of rich leather-bound books. As Amanda skimmed over them quickly—literally volumes of them all of a legal or electrical nature—a chill gripped her. She felt like she was invading Jonathan Brisbane's privacy, despite the many years he'd been dead.

Walking in farther, she realized that the fire in the fireplace opposite the wall of books had only recently died out, its embers still faintly glowing. Perhaps someone had recently been working on the restoration of room. The thought and prospect of possibly getting caught made her shiver and, as she zeroed in on a last look through the viewfinder, her eyes spied a book that lay open on the credenza. Her curiosity immediately aroused, Amanda focused the camera lens in a tight close-up. Beside the book was a daguerreotype in a silver frame of two men shaking hands. She recognized one man as Thomas Edison. She assumed the other man was Jonathan Brisbane. He certainly was handsome. His flashing smile seemed to curl around the corners of his mouth as if he had a great secret he could not share.

Reluctantly pulling herself away from the photograph, Amanda aimed the camera down on the open page of the journal. Bold, dark script met her eyes. The society was obviously doing a wonderful job in this wing. The ink on the page actually looked newly dried, and the page was white in contrast to the yellow, aging documents in other parts of the house. She eagerly read the first paragraph.

"April, 1884. There is much excitement since my return from Menlo Park.

"Edison never ceases to amaze me! The magic of his electric lights at Menlo Park raised my spirits! But what can I do to stop the thievery around him? Alas, the Edison Electric Light Company is still plagued by patent thieves. I must keep a keen eye on the enemy camps..."

"Who are you, sir? And what are you doing in this room?" demanded an angry voice from behind her.

Sir? Embarrassed at having been caught, Amanda flinched and turned slowly, the video camera still on her shoulder, its red light blinking rapidly into the handsome face of...Jonathan Brisbane? Realizing the man must be a docent of close resemblance, Amanda still could not stop the trembling that made its way throughout her body. To her surprise, his hands shot up into the air in surrender!

As she adjusted the camera away from her shoulder, her fedora fell off her head and her long curls fell loosely around her. They stared at each other for an agonizingly long moment.

"A woman? They sent a woman to spy on me?" His face turned a deep crimson and the muscles in his cheek worked into an angry twitch. "How dare they!"

"Excuse me?" Amanda asked, having found her voice. "Don't you think you're taking this reenactment a bit too far?"

"Stop babbling and tell me who sent you! Was it Swan? Or perhaps Verdine?"

Hands still raised, he slowly moved around the desk and closer to Amanda.

Feeling immediately threatened, Amanda raised the camcorder onto her shoulder. "Come one step closer and I'll shoot!" she shouted. Why on earth had she said that? She wanted to laugh at the ludicrousness of the situation, but became wary as he froze in front of her, hands still in the air.

"It appears, Madam, that you have me at a considerable disadvantage. Though I must say I've never seen such a weapon before."

Weapon? Amanda kept filming, not sure what to make of this man. Another long silence allowed her time to reflect on his tall, athletic build. She slowly panned down the length of his body to his strong muscular legs, moving up to his broad chest that pulled at the material of his white shirt, before moving up to his face. Zooming in for a close-up, she stared at the thick, beveled lips, the neatly combed black hair that reached past his ears and covered his neck; over to the flashing green eyes. God, he was handsome...and angry! She let out a sigh and as she started to move the camera away from the agony of her sight, she slipped on her fedora. He lunged forward, catching her and the camera in one quick motion.

"So, now the tables are turned, Madam!" He held the "weapon" out of her reach with one hand, the other holding both of hers together around her back at the waist.

Jonathan Brisbane inhaled her lovely scent as she struggled in indignation. Such a slip of a girl, he thought. When she had first turned around and he had met the softness of those dark eyes, he was disappointed to think a man could be behind them. His gaze lingered on her soft brown hair as a curl brushed against his cheek. Pressing her thighs against him in those outrageously tight trousers proved to be too much. Reluctantly but forcefully, he pushed her at arm's length. She may be a woman, but she was still a spy!

CHAPTER FOUR

Try as she might, Amanda could not free herself from his grasp. "Look, whoever you are—"

"Jonathan Brisbane."

"Yeah, right. And I'm Nancy Drew!"

He reached over to his desk drawer, one hand still tightly grasping her wrists, and opened it carefully.

"There's been a mistake," she pleaded.

"And you have made it, Miss Drew."

"No, no!" she screamed in frustration. "My name is Amanda Lloyd."

"Ah, yet another alias!" He pulled a pistol from the drawer and held it against the small of her back.

"Until I decide what is to be done with you, spy, you will remain here."

"I am not a spy! I demand to see someone in authority."

"You are in no position to make demands, Miss... Drew or Lloyd...whoever you are." Moving backward, he pushed her into a chair and held the pistol pointed at her.

"You can't be serious!" She rubbed her sore wrists angrily.

A soft knock at the door startled them both, but Jonathan managed an authoritative "Enter!" without unlocking his gaze.

The servant entered the room guardedly and closed the door. "Is there anything I can do?" He stopped abruptly, his eyes fixed on Amanda who bore all the signs of a seething crazy woman.

"Not another one! Don't you people ever stray from your script?" Amanda shouted. "You're all nuts!" She began to move from the chair, but Jonathan held his pistol steady.

"Get some rope from the desk, Alan, and make sure this spy is bound tightly."

Alan drew himself up and did as he was ordered. "Spy, sir?" he asked, returning with the rope and approaching Amanda warily.

"That is correct. I found her in this room rifling through my journals on Mr. Edison."

Shaking his head in quiet reprimand, Alan tied Amanda's hands around the back of the chair. As he reached down to her feet, she kicked him. Alan's eyes widened and he turned questioningly to his employer. "Quite a spirited young woman," he commented.

Jonathan shook his head. "Take her weapon and whatever else she has to my safe," he instructed, the pistol at his side now that Amanda was securely bound.

"You're both crazy! Untie me, damn you!"

Jonathan ignored her pleas. "See to it that a room on the second floor is prepared for Miss...Lloyd's comfort."

Amanda's eyes narrowed and she glared at Jonathan as she struggled against the rope. Frustrated, she stamped her feet in a vain attempt to wiggle free.

"Excuse me for asking," Alan put in, "but how will you explain her to Mrs. Brisbane? She's due home from services fairly soon."

Mrs. Brisbane? Amanda felt her heart sink. Not only was he handsome, but also married. He was crazy, certainly, but perhaps it was temporary.

Jonathan's face interrupted her thoughts as he knelt down in front of her, his pistol relaxing on his knee to show he meant business. "You are certainly a fortunate spy." He flashed her a smile. "If you act appropriately some leniency will surely be afforded you." He pushed her fedora down onto her head, smashing her bangs into her eyes.

"I am not a spy," she said through clenched teeth before blowing at the bangs.

Jonathan turned to Alan. "We'll leave her here awhile. See that Renee finds something suitable for her to wear. She must look the proper lady for her presentation to Mrs. Brisbane."

"Proper lady, my eye," mumbled Amanda.

CHAPTER FIVE

An hour later, Amanda Lloyd found herself facing the lovely canopy bed and Aubusson carpet she had admired a few scant hours before.

Be careful what you wish for, she scolded herself.

Renee was a sweet French girl. Amanda figured her to be no older than eighteen. Her arms laden with clothing, she curtsied sweetly when she came into the room. Amanda scowled; stupefied by the frilly white dress, pantalets, camisole, and stockings that Renee laid out on the bed. Maybe she should play along. These people were obviously very dangerous, though this young woman didn't appear to be a threat. She seemed so…delicate…was the word that came to mind. Her auburn hair was in a neat little bun that was gathered into a net, her eyes almost doe-like in their innocence. She was wearing a long rose-colored cotton dress with a white apron layered over it.

Yes, Amanda thought, it would be in my best interest to go along with this charade. Maybe this Renee could eventually prove to be her ally among the lunatics.

"I suppose I have no choice," Amanda said with a sigh.

"Pardonne?" Renee's accent was light and high pitched. "You do not wish to meet Mrs. Brisbane in… feminine clothing?"

Amanda cringed as she unzipped her pants and pulled them off. "I can't believe anyone would marry that horrible man," she offered, her hands now shedding her blazer and blouse.

Renee stared at Amanda, her mouth open wide at the astonishing under things. Maybe they were the rage in Paris, though she had her misgivings.

"He's rude, arrogant, conceited, and a thousand more things I can't think of at the moment," continued Amanda. "He's lucky to have any woman marry him."

A blush crossed Renee's cheeks and she laughed softly. "Mr. Brisbane is not married. I speak of his mother!"

Amanda stopped ranting and simply stared at Renee. She could not explain why, but she found herself relieved by this information. She put on the lacy undergarments and allowed Renee to assist her into the frilly white dress—if only to stifle the young girl's objections.

"This dress is much too tight. How people wore this stuff is beyond me. It's a good thing women have finally exercised their rights," she grumbled.

Renee's eyebrows were knitted together in confusion.

"This dress is too tight," Amanda repeated. "How am I expected to breathe!"

Renee shook her head and came closer, adjusting the ruffled hem out of habit. "It is a good thing we did not use the corset."

"Whose dress is this, anyway?" Amanda asked as she seated herself at the vanity, her ribs aching with each intake of breath.

"Margaret, the parlor maid." Renee took Amanda's thick hair into her hands and pulled it back, bending slightly to look around her into the mirror. "Upsweep?"

Amanda nodded. "Sure, why not."

Though tempted to try to get to her purse and video camera, Amanda knew it would be an impossible task. Not only was she not sure what third-floor room it was in, but the man insisting he was Jonathan Brisbane had informed that Alan person to put them into his safe. Breaking into a locked safe would be impossible. She would just have to wait until she got out of this house and back into reality. Once she got hold of the authorities, she was sure to get her belongings back. Wouldn't the insane Brisbane impersonator be in for a surprise then!

Slowly and carefully, she descended the grand staircase, one hand lightly holding up the long hem of the dress that was rapidly cutting off circulation. Her knees weakened with each step. This was the Brisbane mansion all right, but there were subtle differences. Like the walls, they were floral print with wood only as a border. That couldn't be right. Reaching the bottom stair, her eyes scanned the entrance hall and she groaned. This couldn't be right either. Where were the shadow boxes and the plaques? Where were the docents, for that matter? Someone, a curator, an office manager, anyone! And there were no benches on which to rest during the tour.

What the hell is going on?

Straight ahead of her was the front door. Frightened, yet relieved, she headed with mixed emotions straight for it in quick, hasty steps over the new Oriental carpet. *Freedom! Soon this nightmare will be over!* Opening the door with shaking hands, she stepped out into...

The nineteenth century?

A carriage with liveried footmen clip clopped along the cobblestone street in front of the house. Amanda looked to the right—no cars, not even her own. With a catch in her throat, her hand flew to her mouth and she promptly...fainted.

CHAPTER SIX

Jonathan Brisbane had sequestered himself in the front parlor with a glass of brandy as he tried to figure what action he should take. This woman calling herself Amanda Drew, or Lloyd, appeared to be quite out of her senses, and if that was so, she was certainly a threat to his dear friend, Edison. Above all, his allegiance was with Edison and the inventor's ongoing projects. Of course, all would have to wait until his mother's return from church. What would he tell her? She would never believe the woman to be what she was—never believe that such a soft creature could be a spy. Before he was able to contemplate further on the subject, a scream rendered him into action and he ran from the parlor to find Margaret and Alan bending beside someone by the open door.

So, Miss Lloyd had tried to escape! Her actions clearly brought forth his rage and he pushed the servants aside and swept her up into his arms.

"I think she fainted, sir," commented Alan.

Jonathan instructed them to summon Renee as he rushed up the grand staircase taking the stairs by twos, the limp woman sagging lightly in his arms. Renee joined him in short order with a basin of cold water and a small cloth. Jonathan gingerly placed Amanda on the bed as Renee folded the soaked cloth and pressed it to

Amanda's forehead. She knew better than to question her employer, merely observing him as he glared down at the impossible woman who was putting his household through such inconvenience.

Hearing Amanda moan, and not wanting to pursue the matter in front of his staff, Jonathan abruptly left the room.

Amanda cautiously opened her eyes. "What happened?" Seeing Renee, she didn't know whether to laugh or cry. She was still here!

"You fainted. Mr. Brisbane carried you back to the room."

"You mean he touched me!" She raised her head from the pillow, and struggled to get up.

Renee gently pushed her back. "You fainted," she repeated.

Amanda sighed and bit into her lower lip, nearly drawing blood in frustration.

"What year is it?" she finally asked.

Renee cocked her head slightly at the question, thinking that perhaps Amanda had hit her head when she fainted. "Year?"

"Please...tell me...what year is it?" Amanda pleaded.

"It is 1884, of course. April the sixteenth, eighteen hundred eighty-four."

CHAPTER SEVEN

Down in the front parlor Jonathan paced back and forth in front of the fireplace, a second brandy already in his hands, when his mother swept into the room from services at the church.

"I see you've started the spirits early this evening," she stated in mild reprimand.

"You labor too hard, Jon. You would see much benefit to your disposition were you to set aside one day for the Lord," she affirmed while placing her Bible on the small table beside her favorite wingback chair.

Jonathan stopped his pace and swallowed the remainder of his drink, his brow wrinkled, his mind somewhere else. Instinctively, his mother came to his side and placed an arm on his shoulder.

"What is it? You appear quite in another world." She sat down in her chair and waited for the explanation she was confident he would afford her.

Jonathan turned and acknowledged her with a kiss to her cheek. "Sorry, dear. But, we have a houseguest, a visitor dispatched to us by Mr. Edison," he lied.

Vivian Brisbane smiled brightly, her eyes wide in anticipation as to the identity of the visitor. "Who?"

Jonathan hesitated a moment, hating the lie he was forced to embellish. "A young woman—distant cousin, I believe. She goes by the name of Amanda Lloyd."

"How refreshing! It has been too long since a young woman was in this house."

Leisurely, she removed her long dark gloves, finger by finger. "When will I have the pleasure of her acquaintance?"

"Soon." Jonathan sat down in the chair across from her. "It seems an accident befell her and—"

"Accident? Is she all right?"

"She fainted." He drew in a deep breath before continuing. "Renee is attending to her in one of the upstairs bedrooms."

Vivian rose immediately. "I shall go to her. Surely she is in need of motherly attention," she commented, her voice excited at the prospect of meeting a relative of the esteemed Mr. Edison. "We must make her feel at home."

"Mother, please, she's fine."

"I shall go to her just the same."

Jonathan deferred to her wishes and Vivian made her way up to Amanda's room, leaving a stewing Jonathan rocking his head in consternation.

CHAPTER EIGHT

Upstairs, Amanda tried desperately to understand the people in this house—to understand the very year Renee insisted it was. But, it couldn't be 1884! It was impossible to be 1884! The door opened and a tall, formidable woman sailed confidently into the room, dismissing Renee and taking command.

"I am Vivian Brisbane, my dear. I'm Jonathan's mother. I am so pleased to have you as our guest. Mr. Edison is a frequent and welcomed visitor to Serenity. How are you feeling?" she continued without pause.

Amanda looked at the imposing woman whose soft features were in direct contrast and could only be described as kind. She wore a beige tailored suit with a long accordion skirt, a large white cameo pinned at her throat. Her hair was black with a touch of silver at the temples, and it was pulled away from her face in a neat chignon.

Amanda smiled, warming to the woman whose bright blue eyes glittered with concern; a concern she remembered seeing in her own mother's eyes. Realizing an uncomfortable amount of time had passed since Mrs. Brisbane's question, she tried to raise herself up to reply, but the tight dress sent her reeling back down against the soft cushions.

"Oh, dear!" Vivian came closer to the bed. "What is that you are wearing?" she asked, a finger to her temple in hazy recognition. "Goodness, I know I have seen that dress before. Never mind, it's much too tight. We must take it off you immediately." She called to Renee through the open door.

"Madam?"

"Help me remove this dress, Renee, before the poor girl suffocates."

Together they unsnapped the dress, leaving Amanda in the light lacy undergarments. She let out a long, deep breath.

"Oh, thank you so much."

"You are quite welcome...Amanda, is it?"

Amanda nodded.

"Well, my son informs me that you will be staying for a while. Where is your trunk?"

Staying for a while? How long, she wondered. And what was he up to?

"Trunk?"

"Never mind," Vivian raced on. "I'll have Lottie take care of a wardrobe until we discover the whereabouts of your own."

"Lottie?"

Vivian smiled. "My seamstress," she answered while fussing with the bed covering and drawing the quilt comfortably up to Amanda's neck. "How old are you, dear?" she asked suddenly.

"Twenty-seven."

Vivian's hands reached out to dislodge the comb holding back Amanda's long hair, her hand lingering as she brushed aside a tendril. "You know, I would have had a daughter your age...had she not succumbed to typhoid."

"I'm sorry."

"Well, these things happen," Vivian reasoned while holding back the water building behind her lids.

"Not in..."Amanda almost said, my time but caught herself. "I mean, I lost both of my parents."

Vivian's hand flew to her lips. "How dreadful! Then you must be all alone. Except, of course, for the kindness of your cousin."

"Cousin?"

"Mr. Edison."

Feeling the conversation was turning toward a topic she wished not to pursue, Amanda gave the subject a turn. "I should think your son is enough to handle!"

Vivian smiled. "Jonathan can be cantankerous, but he's really a gentle soul." Amanda left things at that. How could she possibly tell this amiable woman that her son was crazy? That "gentle soul" had held a gun to her and mercilessly tied her to a chair. No. She wasn't going to say anything to anybody until she found out what was going on here.

CHAPTER NINE

It didn't take Vivian Brisbane long to send up a dress more suitable to Amanda's measurements. This Lottie was apparently a remarkable seamstress, though Renee suggested that it was more likely that Lottie had a pattern already prepared. Amanda nodded as she allowed Renee to again aid her in dressing.

Renee's assessment was quick as she once again fashioned Amanda's hair into an upsweep of cascading curls held back by two large ivory combs. "Most likely this was to be one of Miss Susan's dresses."

"Susan?" Amanda looked at her, meeting her gaze through the mirror of the vanity.

Renee nodded. "Mrs. Brisbane's daughter. You are much closer to her size. She, too, was small in height... and full of body."

Amanda laughed. Indeed, for a woman of merely five foot two, her breasts were large, and that suited her just fine—as did the lovely and comfortable dress. Again, Renee yielded to Amanda's wish to not wear the corset, and they compromised with Amanda wearing the pantaletes because Renee saw Amanda's scanty bikini briefs as simply unacceptable.

Rising slowly, Amanda twirled around, the layers of silk folding over with each other like the petals of a flower. The dress was pink with tiny rosebuds laced throughout in random design. It did not come as high to her neck as the other dress, instead accentuating her ample bosom in a square chest line.

"How do I look?" She asked while adjusting the frilly ends of the sleeves that neatly met her hands.

Renee thought about this a moment. "You certainly do not look like a spy," she said seriously.

"Who told you that? Mr. Brisbane?"

"Are you, Miss Amanda? A spy, I mean?"

"Mr. Brisbane seems to think so."

Renee began to make the bed, puffing up the pillow with ease. "Well, you do not look like a spy," she decided. "You look lovely, Miss Amanda. Mr. Brisbane will be quite surprised and pleased."

"Who cares what he thinks?" Amanda said sharply.

Renee blushed. "I do not wish to anger you, Miss Amanda, but we dress for the pleasure of the man."

"No, no, Renee. Women should dress to please themselves," she corrected.

"Pardonne?"

"Never mind. I guess I should go down to dinner."

"Dinner is over, Miss Amanda. Supper awaits you," Renee answered in confusion.

"Whatever." With the lift of her hem, Amanda left the room and gingerly took the steps of the grand staircase.

CHAPTER TEN

Already seated for supper, Jonathan and his mother were exchanging disagreeable words in the main dining room.

"I wouldn't become too attached to this young woman," he commented briskly. "I doubt she will be with us for too long."

"Nonsense!" Vivian replied while placing her cloth napkin on her lap. "Our home is open to her for as long as she likes. Besides, I don't think the poor girl has anywhere else to go."

Jonathan groaned. Introducing his mother to the devious young woman was obviously a mistake. But, what choice had he? He listened without comment as Vivian rushed on.

"She told me herself that she lost both her parents. That is probably why Mr. Edison sent her. And we owe him, Jon. He's your most prestigious client and a dear friend. He is always busy and probably doesn't know what to do with her." She picked up the crystal goblet of water and sipped. "After all, since Mary took sick he has three children to contend with, poor dear."

Jonathan took this information in slowly. Poor Edison. He wished this Amanda Lloyd problem had not come to light at such an inconvenient and difficult time in the life of his friend. It angered him to think of all the discomfort she had caused since her arrival. Though he hesitated to do so, he would eventually have to wire Edison. He was certainly obliged to warn him against this latest deception to sabotage his work.

Amanda glided into the dining room, the soft velvet slippers like pillows on her feet. She marveled at the table, set exactly the way it was when she had filmed it on the tour.

It was waiting for me!

Conversation ceased abruptly, and whether it was the manner in which he was raised or her beauty, Jonathan found himself rising to pull out a chair for Amanda, his pulse quickening at her closeness, his heart hammering lightly. He suppressed a smile and offered her the chair with a grumble, casting a wicked compliment from his mind before it could reach his lips. He must not succumb to her charms. It was important, for Edison's sake, that he maintain his wits about him.

"Miss Lloyd, I trust you are feeling better?" he asked while taking his seat at the head of the table.

"Oh, Jon, her name is Amanda," Vivian put in. "There is no need to address her so formally. How are you, dear? You do look lovely"

"Thank you, Mrs. Brisbane."

Jonathan watched her carefully and shook his head with impatience.

"Vivian...please call me Vivian."

"Vivian, you have a lovely home." Amanda all but ignored Jonathan, a difficult task, considering how handsome he looked in his charcoal suit.

Ruth, the cook at Serenity, had prepared a small feast of welcome: honey glazed ham, potatoes, an array of heavily seasoned vegetables, and a specially whipped dessert for Mr. Edison's "cousin." When Amanda asked for the recipe, Vivian was quick in explanation.

"Oh, dear me, Ruth would never divulge her culinary secrets!" She laughed softly thinking of the forceful Ruth who ruled the kitchen as she would a regiment, and who kept her recipes hidden in the vault of her mind with no other keeper to the key.

Amanda smiled. "Well, it is all really delicious. Please tell her I appreciate it." Vivian nodded.

Jonathan had been quiet during the meal, right through to the strong coffee and the side of brandy. Without explanation, he rose from the table abruptly, still deep in whatever thoughts had claimed him through supper.

"Jonathan?" Vivian questioned, more with her eyes than further words.

"Cheroot," he replied. "I'm going to step outside for a smoke." He pushed his chair in and moved from the table.

"It would be nice for Amanda to see the gardens at sunset, Jon. You would like that, wouldn't you, dear?" she asked Amanda.

Jonathan shot Amanda a look that clearly expressed his desire to be alone. He'd be damned if he would allow her outside the confines of the house where she might be likely to flee. It would be impossible to justify such an action to Vivian. His brow furrowed and he raised an eyebrow to Amanda in challenge.

"I think I would like that very much," she responded, accepting his challenge.

Upon reflection, Jonathan again deferred to Vivian's wishes. Reason dictated that it was highly unlikely that this wisp of a woman would escape as night was approaching, and on foot. Stiffly and politely, he ambled over to Amanda.

"Shall we?"

She nodded and could have sworn Vivian winked at her as the two walked out of the dining room.

"Don't forget a shawl, dear," Vivian called. "There is one on the rack near the back door."

They stood together on the white-posted porch that overlooked the sixty-five acres that framed Serenity. Amanda closed her eyes and breathed in the cool night air, Vivian's shawl wrapped comfortably around her. The herbal blends in the garden claimed her at once, delightfully assaulting her senses. She smiled inwardly. Was she really here, in 1884, living with the Brisbane family? She turned and looked at Jonathan as he drew a gold case from the inside pocket of his jacket, clicked it open and pulled out a cheroot. Soon he was inhaling the flavor, smoking in silence.

"Shall we walk?" He did not wait for her answer as he stepped down from the porch and moved along the stone path toward the gardens. Amanda followed, swiftly jogging to catch up with him and silently cursing the long hem of her dress.

"Do you mind if we stroll rather than run?" she asked, her breathing ragged from trying to keep pace with him.

He stopped and stared into her eyes. They were certainly pretty eyes, he thought. So dark they appeared onyx and were framed by dark lashes. He shook his head and found himself once again casting away a compliment from his mind.

"You may have my mother fooled, Miss Lloyd, but I wouldn't become too comfortable here." He began to walk again, more slowly, reluctantly offering his arm, as he would have afforded any other woman.

Recalling the etiquette of this century, Amanda reached up a hand and lightly placed it on his arm.

The warmth of him was a startling contrast to the cold strength of that very arm as it had held her at bay in his office earlier. Her hand trembled along with the rest of her and she drew the shawl closer to her body.

"Cold, Miss Lloyd?" he asked. "Maybe we should return."

"Amanda," she whispered. "And, no, I'd very much like to see the gardens. I've learned so much about them."

"I'm sure." His answer was short and accusing.

"What's that supposed to mean?" she snapped.

They stopped near the greenhouse, just ahead of the white picket fence that surrounded the rows of roses, carnations, and borders of Japanese quince. Jonathan released his arm and began to pace back and forth, his hands clasped behind his back, fingers laced tightly together.

"Are you going to tell me who hired you?" he asked, still keeping his pace.

Amanda sighed loudly and looked to the brilliantly red setting sun. It would be a hot day tomorrow, especially for early spring. "No one," she finally replied.

"Well, it's beyond me how you can manage to get by the hounds—"

"Hounds?" Amanda leaned her back against the fence for support, her hands grasping the wood so hard her knuckles turned white. She stared at him with wide alarming eyes.

Jonathan stopped pacing and looked at her startled expression. She posed a delightful picture with the sunset behind her, her dark hair gently blowing in the breeze, eyes wide, and lips so full and partially open that he wanted to claim them to his own. God, but she was beautiful! The temptation to gather her into his arms and still her fear was almost too much for him, but rather than do so, he simply grinned.

"You must be very clever. Perhaps you slipped them meat at their hungriest?"

"I..." Amanda began, but knew her explanation would fall on deaf ears. He was obviously goading her, and this simple stroll along the property was fast becoming an interrogation.

Amanda's fears had more to do with survival in this century—which she was now sure was real—than with the hounds Jonathan so conveniently mentioned.

A slight breeze brushed through the trees and sent her skin to tingling. Jonathan moved closer to her until he was right in front of her, deciding he would like to know more about Miss Amanda Lloyd, and maybe it would be more fruitful to gain her trust rather than frighten her. She was, after all, a woman. Yes, he thought, women were more likely to bear their hearts when not on guard, and spy or not, Amanda Lloyd was certainly a woman. He swung open the door to the greenhouse and gingerly stepped in. Amanda kept her eyes on his every move.

Jonathan carefully removed a flower and came back to where she stood. "Gardenia," he related softly as he pushed it gently into her hair, their bodies so close he nearly touched hers as he placed one arm on either side of the fence and trapped her between them.

Amanda tried to turn from those penetrating green eyes but found herself mesmerized by them. Slowly, he leaned forward and lightly kissed her lips. When he pulled back, her eyes were still closed and he suppressed a smile.

"Forgive my indiscretion, but I was, for the moment, swept away by your charms."

Confusion reigned supreme for Amanda. *What was this man up to?* Though it was a light kiss, she found herself yearning for more. Tearing herself away from his gaze, she turned her back on him and looked to the sunset, still captured within the circle of his arms.

"What if I were to tell you," she began, eyes held fast on the orange-red sun as it slowly set, leaving a spray of color in its wake. "...that I am from the future?"

Jonathan laughed heartily, his lips grazing her soft hair as his breath moved through the strands. He was finding the closeness of her unbearably delightful and though they were playing a dangerous game, he did not intend to lose.

She spun around defiantly. "You believe in Edison's light!" she defended.

Jonathan drew back and shook his head. "There is no comparison. Time travel is a fictional means of transportation, my dear Ms. Lloyd."

"I used to think so," she mumbled as she turned away from him and started back to the house.

"Used to think so?" he called out to her, his laughter carried along with the gentle breeze.

She didn't look back as she ran with quickness into the house, never stopping until she was safely in her room.

CHAPTER ELEVEN

Parting the heavy drapery, Amanda leaned her head against the cold glass of the window and watched Jonathan walk briskly up the path. Had she really brought up the seemingly inconceivable concept of time travel? She found it hard to believe herself, and she was here! How then could she expect him to do anything other than laugh? In his eyes, she was a spy, and surely, after tonight, she was also a crazy spy. *And that kiss! What was that all about?*

The knock on the door jarred her thoughts. She was happy to discover her visitor to be Vivian Brisbane, who swept gracefully into the room aided by a candle glowing within a hurricane lamp.

"Well, dear, how was your walk with Jonathan?" She set the candle down on the dresser and smiled hopefully.

Amanda moved from the window and returned the smile. "Fine."

Vivian walked to where Amanda had been standing and drew the drapes closed.

"You know what you need, dear?"

"I'm afraid to ask."

"A party!" Vivian gushed.

Amanda sat cautiously down on the edge of the bed. "A what?"

"A party, Amanda...a little fun!" Vivian sat down beside her. "And I have just the one in mind!" She beamed and took Amanda's hand into her own. "It will have to be a special theme, of course. I've been wanting so much to contact Madame Winston."

"Madame Winston?" Amanda shrugged in question.

"Yes. The spiritualist medium. You know...a psychic. Surely, you have heard of her. She hails from England, but I believe she's in America at this time." Vivian didn't miss a beat as she began to mentally prepare her party. "We could probably get her here for the next weekend, though it is short notice." She put a hand to her temple and tapped it several times. "I'm sure she will accept."

"Next weekend? If I'm still here," Amanda said, more to herself than to Vivian.

"Don't be silly, of course you will be here." Vivian rose abruptly and walked to light the lamp by the bed before picking up her own. "My suggestion to you would be to soak in our wonderful alabaster bathtub before retiring. I assure you it is a luxury you will enjoy. We are so fortunate to have indoor plumbing, you know."

"Thank you." A bath would certainly calm her nerves and ease her out of the depression that had draped over her since her curious confrontation with Jonathan in the gardens. She recalled that special tub with its golden knobs when she had taken the tour. "I believe that would be just what I need."

"I'll send Renee up with fresh towels and a nightgown. Oh, and some lavender beads for the bath." She paused by the door. "Good night, Amanda. I'm so glad you are with us."

Amanda smiled. "Me too."

Soaking in a tub had always been a pleasing experience for Amanda, but soaking in the long alabaster one with the gentle lavender beads while surrounded by candlelight, only made the experience even more wonderful. She was soon able to leave the stress of the day easily behind her. Leaning back, she dipped her body into the rippling water, her hair fanning out behind her head as the steam rose to the surface. Her thoughts drifted back to Jonathan and his kiss. What was going through the man's mind? One minute he was accusatory and the next, romantic.

As her hands began to wrinkle in the water, she realized it had turned cool and her body began to shiver. They had indoor plumbing, but heat was another thing. She climbed quickly out of the tub and rubbed her hair vigorously with a towel before tossing on the white wrapper Renee had left. *My kingdom for a blow dryer*, she thought dismally while padding her way across the cold marble floor and out to the hallway. *Damn!* Why hadn't she remembered her slippers! She couldn't wait to get back into the bedroom and the warm bed she knew awaited her.

* * *

He had yet to step out of the darkness, content to stand quietly in the hallway watching her. He stared, unblinking. Looking at her now, fresh from her bath, Jonathan could almost believe that Amanda Lloyd was indeed from another world. One not of earth, but of heaven, for she looked like an angel; the soft curls framing her face, shimmering golden by the lamps' light, the white wrapper trimmed in gold, generating a vibrant aura around her delicate form. He could not move—was frozen to the floor as if his feet had been poured into cement. When she moved past his dark corner, her lavender scent embraced him. It was at that very moment in time that she crept into his heart, and it was all he could do to compose himself and still the trembling within him.

"Amanda," he whispered as he stepped out and touched her arm.

Startled, she raised the lamp and peered through the light with frightened eyes.

"Jonathan!" It was more an intake of breath than his name.

Their eyes locked and several moments passed before either could look away as a surge of energy passed through them. She found it almost impossible to draw her eyes from his gaze.

"I wanted to ask you," he began softly, reluctantly removing his hand. "Would you like to accompany me into town tomorrow? You rushed off so quickly that I feared I may have offended you."

What spell had she cast, Jonathan thought suddenly. Why then did he feel he had lost before the game had even begun? He watched her eyes narrow suspiciously and the spell, for the moment, was broken.

Offend me? When had the tables turned? Since when had he become the offender when she was clearly the intruder...the spy, as he had insisted? She stared into his eyes in search of the answer.

"Will you join me tomorrow?" Uncomfortable with her scrutiny, he cleared his throat loudly.

"I....don't know." She shook her head. "Good night, Jonathan."

Rushing into her room, she closed the door behind her and leaned her back heavily against it as she listened to his footsteps disappear down the hall. It was only when she heard his door softly click closed that she realized she had been holding her breath. Letting out a rush of air, she walked over to the night table and set the lamp down with trembling hands before collapsing onto the bed. Pushing her legs under the covers, she drew the soft downy quilt up to her chin. Her eyes burned and she knew her cheeks were flushed. *What the hell is happening to me?* Who was this intense and provocative man? And why did he stir such yearning within her? She lay back with a sigh, surprised to find her cheeks wet. No man had ever made her cry—not that there had been many in her life. What was he trying to do to her? Was this tenderness his means of torture? Turning on her side, Amanda punched her fist into the feathery pillow in frustration. Well, it was working!

* * *

Sleep refused to welcome Jonathan as he fought with his feelings. He had to find out more about this woman who called herself Amanda Lloyd. Never had he lost his resolve over a woman before. The need to know her kept him tossing and turning. It was beyond reason!

Donning his trousers, he lit a lamp and quietly made his way up to the third floor. Stealing into the room where he had secured her weapon and tapestry bag, he locked the door behind him. He put the lamp down and knelt before the safe, struggling to recall the combination, faltering several times before gaining access to its contents. Steering clear of her weapon, he reached for the bag and pulled it out. He was surprised to find it had no drawstring, but was held together by two long black strips of...what? He had never seen it before. Magically, they fastened to each other and he found the bag opened by pulling the strips apart, and closed by pressing them together. He sat mesmerized on the floor as he played with the mystical fasteners.

Jonathan knew he was invading Amanda's privacy, yet, he felt a certain loss of control as his hand dipped into the pouch and he pulled out the first thing he touched—a short black canister no larger than his forefinger. He surveyed it curiously. At the top was a white button with the word "press," printed on it. Perhaps it was some sort of perfume. Rolling it over onto its side, he read the name of the manufacturer.

MACE...and pressed the button.

Behind a locked door in a room on the third floor of the large mansion, no one heard Jonathan Brisbane's startled cry as he dropped the canister and pressed his hands to his eyes in terror.

CHAPTER TWELVE

Jonathan had spent the remainder of the night flushing the poison from his eyes; inwardly seething and hating Amanda for the pain she had caused him. How foolish he had been to allow himself to fall under her spell! She was obviously far more dangerous than he had imagined. His only relief was that he had not touched her weapon, for today he could be dead!

In his nightshirt, he filled the basin once more with cool water; the morning light stung sharply, but at least his eyes no longer felt on fire. Would he go blind? He cursed himself once more for his stupidity as he felt the cool water wash through them. God, how they ached, so much so that his head accompanied them like a throbbing symphony of pain.

The last to arrive at the table, Jonathan silently seated himself opposite Vivian. He did not acknowledge Amanda at all. It wasn't until he raised his head from his coffee cup and glared at her that she became aware of what had happened.

He found my Mace!

"You look tired, son. You must get more rest," reprimanded Vivian.

He mumbled something incoherent and continued to glare at Amanda.

Though she felt he deserved some discomfort for invading her privacy, Amanda knew he was in pain, for Mace was powerful in warding off an attacker. It was obvious from Jonathan's red-rimmed eyes that he had sprayed a good dose into them. What else was in the purse, she thought, for in her haste to leave for the museum with Carrie she couldn't remember. Her habit of tossing last minute items could certainly prove dangerous to a nineteenth-century man. God knew what further harm he could cause himself with his snooping. Whether he believed it or not, she had to explain this journey she had taken through time. She had to convince him that it was surely possible, even if she was having trouble with that concept herself. Had that only been yesterday? Lost in thought, she did not hear Vivian address her.

"Amanda, I want you to accompany Jonathan into town and purchase what you need on our account."

Amanda looked up. "That's very kind of you, but I don't think that's necessary."

"Mother," Jonathan interrupted, "I have no intention of taking Miss Lloyd along with me today." He placed the cup down into the saucer so hard it shattered.

"Jonathan!"

Amanda groaned. He was back to calling her "Miss Lloyd" and it didn't take a genius to see the hate and anger behind his tortured eyes. Had last night been a dream? No. His eyes clearly revealed that any trust he had felt had been dissolved in a haze of Mace and she could only imagine his pain, or what consequences it would bear.

"Son, your manners are inexcusable! Amanda is our guest."

"I have business in town."

Vivian rose angrily, her hands taking on a life of their own as they fluttered about nervously. "You are behaving quite strangely. You know that I will not tolerate rudeness to anyone who is our guest. You will take Amanda into town," she confirmed.

Jonathan rose as she turned from the table, his napkin slipping from his lap. "Mother—"

"I am planning a party," she said, dismissing his rebuttal, and discounting the subject once and for all. "I am inviting the renowned psychic medium, Madame Winston for the weekend. Amanda will need a wardrobe. I won't have her walking around in Susan's outdated dresses."

Beginning to lose her resolve, she bit her lower lip and Jonathan saw her shoulders begin to shudder. Vivian Brisbane was on the verge of tears and he did not want to cause a scene. Certainly, he did not want his mother to dwell on Susan's death, especially since she had been so long in accepting it. Enough pain had been caused thus far, and he would spare his mother at all costs. Reigning himself in, Jonathan nodded to her.

"Forgive me, Mother. It is never my wish to cause you distress."

Vivian nodded and left the dining room.

CHAPTER THIRTEEN

Amanda looked down at the second of Susan's dresses and frowned. Vivian had been quite upset, and though she didn't want to abuse the woman's kindness, if seeing her in these dresses was painful then she had no choice but to purchase others.

"The carriage is waiting. I suggest you make haste."

The harsh tone in Jonathan's voice alarmed her. Her first carriage ride in the nineteenth century was not going to be a pleasant one. She nodded and pushed herself from the table. Renee met her in the hallway, a light spring cape in her hands. Amanda forced herself to smile a thank you as Renee slipped it over her shoulders, and faced the front door for the second time.

Jonathan stood near the luxurious carriage snapping out orders to his liveried footmen. He looks so handsome in his blue morning suit, Amanda thought. The color enhanced the blue of his wonderful eyes. *His eyes! Oh, God, how am I going to explain this?*

Impatiently tapping his foot, Jonathan held open the door to the carriage. His guard was up now, for sure, and he narrowed his eyes in her direction as if to dare her to try to escape. Lifting up the hem of her dress, Amanda took swift steps to the carriage. Jonathan did not assist her into it, merely nodding for her to get in quickly. He wanted this day to be over with. He thought he would be done with this woman of deceit, only to find he would have to appease his mother and allow Amanda to stay for this blasted party at week's end. With a growl, he slammed the door shut and instructed the driver to move on with the tap of his cane to the roof.

Amanda had dreamed of such a ride—sitting in a horse-drawn carriage, a handsome man by her side—but it was to remain a dream. The ride was bumpy, along dirt roads and cobblestone streets that jarred her body against the walls of the cab. And the man, though handsome, sat across from her and refused to even look at her. As she gazed out the window, the thought occurred to her that she could be filming history if only she had her camcorder. There was so much potential in preserving something of the past that might one day be found in the future. A depression washed over her and she took no pleasure from the sights outside the window. Here was a chance in a lifetime and it was slipping through her fingers.

"It's written all over your face, you know," she said suddenly.

Jonathan jerked his head up and immediately ran his hands over his face.

Amanda laughed. "Not literally, Jonathan. I only meant that I know you rifled through my belongings." That sounded better, she thought. Rifling was certainly a good word to describe the intent.

"What is this talk...some sort of spy code? You do speak strangely at times."

Amanda sighed loudly. Conversation was not going to be easy. "Oh, back off, Jonathan. You were wrong and you know it."

He pushed himself deeply against the back of his seat. "And where shall I back off to?" he questioned.

"We are in a moving carriage together, not by choice, I assure you."

"Again, I did not mean it literally. Oh...never mind." He was making her angry and she truly didn't want to be.

"No. Let us pursue this further." He shifted in his seat and leaned forward, his hands resting on his knees. "I believe I was justified in my investigation of your personal items. You are an intruder in my home—"

"In your time," she corrected, her hands twisting nervously in her lap. "In your time," she repeated with emphasis.

Jonathan rocked his head back and forth, his lips curling into a sneer. "So, we are back to that, are we? Time travel?" He arched an eyebrow mockingly. His first assessment of her had been correct: she was simply out of her mind, and lunacy was apparently a prerequisite for the spy business. "And what time, pray tell, do you hail from, Miss Lloyd?" His eyes lit up in anticipation of her answer.

He was goading her, she knew. She certainly couldn't blame him, but felt as if he had slapped her in the face with his laughter. Undaunted, she drew herself up indignantly.

"Two thousand eleven," she replied firmly.

His eyes narrowed and his laugh was now full from deep within his chest. She couldn't tell whether the tears in his eyes were from his ordeal with the Mace, or because of what she revealed. Frankly, she couldn't blame him for laughing. Shaking his head, his eyes roamed her in inventory. Several combs held up her hair, the long dark strands curling down to her shoulders and held in place by a large green-feathered hat. Her dress was Susan's last walking dress; forest green with mint green stripes. He looked down at her small white-gloved hands as they fidgeted in her lap, then back up to her eyes, which were wide, the pupils dilated; then down to her nose and chin, haughtily pointed in indignation. *The lips...never mind the lips*, he thought, hating himself for staring.

"Two thousand eleven. Well, I must say, the women of your time wear dangerous perfume!"

"That was Mace, you idiot! It's for self-defense."

"How dare you insult me! I am not an idiot! I am fully educated and a prominent barrister."

Now, it was Amanda's turn to laugh and she could feel his body tense across from her, see the muscles in his cheek twitch and tighten.

"You must have a powerful headache, Jonathan. If you would allow me access to my purse, I have pills that could help you," she offered, remembering the Advil she always carried with her.

"Ha!" he answered, reading her mind. "If you are referring to that bottle labeled *Anvil* then I can only imagine that it is likely to do to my head what your Mace did to my eyes!" He raised his cane, and for a moment, she thought he would strike her. Instead, he rapped on the carriage roof and they soon pulled to a stop.

Amanda tried to hold back her smile, but it was too late, and it only served to anger him even more. He shot out an impatient hand as she alighted from the carriage. Careful to watch her footing, she held her eyes fast on her feet. When she finally looked up, she froze, unable to take another step forward as her eyes widened at the scene before her.

Men and woman scurried along the slated sidewalk, some browsing through store windows, others engaged in conversation. Horse-drawn carriages moved up and down the cobblestone street, picking up and depositing riders. On the corner, two little girls played hopscotch in front of a bakery as the proprietor swept his entrance. Everywhere she looked, she noted the tipping of hats in greeting. Not far from their carriage, Amanda heard a man direct a question to a passing stranger. "Do you know the time?"

"I'm afraid so," Amanda heard herself answer. If ever there had been any doubts that she was indeed in the year 1884, they were finally dispelled. There was no denying it. These people were *real!* The clothier directly in front of her was real, the bank on the corner was real, and the bakery was especially real as the scent of hot-cross buns wafted through the air. She turned startled eyes on Jonathan as he tapped her arm and motioned across the street to a brick building.

"I will be back presently. Our credit is exceptional, so you may feel free to go about your purchasing." He crossed to the other side of the street and Amanda watched his tall form dodge an oncoming carriage before he disappeared into the telegraph office. Amanda took a deep breath, moved from the curb, and into the shop.

* * *

Inside the telegraph office, Jonathan stepped up to the desk and cordially acknowledged Henry Chalmers.

"Ah, Mr. Brisbane, how are you these days?" the man asked. "Haven't seen you in town for a while."

"Business is good, Henry. The wife and family are in good health and spirits, I trust?" He pulled a black book from his breast pocket.

"Very well, sir. Thank you for inquiring."

"Glad to hear so," he said as he drew a sheaf of paper from the desk and dipped Henry Chalmers' feather pen into an ink bottle to begin his communication.

Time travel, indeed, he thought as he tried to focus his mind on formulating his message. *A spy is what Amanda Lloyd is!* He began to write to Edison with every intention of revealing this latest deception when he found himself pausing, pen poised in midair. It would not be beneficial to burden Edison with news of the turn of events while his wife was still so ill. As one of Edison's advisers, he was duty bound to deal with Miss Lloyd without troubling his friend. Quickly, he expressed his prayers for Mary's recovery in his neat bold hand and pushed the paper forward. Henry took it from him and read Jonathan's words aloud for confirmation. Jonathan nodded and paid him, but not before Henry handed him an envelope.

"Glad you stopped by today. You have saved me from having to dispatch this to you."

Jonathan looked up and smiled. He liked Henry Chalmers, whose dark eyes held the wisdom of many years, but whose young face displayed only a mere twenty-five of living. Stuffing the telegram into his pocket, he decided to linger awhile to chat with Henry.

CHAPTER FOURTEEN

Amanda stared uneasily around the shop. How did one buy a dress in 1884? And why was she even here at all? Certainly, she must have a purpose in this time. She glanced nervously around at the bolts of material and layers of lace that seemed to fill every wall and corner. To her left were hats; to her right were rows upon rows of dainty white gloves.
My God, I'm really here...1884!
Noticing the alarmed look on Amanda's face, Ella Crocker, who had been in conversation with Frances West, came around the counter, her long blue skirt swishing as her tall frame made quick steps to Amanda.

"May I be of assistance?" she inquired with eager eyes. She had seen Amanda arrive in the Brisbane carriage and had just been pointing out that fact to Frances West.

Amanda stared at the woman, relieved to see a pleasant smile behind her dark eyes. She was very tall, and her hair done up in the customary bun only made her appear taller.

"I hope so," Amanda replied, deciding to make a friend. "Mrs. Vivian Brisbane suggested I make use of her account for some purchases."

At the mention of Vivian's name, Frances West joined Ella Crocker with a rustle of skirts, which was surprising, considering the woman was aided by a delicately carved ivory cane, its head in the shape of an elephant's trunk.

"Word is out already that Vivian is having a party!" the woman gushed. "Frances West," she informed, extending her free hand.

Amanda now turned her attention to the diminutive woman beside the proprietor whose birdlike voice actually managed to rise above the other woman's. She was dressed all in black, from her shoes to her bonnet, which served to accentuate her lightning-white hair.

"Why, yes, that's right." Amanda smiled warmly at the curious woman. "My name is Amanda Lloyd."

"Oh! Mr. Edison's cousin!" Frances West rapped her cane several times, causing both women to jump. "Hop to it, Ella. You have a celebrity in your shop," she scolded.

Ella Crocker fixed her eyes on Frances and shook her head wearily. "Excuse my friend, Miss Lloyd. Word travels fast through town with Frances as its messenger." She set a look of gentle reprimand on Frances. "What would you be needing? I have some taffeta and silk that just came in."

"Would it be an imposition if I left the details up to you?"

Ella Crocker could not conceal her smile. At last, an opportunity to freely spend some of the Brisbane money without Vivian's direction!

"How many dresses?"

"Not just dresses. I will need an entire wardrobe."

The women looked questioningly at each other and Amanda thought she had said something out of turn. "My trunk, you see, has been lost. Mrs. Brisbane suggested I purchase what I need and repay her at a later date," she explained.

"Isn't that just like dear Vivian," Frances offered, winking at her fortunate friend as she imagined the wardrobe sale.

Ella was already behind the counter drawing up a list and Amanda rushed forward, Frances close on her heels.

"I'll make up the order and have it delivered to Lottie on Wednesday," said Ella of the confident seamstress at Serenity. "If there is anything you are not happy with, please return it at your convenience."

"Of course. But do you have a dress or two on the premises for me to take with me?" Amanda asked. Ella looked up from her list. "Surely, Mrs. Brisbane would wish you to have your clothes especially designed by Lottie," she remarked incredulously.

"Yes, but I need something to...hold me over."

"I'm afraid not."

Frances West leaned forward, rapping her cane for attention. "But you do have dresses in your inventory; two that I can think of."

Aware of the dresses in question, Ella looked up at Frances with flushed cheeks, and when she spoke, it was through pursed lips. "I don't think..."

"Will they fit me?" Amanda interrupted, uncomfortable with their exchange and anxious to get this over with.

"The dresses were never picked up," Ella stiffly replied. "I suppose it would be all right," she decided.

Frances West nearly sneered as the frowning Ella made her way behind a curtain to the back of the store. At least her friend would be rid of Lavinia's garments. Besides, they would look very lovely on the pretty Miss Lloyd.

"This party is a long time coming. I am sure it will be wonderful," offered Frances.

Frances smiled sweetly at Amanda, who was beginning to feel the shop closing in on her. This was too much for one person in one day.

Ella returned with the dresses in short order and informed Amanda that she would adjust the Brisbane account and have the material delivered no later than Wednesday. As Amanda exited the shop with her purchases, she heard Ella's voice rise in consternation.

"That was insensitive of you, Frances. She obviously doesn't know of Lavinia or the scandal. Poor Jonathan," she said with a sigh.

CHAPTER FIFTEEN

On the steps of the telegraph office Jonathan watched his footmen gather Amanda's purchases from her, his gaze all absorbed on the excitedly pretty picture she made. He shook his head; if only it were that easy to shake Amanda Lloyd from his mind, or the feeling of yearning that lent itself whenever she was near. He had all but forgotten the telegram in his breast pocket and was reaching for it when a hand touched his arm.

"Jonathan Brisbane, old pal!"

Startled, he turned to the man addressing him. "Linwood Crane! It's been awhile!" The old friends shook hands and Linwood's eyes followed Jonathan's line of vision, both men watching as Amanda hurried across the street.

"Hello." She smiled at the handsome man with Jonathan, so in contrast was he that one would be hard pressed not to smile at him. The eyes surveying her were blue against golden blond hair that curled at the nape of his neck; his face bare, except for a neat blond mustache. Though slightly shorter than Jonathan, he was solidly built. *One was silver and the other was gold....*The childhood phrase sprang immediately to mind.

Linwood Crane flashed his most winning smile, gathered up her hand and kissed its glove. "Charmed." He looked to Jonathan for introduction.

"Amanda Lloyd, allow me to present Linwood Crane, an old friend of mine."

"It's a pleasure to meet you, Mr. Crane."

Linwood took off his hat and bent again to her hand. "I assure you the pleasure is all mine, Miss Lloyd." He gave Jonathan a playful punch on the arm and raised an eyebrow. "Where have you been hiding this delectable beauty?" he asked, his eyes lingering on her until Amanda felt herself blush.

She had done more blushing in only twenty-four hours of 1884 than she had in her entire life in her own time! Her mother's wisdom slipped to mind once again. She had always said that women had given up something in their plight for equal rights, and that "something" Amanda decided, was chivalry.

"Are you from the South, Mr. Crane? I detect a light accent."

"Why yes, how perceptive of you."

Jonathan gritted his teeth in irritation. *Perceptive?* It was flirtatious stupidity and he was becoming downright angry at having to listen to their mindless prattle. With furious fingers, he tore open the telegram. All at once, his face turned the color of chalk, his eyes straining in disbelief at the words on the page.

"Not bad news, I trust?" Linwood put in quickly. He'd had enough of the never-ending gossip surrounding Jonathan. His friend did not deserve pity for his predicament, for it took a courageous man to withstand the turmoil directed at him.

It was several long moments before Jonathan spoke and it took all his effort just to voice a very slow, "No..."

Amanda looked from one man to the other and could sense something uncomfortable pass between them.

"Linwood," he said, his tone easy, but unconvincing, "you must come to Serenity this weekend. We are having a party. Mother is having the invitations dispatched as we speak. I have no doubt you are foremost on the list." He patted his friend on the back.

Linwood laughed, feeling slightly relieved. A party was certainly a good sign, and one that spoke of matters having improved at Serenity. "Are we marking a special occasion?"

Jonathan offered his arm to Amanda and the three started down the steps. "Miss Lloyd is a distant cousin of Thomas Edison's."

"I had no idea," Linwood replied in all seriousness, afraid he may have made a mistake in toying with her earlier. "Your cousin, Madam, is a genius."

They crossed the street and stopped when they reached the carriage. Amanda yanked herself away from Jonathan.

"Please, call me Amanda. I'd prefer it," she responded, easily dodging any questions regarding her so-called cousin.

Linwood nodded and turned again to Jonathan. "I look forward to your party and thank you for the invitation." He shook Jonathan's hand and tipped his hat to Amanda. "Until then."

CHAPTER SIXTEEN

"Well, you certainly made a perfect fool of yourself with Linwood Crane," Jonathan commented coolly as the carriage lobbed along the bumpy roads back to Serenity.

"Excuse me?" Amanda looked away from the window and directly met his eyes. "You have no right to speak to me that way. Who are you to pass judgment?"

"Your keeper, Miss Lloyd. You are my prisoner until I decide your fate."

"My fate is not in your hands!"

"That is where you are mistaken. You are a spy—an intruder in my home."

"In your *time*," she mumbled.

Jonathan grinned and nodded. "Ah, yes. How could I forget? You hail from the future," he taunted. "It slipped my mind completely. Some people hail from Maryland, Virginia, or even Washington...but not you, no...you hail from the future!" His laughter was near tears again.

"I wish I had been the bearer of that telegram," Amanda snapped, "that wiped that smug smile from your face!"

If she were a man, he would have struck her, and as Amanda noted his body stiffen and the blood rush to his cheeks, she felt her heart pound rapidly in real fear.

She hadn't planned for the words to come out that way. Maybe the telegram held some terrible news. Maybe it was so terrible it would hurt the people at Serenity; and what might bad news do to the wonderful Vivian? She wanted to apologize, but when she opened her mouth, nothing came out. Her thoughts drifted back to the women in the shop. What had they meant by their remarks? *And who is Lavinia?*

It was not Amanda's outburst that had angered Jonathan, but the remainder of the telegram and the distress it would issue. *Lavinia!* He closed his eyes tightly, his mind racing at ways to avert what surely lay ahead. How would he break the news to his mother? Vivian would be livid.

Amanda stared openly at Jonathan, hoping to read what thoughts he was lost to. She had chosen a sorry way to find out the contents of the telegram. Taking a deep breath, she bit her lower lip in regret, her eyes still envisioning the look of shock on his face on the steps of the telegraph office.

CHAPTER SEVENTEEN

The house was a bustle of activity. Servants moved about in nearly every room of the first and second floors of Serenity in preparation for the party. Silver was polished, linen pressed, furniture dusted. Caught up in the excitement, Amanda rushed passed them through the grand hallway and up the stairs to her room, anxious to show Renee what she had purchased.

Jonathan, however, sequestered himself in his study on the first floor to secure his privacy. Taking off his jacket, he tossed it over a nearby chair and sank into the soft leather one behind his desk. He took the telegram out with trembling hands and stared down once more at the parchment.

Was the Almighty punishing him? First the spy, and now Lavinia! He had been a good son, a good barrister, and a good friend, he reasoned. In fact, in all due modesty, he believed he had always been a good man, even an honorable one. Amanda Lloyd was trouble; he knew so from the beginning. But Lavinia was trouble personified! Propping his elbow on the desk, he leaned his head into his hand and gently rubbed his forehead. His head ached, worse since the telegram, as so many thoughts raced through his mind.

Lavinia was coming back! Just when he had been sure all was over and done with and that their mockery of a marriage was truly a dying memory, she was coming back. *Marriage*! The very word did not describe life with Lavinia. Less than a year after the nuptials, she had requested a divorce. Lavinia had set a precedent in having a divorce granted her in the state of New Jersey. The very idea made his stomach turn and he felt the bile rise to his throat. Reaching over to the china pitcher, he poured forth water and took a long drink. This could not be happening! He looked down at the page once more, Lavinia's plea for reconciliation as stark and bold as the woman herself. He leaned back into the soft leather and rang for Alan as a thought popped to mind. Had the final documents been signed?

* * *

Upstairs, Amanda was dizzy with excitement as Renee unwrapped her purchases. Lifting one of the dresses from the bed, Renee frowned. Could it be the same? She put down the blue one and picked up the striking red one. Her frown deepened and she turned to Amanda who sat at the vanity unpinning her cumbersome hat.

"Excuse me, Miss Amanda, but these dresses..."

Amanda turned, her smile quickly fading as she noted the alarm on Renee's pretty face. "What's wrong with them?" She joined her by the bed and picked at the silky material of the red dress. "I think this one would be perfect for the party, don't you?" She smiled, but Renee's eyes only blinked several times. "Renee, what is the problem? Please tell me!" She plopped down on the bed. Was it a *faux pas* in 1884 to wear dresses designed for someone else?

Both women turned to acknowledge the light tap on the door. Vivian sailed in and stopped abruptly, her face contorting in suppressed rage.

"My Lord! How did those get into this house?" She walked to the bed and stared down at the dresses as if recalling something Amanda could only envision was positively despicable. She looked from Amanda to Renee who backed away several steps. "Well? I want some answers!"

Renee shrugged, wishing she could shrink from the room.

"I bought the dresses from Crocker's Clothier, Vivian," Amanda explained.

"The audacity of that woman to take advantage of our family this way!" Vivian turned to the bewildered Amanda. "It is certainly not your fault, dear. The Crocker woman probably wanted these gowns away from her establishment as much as I want them out of here." Her face softened and she smiled at Amanda, her hand lightly brushing Amanda's cheek. "Surely you do not intend to wear these? Didn't you order material for Lottie to work on?"

"Yes, of course. But, I planned on wearing the red one to the party."

"I won't hear of it. You will wear a new creation that is designed for you. Lottie will just have to make haste with her fingers."

"Why?" Amanda picked up the red dress. "This would look wonderful, I'm sure. I can't impose on your seamstress on such short notice."

"Lottie is paid well for her services," Vivian replied simply.

Amanda sighed evenly. The blue dress was OK, but she desperately wanted to wear the red one to the party.

"I was told by a Mrs. West that the woman who ordered these wouldn't be coming back for them."

"Frances had a hand in this? I should have known." Without further explanation, she asked Renee to remove the dresses and turned back to Amanda. "I do not expect you to understand, Amanda, and I do not intend to offer explanation at this time." She sat down and gathered Amanda's hands into her own. "You are special, my dear, and you deserve special gowns."

Amanda nodded. It was difficult not to defer to Vivian's wishes. She was, after all, a guest in the woman's home. "Very well," she resigned.

"Good. Now, as you saw upon your return, the staff is busy. Invitations are being dispatched this very day!" She was beaming now, elated at the prospect of a party at Serenity. "We are in need of raising spirits around here."

Amanda laughed. "I hope not the kind Madame Winston is likely to conjure!"

Vivian laughed along with her. "I should hope not!" She patted her hand. "Now, come with me. Ruth heard of your glowing comments on her culinary skills and wishes to make your acquaintance."

※

CHAPTER EIGHTEEN

Not hearing Jonathan's command to enter, Alan opened the study door to find his employer frantically searching the drawers of his desk.

"Is there something I can help you with, sir?" Alan stood by the door for several long moments before his distracted employer acknowledged his presence. When Jonathan finally looked up, it was clear to Alan that something was terribly wrong.

"Come in, Alan, and close the door behind you." Jonathan motioned for him to sit. "I have information I need to confide to you and it is sure to test your loyalty. However, I have no one else to turn to and do not wish to distress my mother." He pushed the telegram to Alan and ran his fingers through his hair.

Alan's gray eyes darkened, and his mouth opened and closed without a word as he took in the information.

"Blasted! I know I secured the papers somewhere!" Jonathan boomed while continuing his search.

"Papers, sir?" Alan finally found his voice, realizing that Jonathan Brisbane surely needed the voice of reason right now.

"The documents, Alan! The documents for the divorce!" He spat the words and looked up through tortured eyes. "They were fully executed; I could swear so!"

In his typical manner, Alan drew himself up and pulled confidently at the hem of his vest. "If you will recall, Mr. Brisbane, you had Mr. Crane take charge of them," he offered in the hope of refreshing his employer's memory.

"Mr. Crane? Ah...yes. But, what was wrong with my own safe?"

"You wanted no further reminder of *her* in Serenity, sir. You were quite adamant..."

"Yes, yes. Well, we must contact Mr. Crane at once. Only today I ran into him at the telegraph office. Get right on it, will you, Alan?"

"Yes, sir, of course." Alan rose, but stood by the chair his hand resting on the back of it.

Jonathan looked up from the mounds of paper on his desk, hastily shoving them back into order. "That will be all, Alan."

"Excuse me, Mr. Brisbane, but what about the spy, sir?"

Jonathan groaned. "She is the least of my concerns right now. I will deal with her eventually."

Though Alan made repeated attempts to contact Linwood Crane, they were futile. The man was out of town for the duration of the week and would not be available until the very night of Vivian's party.

CHAPTER NINETEEN

Amanda Lloyd had never seen a kitchen as large as the one Ruth and her team worked in. Heavy iron pots hung suspended around one wall nearest the brick oven, and running water was piped into a basin by a curious pump. In the center of the kitchen stood two large butcher-block tables where the present activity was taking place. From table to stove to sink to butlery, the steps these people had to take would be exhausting to those in Amanda's indulgent century. She wrinkled her nose dreamily at the welcome blend of spices like vanilla and cinnamon, the pungent aroma of sausages and onion—a virtual potpourri of kitchen magic assaulting her all at once.

Ruth was a robust Irish woman, who, despite her weight, managed her steps swiftly and easily in her efficient environment. Her red hair was pulled severely back into a bun, her entire head covered by white netting. Blue eyes bulging through her plump face, she grinned widely as she noted Amanda's complimentary survey of her kitchen.

"How do you ever remember where everything is?" Amanda marveled. "One could get easily lost in this wonderful kitchen."

"Oh, Miss Amanda, you flatter me." The key ring around her apron jingled noisily as she spread her dough back and forth with a large rolling pin.

"Am I to assume you also know the lock for every key on your ring?" Amanda asked as one of Ruth's assistants placed a cup of tea in front of her and pulled out a chair for her to sit.

"I've been here twenty years and know every key by heart," she answered proudly, her face turning a bright red, which Amanda assumed was more from exertion than flattery.

"Maybe you can show me the rooms on the third floor," Amanda requested as she blew into her cup before bringing it up to her lips. "That part of the house appears to be closed off."

Ruth looked up from her task and pushed the rolling pin aside as she prepared the dough into a round baking pan. "I have no keys for that wing. Alan and Mr. Brisbane have the only ones."

"Why is that?"

"That is the floor Mr. Edison occupies on his visits." Ruth handed the pan to yet another assistant who brought it to her station to fill with fruit, and then began rolling dough again. "Of course, you being Mr. Edison's cousin, I'm sure Mr. Brisbane would give you a tour himself."

"Of course. I should have thought of that," she lied.

Amanda continued to watch the assembly line with interest—the next pie being filled with meat—but did not want to overstay her welcome. Though Ruth had entertained her with polite conversation, it was time she left the woman to her business.

"It was a pleasure chatting with you, Ruth."

Ruth looked up from her work, her apron creamed over with flour. "Come visit my kitchen again, Miss Amanda."

Amanda walked slowly back to the front of the house. Passing the parlor doors, she heard Vivian's voice rise.

"Hasn't she caused this family enough embarrassment and scandal? Why, people are *still* talking!"

"My concerns are not with the thoughts of other people, Mother," Jonathan replied.

Amanda leaned toward the partially open parlor door. Vivian was pacing back and forth, her long blue skirt swishing as she nervously twisted her hands together.

"Well, she is not welcome in this house!" She stopped abruptly, panic ceasing reason. "You must do something, Jon," she pleaded. "You must make sure she does not come near Serenity again."

Jonathan clenched his back teeth together, his jaw tightening at the very idea of Lavinia back at Serenity. "According to her message, she is still my wife and wishes to reconcile." The very word terrified him.

"And what of the documents you mentioned? Surely you have them safely secured?"

"I gave them to Linwood Crane for safekeeping. I do not know what Lavinia is planning, but I intend to prevent her from disrupting our lives again."

Hearing his footsteps move toward the door, Amanda nearly ran up the grand staircase. So, Lavinia had been Jonathan's wife! Maybe that was why God had thrust her into this time. Maybe Lavinia was her mission. She drew in a quick breath at the top of the stairs and gulped for air as she remembered the dresses that had upset Vivian. They obviously belonged to Lavinia, she thought, recalling the conversation she had overheard at Crocker's Clothier. Well, she had to help this family and try to protect them from this woman who meant them harm.

It was then that she made a silent promise to herself to prevent Lavinia from hurting anyone at Serenity. How she would accomplish that, she hadn't a clue. But, how devious could this woman be? Amanda, herself, was a century ahead in that department. Surely, that kind of knowledge accounted for something. Smiling inwardly, she opened the door to her room and changed for supper.

"Where is Vivian?" Amanda asked, uncomfortable at being alone with Jonathan at the long dining table.

Jonathan looked up at her and frowned. "Mother has decided to take supper in her room this evening. Probably the excitement of the party," he offered stiffly. Why did this spy have to look so damn beautiful, he thought. Susan's yellow dress seemed to fit her like a glove—snugly around her breasts and waist. He was sure she wore no corset and silently cursed himself for wondering what was binding her beneath the soft material. Stabbing at his potato, he put his head back down and tried to concentrate on the meal before him. He needed to be strong, and the lovely woman at his table could easily prove a threat to that strength.

"How are your...eyes?" she asked, daintily bringing her wine goblet up to her lips and sipping.

Jonathan glared up at her, his eyes changing from light green to blue to dark gray and back to green in one quick moment. His muscles tightened as he recalled his strange encounter with the poison in her purse. The longer he stared, the more uncomfortable Amanda became, but she did not back down. Her eyes remained locked to his.

"I wish you would allow me to explain."

Jonathan put down his fork. "Miss Lloyd, since your arrival my house has been wrought with unpleasantness. I have no intention of sharing anything of a personal nature with you. Your explanation will only fall on deaf ears." He got up and walked to where she sat, his tall frame looming over her as he leaned in, one hand grasping the end of a nearby chair, the knuckles white as he attempted to control his fury. "You are not here as a guest, but as an intruder. You are only at my table for the sake of my mother. Try to bear that in mind in the future." He started to walk to the door.

"Mine or yours?" she asked.

"Excuse me?" He turned at the entrance and glared at her.

"Whose future are you referring to...mine or yours?"

He slammed the door behind him and Amanda could hear a growl, followed by a loud crash. She jerked her head up and stared, cringing at the door.

※

CHAPTER TWENTY

The material Amanda had ordered arrived on schedule and Vivian immediately put Lottie to work. Once the measurements were dispensed with, Amanda decided to take a stroll in the gardens. The air was crisp yet warm, and it was a fine spring day. The current of air felt cool against Susan's cotton dress—the pink one Amanda had worn on her first day—and she let the breeze gently brush through her long unbound hair. Spying a bench nearby, she sat down and breathed deeply. Yes, there was certainly a drastic difference between her time and this one, and it wasn't just the people or Serenity, but the air! It was pure and clean, and the sky was so much bluer. This would be what she would miss most when she finally left this time; and she was sure she would, once her mission was accomplished.

"Amanda!"

Vivian approached her slowly, and upon closer observation, Amanda noted Vivian's eyes were red and puffy. She occasionally dabbed at them with the handkerchief that twisted in her nervous hands.

"Vivian, are you all right?" Amanda reached out and clasped her hand.

"As right as a mother can be under the circumstances." She sat down beside Amanda on the bench. "For a brief moment as I walked toward you, I thought you were the specter of my Susan. I imagine it is the dress."

"I'm sorry."

"You have nothing to be sorry for, my dear. I just miss Susan so very much."

Tears welled up in her eyes. "It was merely wishful thinking on my part." She blew into her handkerchief and wiped a single tear from her eye before it had the chance to descend onto her lovely blue dress. "Susan and I often sat on this very bench to chat." A smile curled the corners of her mouth as if reminiscing a particularly fond moment.

"You must have loved her very much."

"I love both my children with equal passion, Amanda. My dear Jonathan is a model son and a good man. If only matters were not beyond repair for him, things would be different."

"What is beyond repair?"

Vivian searched Amanda's trusting face. It was unfair to burden her with problems clearly relating only to the Brisbane family. Then, as if on second thought, she began to talk and once her words poured forth, there was no stopping her.

"Jonathan was married, you see, to Lavinia Ashton, a woman from Atlanta. Introductions were offered by Linwood Crane whose family she was visiting in the spring of...'83, I believe it was." She shook her head as if to jar loose the cobwebs of Lavinia's marriage to her son.

Amanda noted the pained look on Vivian's face as the woman embarked on awakening a memory she would rather remained buried. She placed a hand over Vivian's and patted it, a role reversal seeming to take place between them.

"She seemed such a sweet young woman," Vivian continued. "She was shy and coy and quite well mannered too. She set her sights on Jonathan and their courtship was a speedy one. The truth be known, she stole herself right into his heart. Before her month at the Cranes' was up, Jonathan proposed and they became engaged, marrying in such haste that one would suspect a spell had been cast upon them."

Her mouth set into a tight line and her eyes darkened as the memory unfolded. "It was a loveless marriage. From the moment they were united, Lavinia refused him the marital bed." Vivian watched Amanda's eyes widen. "A mother knows," she said simply. "Besides, Lavinia had her own room on the third floor, which was certainly suspect."

Amanda stopped her. "The third floor? But, Ruth told me that floor was reserved for Mister...for my cousin."

"Mr. Edison did not come to visit Serenity after Jonathan married Lavinia, and she was positively shrewish on the matter of separate rooms. Jonathan could not stand much more of her temper and informed the staff of the new arrangements." She shook her head sadly. "Oh, and to think that our poor staff was subjected to such unreasonable demands while under Lavinia's instruction!" She took a deep breath and bit her lower lip as the recall drove itself home for a second time. "Lavinia did not want Jonathan near her—could hardly tolerate being in the same room with him. Personally, I doubt their marriage was ever consummated."

"What changed her?" Amanda asked. "I mean, why marry a man you don't love?" Amanda herself could not imagine any woman not wanting Jonathan Brisbane. For all his suspicions of her, which were justified to a certain extent, he could put his shoes under her bed anytime! *Lord! What am I thinking?* Her heart began to hammer rapidly at the thought of being held in his arms—she could actually see his shoes under her bed. Unwillingly, her hand came up to her chest at the vividness of the picture.

Vivian took her reaction as shock, for which Amanda was grateful. "Serenity," she answered simply.

"Serenity? You mean this Serenity?" she asked, her hand sweeping across the acres in front of them.

"I mean money, my dear Amanda. Lavinia's motive was money. Her family had lost it all in the war. Her intention was to restore her plantation home in Atlanta to its original glory, and for that, she would need a great deal of currency. In short, she was—is—an opportunist with a single goal in mind."

Amanda soaked in this new information and immediately understood why Ella Crocker and Frances West had referred to him as poor Jonathan. Indeed! What rejection he had suffered. What hurt he had endured!

"Did he truly love her?" Amanda found she could not look into Vivian's eyes for fear of the answer.

Vivian smiled, the thought of Amanda's interest in her son coming to the forefront for the very first time. "No," she stated firmly. "Jonathan was swept away by the amorous attention of a beautiful and devious woman. Men are not adverse to flattery themselves, my dear."

"What happened then?" Amanda asked, as she nearly pleaded for the rest of the story.

Vivian stood. "Let's walk."

"Please don't leave the story half finished."

Vivian looped her arm through Amanda's as they strolled lazily up the stone walk back to the house. "Linwood Crane, who had been dismayed by the union, came forth with information that Lavinia was a woman of questionable morals. Jonathan confronted her, appropriately during a thunderstorm, though the storm inside the front parlor was far worse, I assure you. He felt betrayed and he was finally convinced that money was Lavinia's only reason for marrying him, and he told her so. She laughed at him, verbally taunting him with details of her affairs, right to his face! Soon after, Jonathan informed her that he had closed out all of her financial accounts in town. Lavinia sought a divorce."

"That was a good thing, wasn't it?"

Vivian looked over at her curiously. "On the contrary. It just isn't done, Amanda! Surely you should know that."

"Yes, of course," Amanda apologized, deciding to keep such opinions to herself.

"It was a terrible scandal," Vivian continued. "Lavinia left that very night and we never saw her again. The only time we heard from her was through her representative of counsel when the documents arrived formally requesting Jonathan to divorce her."

"On what grounds?"

"As audacious as it appears, she claimed her husband did not fulfill his marital duties."

"How dreadful!" *The bitch!*

"Now you understand why I reacted in alarm when I saw the dresses you brought home."

Amanda nodded.

"Lavinia tried to retrieve them from Ella Crocker's shop, but without credit she was forced to leave them behind." Vivian pursed her lips tightly together. "The red dress, in particular. It wasn't much, but for Jonathan there was some revenge in that action."

They had reached the house and Vivian thought it prudent to end her soliloquy. "Enough, dear." She patted Amanda's arm. "That's all I have to say..."

"No, there's more."

They entered the house and stood inside the front hall. Vivian turned and stared at her. "Now, it is I who does not understand."

"You were crying, Vivian. I think Susan was only part of the reason." She hesitated a moment, her voice a whisper. "I know about the telegram."

The statement wet Vivian's eyes again. "Then you know she is returning, and that she is determined to reconcile," she whispered in return.

"But, how? They are divorced."

"Jonathan gave the documents to Linwood Crane for safekeeping and in order to prevent Lavinia from coming to Serenity, he must have them in his possession."

"Surely, that isn't a problem?"

"Jonathan informed me that he dispatched word through Alan, but Linwood is out of town. Word won't reach him until he arrives for the party."

"Alan should have left word..."

"No! Dear me, we have had enough scandal in this family. The news would travel quickly and refresh the gossip in town."

Amanda shook her head, at once deciding not to add to Jonathan's grief, no matter how he might bait her. She felt she understood his bitterness—understood more about the man who, she was reluctant to admit, had stolen himself into her own heart. It was a resolution she intended to keep.

* * *

Hidden in the shadows of the front parlor, Jonathan Brisbane sighed inwardly as he listened to their conversation. He found himself torn in his feelings. He knew Vivian needed a friend, preferably a woman, to share her feelings with. And he didn't really mind that Amanda's convenience at Serenity provided that relief. What disturbed him was that Amanda Lloyd might come to pity him, and that was something he would not accept. Not from anyone.

CHAPTER TWENTY-ONE

The rain lightly rapped against the bedroom window like tiny pulsating fingers as Amanda paced back and forth relentlessly across her room. She had chosen to remain in there on this the day of the party, and with the exception of coffee, had refused the meals Renee left on the table outside her door. Her talk with Vivian had been two days ago and by now it was evident that word had not reached Linwood Crane in time to foil Lavinia's pending arrival.

Standing in front of the fireplace, Amanda hugged the blue wrapper around her body. She rubbed her hands vigorously up and down her arms, barely feeling the soft velvet of the garment Lottie had painstakingly adorned with lovely white lace.

She could not shake the chill from her body. The rain only made her feel colder, the fire hardly capable of casting away the feeling of foreboding that had assaulted her from the moment she opened her eyes.

Surely, there must be something I can do, she pleaded with herself for the umpteenth time; some way to make Lavinia think twice about remaining at Serenity. If she could just get to her purse, she might find something in there to squelch Lavinia's triumphant return. Her features contorted as she screwed up her face in displeasure. Jonathan would never allow it.

So, what do I do now, pace around this damn room and stare into the fire for answers? Fire. Red. The dress!

"That's it!" she shrieked, stopping her pace. "I'll just have to fight fire with fire—1884 style!"

As if in confirmation, the rain stopped its infernal battering against the window as the sun peeked through a dark cloud. Though she knew Vivian would disapprove, she rang for Renee and requested the red dress.

"She will understand, Renee," Amanda explained at the look of uncertainty on the young woman's face.

"Well, I don't." Both women turned to find Jonathan standing at the open door. With a nod to Amanda, Renee slipped past. "May I come in?"

"It's your house." Amanda sat down in the green wingback chair and self-consciously crossed her legs, unaware of the wrapper sliding open.

Jonathan stared at her a few moments, his eyes unwillingly traveling down to the white skin of her exposed legs. He cleared his throat and closed the door soundly behind him. Amanda followed his eyes and silently cursed herself for feeling so nervous. Why had he shut the door? Certainly, it was not proper for him to be alone with her in the bedroom. Then she remembered her promise to be kinder, and to not let him best her into an argument. She stifled her objection.

"What is it you don't understand?" she asked instead, her smile warm and inviting.

He hadn't expected the smile, and could not prevent the one he returned. She looked so damned sweet when she smiled, and the wrapper draped her sweetness in a blue light, her hair flowing loosely about her shoulders like a dark silken cape.

"I don't understand why you have not chosen to take your meals with us," he answered, trying hard to sound impatient. And, indeed, looking at the beguiling picture of her made that very difficult.

Amanda sighed evenly. "I'm sorry, Jonathan, I just don't have an appetite."

He walked farther into the room until he was standing right in front of her. She stared innocently up at him. Slowly, he encircled an arm on either side of her chair and leaned into her, his face mere inches away. She felt her body tense as his eyes locked to hers.

"What are you up to, Amanda Lloyd." It was more a whispered statement than a question.

Since Vivian's heart-wrenching tale, Amanda was seeing Jonathan in a new light—seeing softness behind the sober facade. He looked so crisp and clean in his light gray suit. Leaning in the way he was now, Amanda could smell the faint scent of bay rum. What a gorgeous man, she thought as her pulse quickened at his closeness. When God created Jonathan Brisbane He knew exactly what he was doing.

Amanda could not help what she did next as she slid her hand shakily up to his cheek, and then tenderly traced her palm down the side of his handsome face, around his angular jaw. His own hand reached up and held hers in check, the contact of fingers against fingers sending tiny electric currents through her body. Gently, he brushed his lips against hers and Amanda found herself holding her breath in anticipation. He did not disappoint her as his kiss deepened and she could sense his desire as his lips burned against hers.

Jonathan broke the kiss and Amanda opened her eyes to find him standing upright, his hands in his pockets, his eyes nervously inspecting his shoes.

"I'm sorry," he whispered.

"Don't be," she squeaked, her breath returning in a rush.

Looking up, he laughed. "You are a curious woman, Amanda Lloyd, albeit a beautiful one."

She smiled. "Thank you, I think." She stared waiting, for what, she wasn't sure. Right then she felt so very vulnerable, so torn between conflicting emotions. She could sense the same discomposure in Jonathan as she watched him draw a watch from the front pocket of his vest and flip it open.

"It's nearly five. Madame Winston will be arriving soon. I...I'll leave you to tend to your toilette," he stammered, the statement prophetic as Renee called gently through the door.

Jonathan opened it and could see the blood rush to Renee's embarrassed cheeks as she glanced from one to the other.

"Excuse me, Mr. Brisbane, but..."

Jonathan put up a hand to silence her, his mood quite light considering his circumstances. "I was only here a moment, Renee, and I am leaving." He rubbed his hands together briskly. "We're having a party at Serenity!" He grinned, then, and gave Renee a wink, catching the young woman off guard, never once noticing the red dress in her arms.

As he looked back at Amanda, his grin widened and he shook his head. No woman had a right to look that beautiful. Reluctantly, he pulled his eyes away and left the room.

Remembering his kiss, Amanda smiled. *Don't beam me up yet, Scottie.*

CHAPTER TWENTY-TWO

In Amanda's time, psychic mediums were plentiful and popular. So popular that two psychic mediums even had television shows where they acted as willing hosts to spirits who popped in and out looking for validation. Amanda herself had sought one out after her parents' fatal accident, but her experience had been brief and inconclusive in its results.

In this century, the "real" psychic medium was revered because it was the beginning of the spiritualist movement and many were discovered to be frauds. Amanda vowed to keep an open mind, as even in her time Madame Winston was legendary. Though she knew little about Madame Winston's life, what she did know indicated that the medium's reputation was beyond reproach.

An Italian who married English nobility, Madame Yolanda Winston was highly respected and instrumental in aiding Scotland Yard. Her impressive career already spanned thirty years. A tall, solid woman, the medium was not what Amanda had expected. Dressed entirely in black, her hair was uncharacteristically short and sprinkled with gray; her face white and smooth against plump pink lips. But, it was her eyes that were disarming. They were a deep emerald green that seemed to sear right through whatever they looked at.

"Amanda Lloyd, allow me to present Madame Winston."

Jonathan had to nearly push Amanda into the front parlor, but not before he whispered, "You look absolutely enchanting" into her ear. He watched her exchange with Madame Winston with keen interest, wondering what the renowned medium would think of his beautiful presumed time traveler. His smile gave Amanda confidence and she shot out her hand to the imposing medium. Vivian clucked when she eyed the dress; through she had to admit it certainly looked lovely on Amanda.

Madame Winston stared deeply into Amanda's eyes. "Miss Lloyd," she slowly acknowledged while clasping both her hands over Amanda's. "I understand you are a cousin of Mr. Thomas Edison."

Amanda felt her throat closing up at the lie Madame Winston had been told. Behind her, she heard Jonathan snicker.

"Madame Winston, it is an honor to meet you." Her voice shook as she became increasingly uncomfortable with the woman's hold on her hand. Amanda was sure they would have stayed that way had Alan not announced the arrival of other guests.

"Your journey has certainly been a long one," Madame Winston commented, patting Amanda's hand in a knowing manner. "I suggest we begin as soon as possible." She turned from the startled Amanda as Vivian introduced her to the new arrivals.

Jonathan watched with renewed interest as the color left Amanda's cheeks, the medium's words hanging questioningly in the air.

Could this woman actually sense—*know*—that she did not belong in this century? For reasons she could not fathom, something familiar had passed through

Amanda at the woman's touch; something she could not identify.

"Amanda!"

She turned around at the greeting to find Linwood Crane standing beside Jonathan, both men dressed in black evening clothes and equally handsome. A smile claimed her lips at the obvious rivalry between the two friends. They must have had some battles in vying for female attention, she thought wryly.

"Linwood, how are you?"

"Wonderful, now that I've seen you! You look positively ravishing!" He leaned forward and kissed her hand.

Jonathan groaned loudly and rolled his eyes. "Excuse us," he interrupted. "Linwood and I have some business to discuss. We won't be long."

Amanda nodded and was swiftly swept away by Vivian who looped her arm through Amanda's to introduce her to the other guests. She reacquainted herself with Frances West and was introduced to her stuffy husband, Gerard, a man quite hard of hearing. The others became a blur of names for Amanda as Vivian hastily introduced her. There were the Van Treeses, the Warners, and the Bakers. *All we need are the candlestick makers*, Amanda mused.

The rain descended once again as a light patter tapped against the windows. It seemed that no matter when Amanda glanced her way, Madame Winston's eyes were on her and she would nod, increasing Amanda's discomfort.

* * *

Jonathan wasted no time in getting to the point once he and Linwood were safely behind the closed doors of his study. "Alan tried to get word to you all week," he explained, motioning for Linwood to take a seat.

"I was away on business." He watched as Jonathan reached into his desk, pulled out the telegram, and pushed it forward. Linwood shook his head. "I have a feeling I know what it says."

"Read it." He leaned back in his leather chair as his mind once again tried to come to terms with the telegram.

Linwood scanned it quickly. "Lavinia is out of her mind," he confirmed through clenched teeth.

Jonathan leaned forward, his hands clasped confidently in front of him. "I trust you have the documents secured?"

Linwood slowly folded the telegram and shook his head. "No," he said simply.

"What do you mean, no?"

"There was a small fire," Linwood began. "The wall safe was destroyed. All my papers went up in flames."

"Are you telling me that my divorce decree is gone?" Jonathan asked, incredulously.

"Yes. My business trip had much to do with what was lost." He sighed evenly. "I had hoped to secure a copy of your documents before you were aware they were missing. Unfortunately, it will take at least two weeks before they arrive."

"Two weeks!" Jonathan pulled his fingers through his hair. "Two weeks with Lavinia is enough to kill the strongest of men." He slammed his fist on the desk.

"Jonathan, calm down. You are still divorced from her. It is only paper we are talking about."

Slowly, the muscles relaxed in his face. What good would it do to be angry with Linwood? It was his own fault for not keeping the documents under his own roof.

"Who is suspect?" he asked, for he did not believe the fire was an accident.

"How did you..." Linwood stared into his friend's eyes. "Rachel, the upstairs maid, I should have known. She was Lavinia's trusted servant while in your home."

"I interrogated her at great length."

"And no doubt you discovered Lavinia paid her handsomely for her deed, is my guess." Jonathan frowned. "What good does that do me now?"

Linwood smiled sheepishly. "She told me of Lavinia's plan to return to Serenity tonight. While away, I managed to, well, let's just say I made certain her arrival would be delayed a couple of days while she scrambles to locate her trunk."

Jonathan actually laughed out loud at his friend's boldness. "Good man! A reprieve will at least buy me some time." He rose and walked around the desk. "Then let this séance begin. Maybe the illustrious Madame Winston can provide us with some answers." He smiled at the thought and patted Linwood on the back as the two left the study to join the party.

CHAPTER TWENTY-THREE

The windows rattled as the wind whipped the rain against the house, bearing down on it in torrential fury. The small group gathered around the circular table in the ballroom to begin the formal séance. White candles had been strategically placed along the sideboards and in windows. The candelabra on the table cast a mystical glow upon the room, embracing its occupants in gloomy shadows. Madame Winston sat down and pointed for Vivian to sit to her left; next to her was Linwood, and beside him, directly across from the medium herself, Amanda. Jonathan sat to Amanda's left, then Frances and Gerard West, the Van Treeses, the Warners, and completing the circle, the Bakers.

Though in her own century Amanda did not take the spiritual realm of prophesy very seriously, in 1884 they apparently did, as she scanned the somber faces of the true believers around her. In truth, she was not entirely skeptical, for she could certainly not explain the very fact that she was living in the nineteenth century!

"Please join hands and do not break the circle," Madame Winston instructed.

Flanked on either side by Linwood and Jonathan, Amanda felt a sense of relief wash over her as each clasped hands. Madame Winston took a deep breath and closed her eyes.

"We ask our angels and spirit friends for guidance, and to protect us from the darkness beyond our vision."

A silence fell over the room as Madame Winston's head rolled from side to side and her body relaxed. Frances West nervously giggled.

"Ssh!" Vivian softly scolded.

Frances stifled her nervousness and primly set her mouth tightly closed, a difficult task for the normally wordy woman. It was several long minutes before the medium spoke again, eyes still closed.

"Frances West, hold your tongue and refrain from gossip," came the stem reprimand. "If you do not heed the words of your guide you will regret your interference in the lives of others."

"Humph!" Frances did not take this information kindly and did not like being the center of attention. "She's just guessing," she remarked in a whisper into Gerard's deaf ear.

Once again, Vivian hushed her.

"Linwood Crane, you have exercised good judgment. The guides tell me you have detained the deceiver," continued Madame Winston.

Thunder silenced Linwood's rebuttal and everyone but Jonathan jumped at the roar as a bolt of lightning sliced by one of the windows. Linwood's body stiffened and Amanda could feel his hands sweating over her own. The medium's eyes remained closed though those around her squinted into the partial darkness in search of her expression. She had none. She had not even flinched. Amanda glanced over at Jonathan whose resolve was as cool as his hand.

"Vivian, you are too kind," Madame announced. "The guides warn you to keep up your guard. And Jonathan, you must beware of the deceiver as well, for she knows you from a mutual past and is returning to reclaim you."

Jonathan's hands tightened over Vivian's and Amanda's, both women looking over at his face, which clearly displayed his displeasure at this declaration. He was about to break the circle when Madame Winston's voice stopped him, her eyes flying open and searing straight through to Amanda.

"You...Miss Lloyd...are...a...stranger," she said with slow and deliberate words. "You know too much and that is because you have no...future." Her green eyes held Amanda's compassionately.

Amanda's face blanched and a silent alarm went off in her head as her hands began to tremble. All eyes turned toward her as the medium continued.

"You have a mission here, though the guides are not clear on what that mission is. You must keep up your guard, for the deceiver will despise you. This warning comes from one who loves you."

"Who?" It was Vivian's voice that rose softly in question.

Madame Winston's eyes never left Amanda's as she spoke the name clearly.

"Kendall."

Amanda winced at the mention of her mother's name—a mother who had yet to be born, let alone, die! With a swiftness born of panic, she tore her hands from both men, broke the circle, and ran from the room and up the grand staircase before anyone could stop her.

"I imagine Amanda found the session disagreeable," apologized Vivian as Alan pushed the gas lamps up to fully light the room again. "Who is Kendall?" she asked while leading the group into the dining room for refreshments.

The medium offered no reply.

"Maybe I should go to her," Vivian fretted.

"She needs time to herself," replied Madame Winston. "Leave her to her thoughts."

There was much mumbling from the Van Treeses and the Bakers who felt decidedly cheated.

"Breaking the circle was a selfish act," complained Mrs. Van Treese.

"Yes," agreed Mrs. Baker.

Madame Winston shook her head wearily and requested a few moments in the parlor to compose herself. Jonathan was quick to offer assistance. She linked her arm through his as he led the way. He was anxious to be alone with the woman who so blatantly spat out his circumstances and had forced Amanda to flee. He sighed inwardly as he remembered the look of horror on Amanda's face. He would have to deal with that later. Right now, he wanted some answers.

Yolanda Winston sat into the soft wingback chair in front of the fireplace, her weight heavily leaning into the cushions. Jonathan poked at the fire; the burning logs crackling in an instant.

"That was certainly an impressive performance," he remarked before sitting down in the chair opposite her.

"Performance?" She drew herself up, clearly insulted. "I am not an actor, Mr. Brisbane. I have the gift of second sight and I use it to help others."

"Forgive me, I meant no disrespect." He leaned back comfortably and drew out a cheroot from his pocket, his look to her a question of permission.

She nodded.

"Thank you." Puffing quietly, Jonathan waited as the woman took in several calming breaths. "Tell me, Madame, what is your impression of our Miss Lloyd?"

"She is a lovely young woman," she replied while opening the small pocket purse at her waist and removing a small string of prayer beads. "My way of thanking the Lord," she said smiling in explanation.

Jonathan nodded and waited a few moments before asking his first question. "You said Miss Lloyd knows too much. I thought that odd." He leaned forward and made eye contact. "Is she, perhaps, a spy?" Asking the question no longer seemed important, as in his heart he was finding it difficult to believe it himself, yet he sought this woman's confirmation.

Madame Winston merely smiled.

"You know...she claims to be from...the future. What do you make of that?" He watched her face carefully. If she was surprised, she did not show it.

"I think, Mr. Brisbane, that she is an honest and trustworthy person. One could learn much from her." Rising slowly, she reached out a bejeweled hand. "It is time we joined the others."

* * *

Upstairs, Amanda paced in front of the fire in agitation. *She knows! Dear God, why did she say I have no future? What mission am I on in this century?* And how, she thought, could Madame Winston know anything of Kendall Lloyd, a woman who did not even exist yet! How could her mother possibly be sending her a message when she had yet to be born? *This is becoming impossible. I have to get my things and get the hell out of here!*

Amanda slowly opened the bedroom door and peered up and down the hallway before stepping out of the room. Laughter lightly drifted up to her from the floor below. At the end of the hallway, she turned the knob on the door leading to the third floor. It had never occurred to her that the door would be unlocked, yet it was, and a feeling of hope lifted her softly up the stairs.

CHAPTER TWENTY-FOUR

Jonathan had excused himself from the gathering and headed directly up to the third floor and the room where he had secured Amanda's weapon and handbag. He stood before his open safe and stared at the contents, Madame Winston's comments echoing in his mind.

What had she meant by saying he could learn much from Amanda? If she was the honest and trustworthy person Madame Winston saw, then she certainly could not be a spy. He strained his eyes as if to see through the large tapestry bag Amanda said was her purse, and shook his head.

Amanda stood by the partially open door watching, unable to look away from where he stood by the safe—her eyes resting only on him, never seeing the room beyond him. She slowly shook her head. So, it had finally come to this: a showdown between them. How else would she be able to retrieve what belonged to her if she didn't confront him? How would she get back to her own time? The last question appeared to have no answer. She was a hostage in time with no one to understand her and nowhere to go. And it was painfully obvious from Jonathan's furrowed brow that he would never believe her. Again, she thought of how she couldn't blame him one bit. The situation was hopeless. Even her plan to rile Lavinia by wearing the woman's precious red dress had backfired; she never arrived according to schedule. Amanda's heart sank, and when she spoke, her soft voice wavered.

"Jonathan?"

Startled from his reverie, Jonathan turned and stared at the beauty standing in the doorway. "Amanda." He stretched out a hand in invitation. "Come in. It is time we talked."

Nodding, she entered the luxurious bedroom and closed the door quietly behind her. "How are you feeling?"

"Disturbed and tired." She stood next to him at the safe, both of them gazing at the contents as if not seeing them. "I was coming for my things," she said simply.

"I know. I suspected you would." He turned to look at her and smiled, his eyes lingering on her slightly parted lips. He wanted to claim those lips again—to feel their warmth against his own. "Perhaps Madame Winston's psychic gifts are contagious."

Amanda turned away and carefully sat on the end of the large canopied bed. The room at a glance was comfortable. Its walls were papered in pale blue with tiny pink rosebuds that matched the curtains and loveseat. A dresser and vanity complimented the rich mahogany of the bed and a stone fireplace stood to the other side nearest a door she assumed was the bathroom. Beside it was another door.

A closet?

"This was Lavinia's bedroom," Jonathan offered in answer to her unvoiced question. "It was the haven she escaped to when she wanted to be alone."

"You mean escape from you, don't you?" Amanda clarified.

"Yes."

"And the safe?" she asked, pointing.

Jonathan laughed bitterly. "For the many jewels she assumed I would lavish upon her."

They fell into silence as the rain continued dropping pellets against the house. Jonathan walked to the fireplace and tossed in several logs, immediately casting the room in warmth. He brushed the soot from his hands, walked to the side of the bed to turn up the lamp, and sat down beside Amanda.

"Who is Kendall?" he finally asked.

"My mother."

"It was her name that caused you to leave the circle."

"I found Madame Winston's statement confusing. It is my belief that a true medium can only receive messages from someone who has lived and then died. What frightened me was the fact that in this time my mother has yet to even be born."

Jonathan took this information in slowly before speaking. "I asked Madame Winston about you."

"And did she confirm your suspicion?"

Jonathan reached out and took her hand into his. "She said you were lovely; that I surely cannot deny." His eyes sparkled as he looked at her. "She told me you were honest and trustworthy and that I could learn much from you. Considering her accuracy in naming Linwood and myself as being involved with a deceiver..."

"Lavinia."

"...I could only believe that what she says of you must also be true."

"I'm to be on guard myself, you know. I wonder why Lavinia did not make her scheduled appearance."

He laughed and she loved the sound as it whispered by her ear.

"What?"

"Linwood is responsible for detaining her. Unfortunately, she will still arrive, but two days later."

"I'm sorry." And she truly was.

"Not as sorry as I."

Amanda swung her legs in front of her nervously. "So, what do we do now? It appears you are stuck with me, as I haven't a clue as to how to return to my century."

Jonathan looked into her eyes. "Show me your proof, Amanda." He paused, his eyes searching hers. "Show me your time," he amended.

"Madame Winston is certainly influential. Are you saying you believe me?"

"Maybe."

Amanda's heart lifted along with her spirits and she gingerly hopped off the edge of the bed and hastened to the safe. Jonathan watched in silence as she pulled out the purse, her hat, and then reached in for... the weapon.

"Be careful," he warned. "It must be still loaded, as I have not touched it since your arrival."

"Of course it is," she answered while taking it to the bed, the oversized tapestry bag precariously dangling from her shoulder.

"And it is also sharp, it says so right there." He pointed to the label.

Amanda laughed. "Sharp is the name of the manufacturer, Jonathan; it's loaded with recording tape, not ammunition," she explained while hopping back onto the bed. "It's called a video camera."

He shook his head in confusion and disbelief as he watched her flip a switch on the side and the screen came to life.

"Video," he repeated. "What is video?"

"Moving pictures."

"But Edison is only working on that now, and it's a secret project of his. You cannot possibly know about it."

"Well, I do...and it's no secret in the future. We've come a long way in technology." Amanda turned the small screen toward him. "Now watch. You will soon see moving images of moments in time that were captured on this film."

Jonathan's eyes widened as the scenes unfolded before him.

"That's my house," Amanda explained.

"Who is that?" He marveled at the clarity of the images as they told their story.

"My roommate, Carrie Stern. She came with me to tour Serenity."

As strange machines moved along the road, Jonathan felt his confusion lead to alarm and then, excitement. Amanda called them automobiles—horseless carriages with motors!

The footage of Serenity was suddenly on the screen, and Jonathan's questions were held at bay as he viewed what appeared to be his home. It certainly looked like Serenity, yet somehow it was different. He felt he was watching a parallel world and his questions spilled out with speed.

"Who are those people and what are they doing in my home? Why are there ropes around my rooms? Why are the servants dressed so strangely?" He squinted for a closer look. "And who in blazes are they? They certainly were not employed by me!"

"One question at a time!" Amanda laughed loudly, delighting in sharing something so profound and new with this traditional man of the nineteenth century. "Those people are called docents. They are like curators. I guess we haven't perfected the dress of your time as well as we thought," she mused.

"They look ridiculous," he mumbled.

"Serenity is a historical site in my time. Visitors pay to tour the house and grounds." She pressed the pause button: a little boy with a lollipop stood in front of a grandfather clock.

Jonathan smiled at the image of the child. "I have never acquired such a time piece," he pointed out.

"Apparently, one day you will."

The scene moved up the stairs to the third floor and Jonathan suddenly stiffened. "Good Lord, that's me! That is the day I discovered you in my office!"

Amanda blushed as her aim had taken in his body from head to embarrassing toe. "Yes, I was still recording when you walked in on me."

"I gather you liked what you saw." It was Jonathan's turn to laugh and tease. "Play it again in its entirety, please," he softly demanded.

Amanda rewound the tape and obliged him with a replay again...and again...and again, until finally instructing him on how to view the footage without her help.

An hour later, he flipped the switch off and turned to her in excitement. "We must show Edison!"

"If I remember my history, Edison won't be perfecting the motion picture until 1889. I don't know why I'm here, Jonathan, but I doubt it's to hasten the development of the motion picture. Trust me."

Deeply in awe of Miss Amanda Lloyd, Jonathan sighed heavily. "You have so much to share. And to think I called you a spy!" Shaking his head, he put the camera down.

"How could anyone expect you to believe otherwise? Until now, time travel was something I read about in books of fiction. If situations were reversed, I would have reacted toward you in a similar manner," Amanda admitted.

Jonathan nodded and reached for her fedora. Delicately, he removed the comb that held up her hair and watched the soft waves gracefully fall past her shoulders. He planted the hat firmly on her head. "The latest fashion for women in your time?" he teased.

Amanda smiled and fingered the brim. "My own personal signature, I'm afraid. I love hats, and this one is my favorite."

He leaned in closer. "Show me more."

"Aren't you tired?"

"Not in the least."

"Well, I'm hungry. I missed Vivian's feast in the dining room and I'm dying of thirst, too!"

Jonathan winked and moved off the bed to a pantry door. Inside, the shelves were stocked with jams and crackers and Amanda licked her lips in delightful anticipation.

"Lavinia insisted on keeping this filled with nonperishable items and Alan kept up with the habit knowing I had the study across the hall."

"Good old Alan!" Amanda was beside him now.

"There is more." He was beaming now. "Though probably a bit warm." A box at the bottom revealed a case of champagne. "Believe it or not, it is much cooler up here."

"I don't believe you, but I'm grateful for it anyway."

He removed a bottle and stepped into the adjoining bathroom for two glasses from the cabinet before joining Amanda who had spread a picnic out for herself on the bed and was opening a jar. As he opened the champagne, a stream of clear foamy liquid shot up into the air and all over her dress. "I'm so sorry! I guess it's still a bit too warm."

Amanda rushed to the bathroom and dabbed vainly at the stain. "It will never come out!" She turned to find him standing in the doorway, grinning.

"Then change into your own clothes, if you will feel more comfortable."

He stood holding her black trousers and white blouse in his hands, his mind vividly reliving the sensuous contours of her slender legs as outlined in the trousers. He desperately wanted to see that again!

Amanda stood staring at him as he laid her twenty-first-century clothing on a chair beside the commode, and slowly closed the door.

CHAPTER TWENTY-FIVE

Jonathan's eyes carefully trailed down the length of the snug-fitting trousers as the material curved around Amanda's slender thighs, rounding tightly down her calf. It was all he could do not to rush up and sweep her into his arms, for the garment and its wearer stirred something fiery within him.

"I would never have believed I would have occasion to say this, but women look quite feminine in trousers."

"I'll take that as a compliment," she said while walking back to the picnic on the bed.

"I meant it as one."

Amanda sat facing him, her legs folded yoga style. After a sip of champagne, she dumped the contents of her purse between them.

Jonathan's eyes widened. "My, my, is all this absolutely necessary?" His hand swept over the pile.

"Not really. But, I live by the You Never Know Code."

"You Never Know?" He popped a small cracker into his mouth.

"As in, you never know what might come in handy." She picked up a small bottle opener. "This opens bottles by removing the cap. In my time, they have twist-off caps but..."

"You never know," he finished, taking the curious object into his hands.

Nodding, she smiled. "You catch on quickly."

His gaze roamed the pile and recognizing the Mace, he frowned. "Is that truly meant for intruders?"

"Yes." Amanda quickly put it aside and watched as he picked up her key chain with a large purple crystal dangling from it.

"An amethyst quartz crystal. It helps to relieve stress when you hold it awhile."

One by one they went through it all: the lipstick, compact, Advil, the guidebook from her tour (the inaccuracy of which caused him momentary distress), blank videotapes, a cigarette lighter (that he kept playing with until Amanda's nerves broke, and which she asked him to stop before the thing lost its fuel entirely), and a battery pack, which she told him extended the life of a battery through electricity.

"To think we will come so far in the future," he mused in wonder.

The last item was her leather wallet, which she allowed him to open. "What are these cards for? This one must be the ruler of the lot," he observed.

She peered over at the MasterCard in his hand. "In my time we pay for things we can't afford on credit by using these cards."

"Sounds wonderfully prudent," he commented, now investigating the actual money behind her billfold.

"Not if you consider the high interest rate the banks charge for their use. The value of the dollar has severely depreciated in my time, Jonathan."

"Well, it certainly looks smaller," he noted while fingering a dollar bill.

Amanda laughed and watched him peruse through until he came upon her driver's license with her picture on it. He leaned over on his side, his head propped up on his hand and looked at it closely. "This likeness does not do you justice."

She leaned in for a look and her long hair fell over them like a tent. "No picture of identification is flattering. You should see my passport!"

He reached up and moved her hair behind her ear, his hand softly palming the side of her face as he moved it away. Slowly, he brought her face down to his and tenderly kissed her lips. They were so close she could feel his heart beating furiously in his chest, or was that her heart? She couldn't be sure, as her own body trembled at his touch as fire fingered up and down her back as his kiss deepened.

"Jonathan..."

"I wish," he said while stroking her thigh, "that Thomas Edison could meet you."

"That would be wonderful, but the honor would be mine, not his. Besides, now is certainly not a good time for him." She turned and stared into his emerald eyes... or were they blue? They changed at such an alarming rate it was difficult to read them.

He nodded and kissed the top of her head. "Yes, and if I know Edison, he has thrown himself into his work in the hope that Mary will overcome her illness and they can take a long leave abroad. Yet, why else would you be here, Amanda, if it is not to aid in Edison's work?"

"If that were true then I should have come to him, and while visiting Glenmont on tour."

"Glenmont?"

"His house in West Orange, New Jersey. The one he will live in with his second family."

"Second family?"

Amanda's hand flew to her mouth, and she immediately regretted what she had revealed. "Oh,

Jonathan, please don't tell anyone of anything I have told you, especially Edison. I have no idea why I'm here, but I don't want to mess with history in the process if I can help it. Please, you must promise."

Jonathan nodded. "I promise. Please continue."

"Well, his wife, Mary, will lose the battle with her illness and Edison will marry again, moving to a new house—Glenmont—and he will have three more children."

"Six children in total?"

Amanda shrugged and snuggled closer to him, as if that were possible. "It's truly a lovely place, Glenmont."

"As lovely as Serenity?"

She shook her head against his chest. "Different... and much darker. Though I'm sorry to say that Serenity will not have all sixty-five acres in my time. Much was sold off for housing purposes."

"My poor Serenity." Jonathan let out a long breath. "My plans are not for her to end up that way. I wanted Serenity to prosper through generations of Brisbanes. I had hoped there would always be a Brisbane living here. As evidenced in your time, I will fail miserably. No matter how optimistic I am during my lifetime, Serenity will be nothing more than a relic of the past and my family will have ended with me."

Amanda propped two pillows behind her and sat up. "I'm so sorry, Jonathan."

She bent over and kissed his cheek. "I hadn't thought of it quite that way." Then it came to her, slowly. "Maybe I'm here for you personally, Jonathan—to get rid of Lavinia and to permanently free you so you will meet someone and have a family."

Jonathan was astonished. Meet someone else? Wasn't it obvious that he had just found the one woman he wanted to spend the rest of his life with? He thought to declare that to her.

"We will never know," he said instead.

"The guidebook!" Amanda scrambled to the pile strewn out at the foot of the bed and picked up a leaflet. "There should be background material in here about who lived at Serenity." She flipped the pages until she came to a picture of Jonathan, the very one taken with Edison that sat in his office. "Here we are... it says that Thomas Edison was a frequent visitor of Serenity...."

"That fact has obviously become common knowledge in your time. My claim to history, I suppose."

Amanda scanned down the page, the last paragraph drawing her into it. "Serenity was once the home of Mrs. Vivian Brisbane and Mr. and Mrs. Jonathan Brisbane."

"Sounds vague to me."

Amanda looked up and bit her lower lip. *So much for historical accuracy!* There was no mention of who Mrs. Jonathan Brisbane was.

"That settles it," she said.

"It settles nothing."

"Whom were you married to?"

"Lavinia, but we divorced."

"Well, something happened to prevent that from occurring because, according to history, you were happily married."

"Then history is mistaken because Lavinia is a terror to live with; happiness is not in her vocabulary. Therefore, I assure you that pamphlet is in error and it settles nothing."

"But, I know from Vivian that you don't have the divorce papers here and that Lavinia is eventually returning to Serenity. Though I know it shouldn't make a difference, Lavinia sounds to me to be a strong-minded woman. There must be something we can do!"

"*We* do not do anything Amanda. I do not want you involved."

"I'm already involved. Besides, how will you explain me to her?"

"A good question." He smiled and tilted her chin up to him with a finger. "Another woman, particularly one as beautiful as you, would undoubtedly conjure up her wrath." He pressed his mouth to hers in a sweet kiss.

Amanda slipped a hand over his chest, her mind wandering back over the events of the séance and the strange warning from the medium. "Speaking of conjuring, maybe Madame Winston can help."

"She is a gifted woman, I will grant you that. The deceiver she refers to can only be one person."

"Lavinia."

He nodded. "Personally, I tend to agree with Linwood's assessment that Lavinia is not quite right in her head."

"How long before the documents arrive?"

Amanda was confident she could endure Lavinia's presence in the house for forty-eight hours if she had to.

"Two weeks."

"What!" Amanda shot up to a sitting position and searched his face for signs that he was joking. Jonathan had to be if he thought she could survive Lavinia that long, not to mention what it would do to poor Vivian. Anything could happen in two long weeks and she dared not think what that anything could be. "Jonathan, you can't possibly be telling me those documents of yours can't get here sooner."

"Amanda, we are not in your time. We do not have steel motor carriages that whisk about on paved roads.

The messenger will arrive in approximately two weeks' time, and bone weary at that."

"I never really appreciated progress before," she replied, leaning her head against his shoulder. "I still think there must be something I can do. First, I think I'll have a few words with Madame Winston."

Crushing her to him, Jonathan kissed her fully and firmly. "First," he whispered hoarsely, "I would like you to have a few words with me."

CHAPTER TWENTY-SIX

"I haven't seen Amanda since she broke the circle—or Jonathan for that matter."

Vivian paced back and forth in front of the parlor window, Madame Winston her captive audience.

Vivian sighed loudly. Everything was off schedule. Lavinia never showed up at the party, and now Jonathan and Amanda had not surfaced for brunch. Vivian felt her sense of order crumbling and the feeling did not sit well with her. Life was a schedule of events and she firmly believed that schedules should be maintained. Besides, it wasn't polite to have a guest—particularly an esteemed one such as Madame Winston—dine alone, and as head of the household, that did not excuse Jonathan from his responsibility.

"Amanda is feeling much better." Jonathan pushed Amanda ahead of him as they joined the women in the parlor.

"My dear, you had me so worried!" Vivian rushed over and gathered Amanda to her bosom. "Are you sure you are all right? You looked positively horrified when you ran off."

"I'm fine, Vivian." Amanda looked over at Madame Winston. "I would like to have a few words with you in private." It was more a demand than a request.

Madame Winston nodded, and in silent communication, Vivian excused herself. With a mutual nod, Jonathan followed and closed the door behind him.

"How do you know my mother's name?" Amanda got straight to the point and watched guardedly for a reaction.

A tiny smile curled at the corners of Yolanda Winston's mouth. "I know your mother's name because I knew your mother."

"That's impossible."

"Kendall Lloyd is—was—my friend."

"My mother hasn't even been born yet so I can hardly see how you could know her!" Amanda announced triumphantly, regardless of how ridiculous the statement sounded.

Yolanda shook her head. "I came here over thirty years ago, in 1854. I had been on my way to Woodstock..."

"What the hell are you talking about?" Amanda's hands were on her hips, eyes wide in disbelief. It made so much sense, yet it just wasn't possible. But, obviously it was possible or she wouldn't be here having this conversation. What wasn't possible was envisioning her mother at Woodstock.

"Nineteen hundred and sixty-nine, my dear." Yolanda watched Amanda slowly slide into the chair as the information began to sink in, her eyes locked to Yolanda's in a connection she could not deny.

"Oh...my...God. You're really from the future? From 1969?"

Yolanda laughed. "You talk like that's something alien to you. You probably know more than I!" With a swish of her long skirt, Yolanda went to the liquor cabinet and poured two shots of whiskey. "I think you're going to need this. I know it helps me."

Amanda nodded and gratefully accepted the whiskey. If ever she needed a drink, it was now. No, it was before, when she arrived. By now, she needed to be injected with the stuff to believe all this was actually happening. The liquor brought her around and she leaned back against the loveseat, her mind racing with questions she could ask this fellow time traveler.

"How did Woodstock turn out?" Yolanda asked. "I had tickets, you know. I never got to stay for the whole thing." Her eyes glazed over as she wistfully recalled that day of her youth in another time. "I was digging the far out sounds of Jimi Hendrix—though I would have preferred to be hearing the other Jimmy, Morrison—and I was smoking a joint and eating one of those magic mushrooms everyone was into, when I found myself in 1854 England." She shook her head. "But that's another story."

"And one I would certainly like to hear. What I really want to know is how you knew my mother."

"Kendall and Willy Boy were in the group I traveled with to Woodstock. Willy Boy had borrowed a van and..."

"Willy Boy?" Amanda knew Yolanda was referring to her father, but he was never a Willy Boy, always a William. He was a very secure, confident, and stringent individual. He was a banker and it always seemed to Amanda that he took that banker's etiquette of stuffiness home with him. It was impossible to picture him as a hippie making his way to Woodstock in a borrowed van to hear rock music. This was her father, for goodness sake!

"It was his nickname." Yolanda moved to sit beside Amanda. "You look exactly like her, you know; your mannerisms and the sound of your voice are alarmingly similar to that of your mother."

"Is that how you recognized me?" This did not surprise Amanda, as many people have pointed that out when her mother was alive.

"I thought Kendall had come back in time, until I saw you reach for a glass. Unlike your mother, you appear to be left-handed."

Still reeling from this new information, Amanda smiled at the obvious clue.

"My father was left-handed, but he sure wouldn't have even admitted to knowing what Woodstock was. Mom, on the other hand, might have told me one day... had she..." The words caught in her throat and she bit into her lower lip to keep back the tears.

"It's OK, honey, cry if you must." Yolanda patted Amanda's hand affectionately. "I had a feeling they were gone. You wouldn't have traveled to this time otherwise. What we have to discover is your purpose here."

"My purpose?" Amanda's eyebrows came together in confusion and concern.

"You are the third one I have met, Amanda."

"There are others?"

Yolanda nodded.

"Tell me, has anyone ever been able to return to their own time?"

"All I can tell you is that you are here for a reason. If that means making your life here in this century, then it is your destiny." Yolanda leaned back and sighed evenly. "The portal to which you gained entrance is still there, Amanda. You can leave any time you wish. The door has always been open and the choice has always been yours."

"If there is a way home, I haven't found it."

"It's there, Amanda. Something is keeping you here and soon you will know what that is. Then you will be able to exercise your true right of choice. But once you make your decision, the door will be closed to you forever."

The two time travelers remained silent for quite some time as Amanda rearranged the order of things in her head. She had come here for a reason and once she fulfilled her mission, she had the choice to go back. It sounded so simple in its logic, yet she doubted anyone in her time would believe her, and certainly only Jonathan believed her in 1884. She would have to keep silent on this chapter of her life regardless of what time she remained in; and that might be OK, if only she knew the reason why she was here!

"Do you think I'm here because of Lavinia?"

"The deceiver?" Yolanda got up and helped herself to the teacart. "As a matter of fact, Amanda, I do," she answered, while stirring in two cubes of sugar.

"No higher mission?"

"I think helping the Brisbane family with Lavinia is a formidable mission."

"I suppose we will soon find out. But tell me something. It's obvious you have made your choice to stay in this time, but don't you miss it—your own century, I mean?"

"I have helped a lot of people in this time with what I know of the future," Yolanda confirmed.

"Is that your mission?"

"For the most part."

"Why did you choose the psychic medium route?"

"I arrived here wearing a granny dress, a shawl, and lots of jewelry. I also had a deck of tarot cards in my knitted pouch. They mistook me for a traveling Gypsy and thought I told fortunes!" She smiled broadly. "I will admit that if there is anything I do miss, it's television and movies."

"Movies, maybe. But, I can do without television. In my time, it's pretty depressing."

"Well, it wasn't too pretty in 1969 either." Yolanda reached over to the teapot and poured. "Have a cup of tea with me, Amanda. You and I have to come up with something for this Lavinia situation and I think I've just the ticket."

CHAPTER TWENTY-SEVEN

"It will never work!" Jonathan sat in the chair at his desk with both hands holding his stomach in laughter.

Amanda glared at him, her hands on her hips. "Well, I don't see you coming up with anything better." She sat down on the loveseat, arms folded across her chest. "Well? Have you a better idea?"

Wiping the tears from his eyes, Jonathan walked over to her and sat down beside her, unable to keep the smile from his lips. He put an arm around her and drew her close.

"I'm sorry, truly, I am, Amanda. But, how do you intend to convince Mother and the staff to participate in this deception? Surely, it will prove difficult."

"Yolanda is explaining the plan to Vivian at this very moment. As for the staff, I should think they would welcome any opportunity to avoid having Lavinia around again."

The knock on the door startled them both as Vivian rushed into the room, her long blue dress scraping hastily against the polished wood floor. "It is worth the effort," she announced. "I have sent for Alan."

Jonathan looked from one woman to the other. It was an insane idea, but apparently, his mother was a participant who was willing to try anything. He shook his head for the umpteenth time. It will never work, he said again, this time to himself, for it would be impossible to convince this band of women otherwise.

* * *

Within the hour, the staff that was employed on the grounds of Serenity grouped to hear Jonathan explain the nature of things, while those responsible for the main house were gathered in Ruth's kitchen to be informed by Alan.

"Pretend we do not see or hear Miss Amanda?" Renee repeated in question. "How is that possible, Mr. Alan?"

"And why would we do such a thing? Has everybody gone daft around here?" added Ruth, her chubby hands firmly on hips as she prepared to strongly disagree with Alan. Certainly, they had heard wrong.

Alan straightened his jacket with authority. "We are not in the position to question Mr. Brisbane. He related to me that it might prove a way to, shall we say, 'dispose of' Miss Lavinia for good." His eyes flickered across the faces of the staff in his charge and he saw the change in their eyes at the mention of the woman's name. Not one of them wanted Lavinia back, and all for different reasons.

"You mean...like she is invisible...like a ghost?" asked Renee, who was in dire need of clarification. As the one in charge of Miss Amanda's needs, it would be difficult for her to perform her duties.

"Precisely." Alan could not believe what he was saying. Not in thirty years of service had he been reduced to making such a ridiculous request of his staff. Taking out his crisp white handkerchief, he wiped his beaded brow. "The plan, you see, is to frighten Miss Lavinia into believing Serenity is haunted."

"By anyone in particular?" asked Ruth.

"The ghost will be known as Ebony, the Woman in Black."

"This will drive Miss Lavinia away, then?" Renee asked hopefully.

"Forever, providing we all adhere to the plan."

"Sounds like a good plan to me, and a most enjoyable one at that," agreed Ruth.

Alan clicked his pocket watch open. "We have about two hours. Mr. Brisbane is counting on us." He clicked his watch closed and made quick steps to the door. "Remember, even if you are alone with Miss Amanda, do not put down your guard. Keep up the charade regardless of the circumstances."

* * *

They sat in the front parlor and waited. It wasn't long before the silence was filled with the sound of horses' hooves stopping in front of Serenity. Amanda parted the lacy white inner panel of the curtain and peeked out.

"Oh, Lord!" she exclaimed in a whisper as she watched the blond woman accept the hand of a liveried footman. Lavinia's large blue eyes moved about in quick survey and she shook her head at the obvious opulence of Serenity. It was a severe error in judgment to have divorced Jonathan Brisbane before she had the opportunity to gain something from the marriage. With the lift of her skirts, she descended from the carriage and briskly walked up to the front door.

Inside the front parlor, Amanda turned alarming eyes on Yolanda. It was one thing to dream up such a scheme and quite another to actually pull it off.

"I don't know about this."

"Don't worry, dear," Yolanda responded. "Now off with you. You know what to do." She shooed Amanda with her hand in a motion toward the door.

Amanda smiled nervously and started out of the room. Jonathan reached out a hand and gave hers a tender squeeze.

"We have nothing to lose," he said, his eyes holding hers for a long moment.

"Amanda! Quickly!" Yolanda whispered urgently.

"I'm going! I'm going!"

Her hand slipped from Jonathan's, and he watched as she ran from the parlor, her sweet lemon scent still lingering in the room. It was not going to be easy for him to not acknowledge her presence—not to touch her—to kiss her. If anyone, he feared he would be the most likely person to betray his feelings in front of Lavinia and ruin the plan.

CHAPTER TWENTY-EIGHT

"Vivian, my dear!" Lavinia swept into Serenity as if she had never left it, and hugged her ex-mother-in-law with a kiss to the air. "Be a sweet and have Alan move my trunks to my bedroom."

Vivian's frozen stare was one of disbelief. Though she thought she knew what to expect, nothing could have really prepared her for actually seeing Lavinia and hearing that shrewish voice barking out commands. It took several long moments for Vivian to regain her composure and remove the startled expression from her face.

"Alan, see to Miss Lavinia's trunk," she requested.

Jonathan walked from the parlor with Madame Winston on his arm, and acknowledged Lavinia with a terse nod.

"And who is this?" she asked warily, her eyes trailing up and down Yolanda in survey. "You look very familiar."

"Allow me to introduce Madame Yolanda Winston."

"Madame Winston? The spiritualist medium?" Lavinia's eyebrows arched high in amusement.

Yolanda nodded. "I am very pleased to meet you, Mrs. Brisbane."

Both Jonathan and Vivian winced noticeably at the "missus." Lavinia, on the other hand, immediately decided to like anyone who addressed her as the mistress of Serenity.

"It's so wonderful to meet you," gushed Lavinia in false excitement. "Have I missed all the fun?" she asked while leading the way into the parlor.

"Madame Winston will be here until week's end," put in Jonathan.

Alan's entrance rescued Jonathan from delivering further explanation. "The footmen are securing your trunk on the third floor—"

"NO!" Both Jonathan and Lavinia spoke in unison, Jonathan for reasons he could not project to the others. That room had become his love nest with Amanda and he recalled the disheveled state they left it in, not to mention the fact that Amanda's personal belongings were secured in that room's safe.

Taking his outburst as an indication that he wanted her in his bed, Lavinia smiled at him in surprise. This was proving to be far easier than she had anticipated.

"Place the trunk in my husband's bedchamber, then."

Jonathan groaned. There was no way he was going to share a bed with the woman. He hadn't during their marriage and he was not about to now, plan or no plan.

"There are several rooms to choose from, Lavinia," Jonathan offered gently. "Perhaps the one down the hall?" He looked to the others, but his mother was speechless and Madame Winston was not in a position to offer an opinion.

Lavinia linked her arm through his and reached a hand up to his cheek. "Darling Jonathan, I understand your reluctance. It has been so very long."

"Yes, well, I believe it more prudent for you to secure another room until we...become reacquainted."

* * *

Amanda's appetite had all but disappeared the moment Lavinia arrived, her thoughts all consumed on whether she could pull this haunting off. Certainly, no one in her time would fall for such a trick. With her doubt came Yolanda's reassurance that people in 1884 were far more susceptible, and she had seen enough herself to realize it most definitely could work, provided everyone kept up with the charade. And that's what worried Amanda most—the others. *What if someone slips up?*

The footsteps in the hall cast away any further thoughts on the subject as the reality of Lavinia's presence put Amanda's inner antennae on full alert. She quietly turned the knob and cracked open her bedroom door.

"Dear sweet Jonathan," Lavinia cooed. "Are you sure about this room?"

Lavinia stood beside the open door and peered in. When she turned to face him, her hand came up to palm his cheek, long fingers tracing a feathery line down the curve of his angular jaw. "I am hoping to put the past behind us, Jonathan," she whispered smoothly, her fingers now playing softly at his collar.

Jonathan's hand came up in reflex and wrapped around hers. "It's too soon, Lavinia." This was damned uncomfortable and he didn't like it. Lavinia wasn't in Serenity more than a few hours and already she was up to her old conniving ways. He looked into those ice-blue eyes and wondered how he could have ever seen any warmth in them. How could he have been so blind?

"Oh, Jonathan," Lavinia whined as she pressed her body fully against his, her arms lacing his neck. "There once was a time when you said I moved the earth for you," she whispered into his ear. "I can move the earth for you again, Jonathan. I can give you the sky and the—"

Jonathan grabbed both her hands with more force than he intended and slowly brought them down from around his neck where they awkwardly remained locked against his chest. Had it not been for the slamming of a door, he would have been obliged to be more forceful, and he was grateful for the interruption.

"What was that?" Lavinia looked up and down the long empty corridor.

"What?" Jonathan's hands fell to his sides.

"That noise." Her hand on the door, Lavinia pushed it open wider and stepped inside. "My imagination?"

Jonathan shrugged. "Good night, Lavinia."

With a slight bow, he left for his own room down the hall, along the way finding it extremely difficult to keep from laughing, knowing full well that Amanda must have misunderstood what she saw.

CHAPTER TWENTY-NINE

The black figure stole into the room and slipped quietly into the closet. Eye level to the keyhole, Amanda crouched down on her knees and waited.

"I swear, Renee, you are as incompetent now as you were a year ago." Lavinia peeled off each finger of her dainty white gloves with a yank, her Southern accent thickening with her anger. "I should think you know my habits to bathe in lavender. I do not abide any other scent in my bath, and because of your incompetence," she drawled, leaning into the girl, "I will have to forego the pleasure of resting my travel-weary body into a proper tub!"

Amanda's hands tightened into fists at her side. The woman was insufferable! She could see Renee begin to weaken as she listened to the girl's broken voice whisper apologies. She slid back down onto the floor until she heard Renee leave, sure that Lavinia would head for the softness of the bed. Peeking through the keyhole again, she spied the lamplight still on and groaned, stifling a laugh at the irony of the situation. She was, after all, doing precisely what got her in trouble in this time in the first place, spying! And sizing up the competition surely didn't help matters.

* * *

Vigorously combing her long blond hair, Lavinia was seated in front of the vanity in a filmy blue nightgown. Amanda couldn't help but notice how formidable this woman really was, with breasts the size of cantaloupes, a tiny waist, and long trim legs that seemed to go on forever. She was certainly the picture of beauty. Amanda blew out her breath and slid down once more to the floor, her back against the cool closet wall. If anything, she could understand the surface attraction Jonathan had been so taken with, but enough to marry the woman? If having been a photographer all these years taught her anything, it was how to read beyond the face. And beyond the high cheekbones, long lashes, and pale blue eyes was a woman of inscrutable character who concealed that side of her well.

The dim light beneath the closet door went black and Amanda heard the bed creak as Lavinia settled herself in for the night. With a trembling hand, she slowly pushed open the closet door and with soft steps approached the bed. She bent over Lavinia's body until her lips were inches away from Lavinia's ear.

"You are not welcome here," she whispered menacingly. Lavinia stirred and moved her face across the pillow in agitation. Amanda leaned in again and repeated the warning in a louder voice, and then scurried quickly to the door, on her way ripping the downy quilt from the bed and away from Lavinia's body. She slammed the door closed to assure herself there would be no way for Lavinia not to wake up. Moving with swiftness back to her room, she quietly clicked her door closed and leaned her back heavily against it. Try as she might, Amanda could not suppress the nervous giggles that poured forth, nor the triumph she felt deep inside. Her ear to the door, she listened, and was not disappointed.

* * *

Lavinia's scream could be heard throughout the house, and the hallway was immediately illuminated as Jonathan, Vivian, and Madame Winston ran out to the source and met up in front of Lavinia's door. Amanda opened her door a crack.

"Someone was in my room!" Lavinia turned lightning-blue eyes on them. The three looked to each other questioningly.

"Who?" asked Jonathan, still in his breeches, his shirt open to the waist.

"How should I know? My God, aren't you people paying attention?" she shouted. "I was attacked! That's right...attacked!" As if this was a sudden realization, Lavinia's hand flew up to her mouth in mock horror.

Attacked? Why that dimwit, I didn't touch her! Amanda looked at Lavinia's rapt audience and raised her eyes to heaven while sending up a small prayer.

Jonathan raised the lamp up to Lavinia's face, then moved back slowly and directed his comment to Madame Winston. "She's come back." It was a statement, for the look the medium gave him was all knowing.

"Who has come back?" Lavinia's hand gripped the doorknob and she leaned her body against the hard wood of the door. "And what would he or she want with me?"

Amanda crossed her fingers behind her back. It was Vivian's move. Having kept silent up to this time her reaction, and subsequent interaction, was crucial for credibility.

Don't blow it, Vivian. This is your big chance...make Sarah Bernhardt proud.

"Ebony," said Vivian softly, her hand reaching out to the anguished young woman. She put an arm around Lavinia's shoulders. "Madame Winston is here to help us with Ebony."

Lavinia stiffened at Vivian's caress and pushed her arm away, drawing her body up with authority. "I'm... fine. Now, who is this Ebony person?"

"We should adjourn to the study. We three need to explain and it is too long a tale for this drafty hallway." Jonathan turned, and by the light of his lamp, led the way down the grand staircase, simultaneously buttoning his shirt with his free hand.

"And that you had better!" huffed Lavinia as she quickly fetched a wrapper and followed the group down the hallway, several times raising her lamp high and peering up and down, eyes searching for her bedchamber intruder.

Amanda lightly clicked the door closed. *So far, so good.*

* * *

"Some mysterious events have plagued Serenity in recent months," began Jonathan, his attention focused on filling goblets with brandy. "These events have forced us to seek the advice of the renowned medium Madame Winston." He handed each woman a brandy before sitting down with one himself.

"Ebony is the woman in black," explained Madame Winston. "She haunts Serenity in grief over the loss of her husband and son...she is a widow of the War." Yolanda eased her back against the loveseat and pursed her lips together tightly.

"It is a pity, I suppose," commented Vivian from her seat beside Yolanda.

Lavinia's goblet stopped at her lips briefly. Taking a sizeable sip, she put it down and set her hands into her lap. At least they weren't shaking now. "Am I to believe we have a ghost living among us?" Her lips curved in a smirk of disbelief.

"An apparition has appeared, yes," clarified Yolanda. "Apparitions are the spirits of people who have died; therefore I doubt you could say Ebony is living among those at Serenity. Walking might be a more appropriate description."

"Whatever!" snapped Lavinia in frustration. "I did not intend to be taken literally, Madame Winston." She folded her arms across her chest and stared at Yolanda until the woman looked away.

Vivian wrung her hands through her hanky before dabbing at her tears. Jonathan saw this as most dramatic, but applauded the action, as it certainly did lend credence to her distress.

"We have been at our wits' end, Lavinia. You have no idea what it is like with that darkly sinister woman walking around." She turned to Yolanda and grasped her hand tightly. "You must do something, Madame Winston. You simply must!"

Jonathan came to Vivian's side to console her. It was a long time before anyone spoke.

Lavinia rose and picked up her lamp. "I suggest we all get some rest. And you," she pointed to the medium, "you must find a way to get rid of this...pest."

Turning abruptly, she walked out of the room and up the grand staircase, her steps quickening the closer she got to her room. Though her heart was beating furiously in her chest, she'd be damned if she would allow them to see her weakness. When she arrived at her door, Lavinia opened it slowly and glanced around the room before running to the bed and crawling under the covers. She left the lamp on high and with a long sigh leaned back against the pillows. A ghost? Surely they're not serious!

"There are no such things as ghosts," Lavinia announced to the empty room.

"Everyone knows that." *Don't they?*

CHAPTER THIRTY

"You are not welcome here!"

Lavinia's eyes shot open, and this time, as the first rays of light filtered through the dark drapery, she was able to see the sinister dark form standing at the foot of her bed.

"W-who are you?" she stammered while trying to tuck the sheet around her ample bosom.

"I'm your worst nightmare," came the deep response as the figure gripped the bedposts on either side and leaned forward.

Lavinia's face blanched and she fainted before the scream could reach her lips.

Amanda brushed her hands together and tapped her fedora in triumph before leaving the room. "That was easier than I thought."

Standing outside Lavinia's door, the aroma of Ruth's morning preparation beckoned Amanda and she sniffed the air with a hungry smile. *I could really dig into one of Ruth's specialties right about now*, she mused. She bent her body over the railing to further inhale the delightful bounty being prepared in the kitchens below.

It was far too early for anyone but the staff to be awake, and Lavinia would be "out" for quite some time. With eagerness, she ran down the stairs and into the busy kitchen.

"Good morning!" Pulling out a chair, she sat down and smiled brightly at the startled staff.

"You should not be down here, Miss Amanda." It was Ruth who quickly poured a cup of coffee and set it down in front of Amanda. "What would happen if Miss Lavinia should happen to come in?" She touched a hand to the knot in her kerchief before wiping her hands over her crisp white apron.

Amanda took a long sip and leaned back. "You make a great cup of coffee." She set the cup down and smiled. "Don't you worry, Ruth; I've seen to it that Miss Lavinia doesn't wake up for some time."

"You don't say!" Ruth's grin matched Amanda's. "Well, then have you a mind for some breakfast? That is, of course, if you don't mind breaking your bread in my kitchen."

"I'd be delighted, Ruth, I'm famished!"

Ruth's round cheeks flushed red and her smile widened. She liked Amanda Lloyd.

* * *

Lavinia woke with a start and glanced around the room, relieved to find herself alone. Had this Ebony person come to her twice in one night? She was sure of it, and if memory served her well, as it often did, the specter was indeed a woman. In trousers, no less! Someone had to get to the bottom of things. She would be damned if she would allow this apparition to frighten her away from Serenity. Directly after breakfast she would speak to Madame Winston and demand the medium do something at once. *Ghosts! Ha! It will take more than the shade of a dead widow to keep me from doing what I came here to do!* It was a bitter vow, and for all to work to her advantage,

Lavinia knew she had to reacquaint herself with the staff and stake her claim as their mistress.

Donning a wrapper, she pushed her feet into her slippers and headed with determination down to the kitchen. To the Lord and Lavinia, she was still Mrs. Brisbane, and God help anyone who got in her way.

"You are serving a ghost breakfast?"

Her eyes averting those of Amanda's, Ruth turned slowly around and faced an irate Lavinia who stood in the doorway with her hands on her hips.

"I beg your pardon?"

Amanda felt her stomach tighten. This was the first confrontation between them in front of others...and in daylight. Pulling the brim of her fedora down lower, she picked up her cup and turned to face her foe, eyes daring Lavinia's in challenge.

"Ghost?" asked Ruth as she finally found her voice again. "What are you inferring, Miss Lavinia? This is my breakfast." Ruth sat down, and dragging the plate toward her, began to eat.

Lavinia could not tear her eyes from Amanda's. "You mean to tell me you do not see her?"

"Who would that be, Miss Lavinia?"

"The woman in black, of course."

"Ah...yes...Ebony." Ruth put down her fork and wiped her mouth with a cloth napkin. "Is she here?" Her eyes darted around her kitchen.

"I'm looking directly at her," Lavinia confirmed while walking closer to the table. "She is right there, sitting across from you."

She pointed her finger, something Amanda didn't like, not in her time or in this one. Her father used to do that all the time—point his finger accusingly as an "I told you so," or "Don't you dare"—and it infuriated her that this woman was doing it now.

"How dare you point your finger at me!" Amanda scolded in a deeply menacing tone as she shot to her feet and looked Lavinia directly in the eyes.

Lavinia recoiled at their closeness, the scent of lemon assaulting her nostrils. *Since when do ghosts smell like lemon?* Before she could speak, Amanda leaned into her.

"You do not belong here. I want you to leave...at once!" she hissed.

Lavinia's head moved so far back, Amanda and Ruth thought it would fall off her neck. Try as she might she could not stop trembling.

"R-Ruth," she stammered. "I-I'll take my meals in my room."

And she was gone, half-running through the kitchen door.

Ruth laughed out loud. "You sure put a scare into her! I was starting to believe you myself."

"It was your performance that was convincing." Amanda reached over and drained the remaining coffee in her cup. "Thank you for the wonderful meal. I need to rest up for the next performance."

* * *

Flinging her fedora onto the bed, Amanda joined it in short order and stretched her body beside it. Though safe in the confines of her room, her heart was hammering furiously. It was unnerving to look into Lavinia's defiant blue eyes. Though Amanda knew the woman was fearful of "Ebony," those eyes played with challenge. And Amanda did not like the direction of that unspoken challenge.

"This is not right," she said out loud as she straightened to a sitting position. "This is toying with people's lives."

And that certainly could not be God's intention. One didn't just travel through time for the sole purpose of disrupting lives. *Maybe Yolanda Winston is wrong. Maybe there is another reason for being here. This just can't be right!*

Rising from the fluffy mattress, her eyes fell upon the hat. Why didn't it look right on the bed? Because it's bad luck, came a reply, her mother's reprimanding voice floating lightly in clear concise words. With the shake of her head, she moved to the window and parted the heavy drapery with a hand. The sun was hiding behind a soft cloud and a light breeze tickled at the trees along the lane bordering the front of Serenity. It looked to Amanda to be a perfect day for a walk. She closed her eyes and envisioned herself on Jonathan's arm, he in a light blue suit, she, in a delicate lacy dress, a parasol above her head. It was so easy to conjure up a vision with Jonathan as the focus. Filling herself with his imaginary scent, she inhaled deeply and opened her eyes.

"Oh...Jonathan." It came as a whisper as her startled eyes took in the scene below. Jonathan and Lavinia, a parasol in her right hand, her left clutching Jonathan's arm, while behind them at a short distance away, walked Vivian and Yolanda. Amanda moved away from the window convinced more than ever that what she was doing was wrong. She did not belong here at Serenity, and certainly, she did not belong in this century. The light tap at the door caused her to jump as Renee silently slipped in.

"Good day, Miss Amanda." Renee crossed to the table nearest the fireplace and set down a tray of silver dome-covered dishes. "An early supper sent up by Ruth," she explained. "And a message from Mr. Brisbane." Digging into her crisp white apron, Renee pulled out an envelope and handed it to Amanda.

Tearing it open with a finger, Amanda pulled out the note and unfolded the parchment. "Mr. Brisbane wishes to meet after sunset," Amanda answered as she quickly scanned the page.

Renee nodded. "I heard Miss Lavinia say she felt safer outside in the light of day, rather than inside Serenity's walls."

Amanda reached for the wine goblet and took a sip. "Surely, I could slip outside and just as easily frighten her."

"I do not know how Miss Lavinia thinks. What I do know is that she told Ruth she has plans. *Oui*. Plans to... how do you say...exorcise you?"

CHAPTER THIRTY-ONE

"Exorcism!" Jonathan had stopped in mid-step so abruptly that Vivian and Yolanda nearly tripped at his heels. "Lavinia, surely you jest."

Lavinia's eyes narrowed and with the flick of her wrist she brought down the parasol, her knuckles white as she gripped the handle tightly to reign in her anger. Jonathan was grateful she hadn't brought it down on his head.

"Am I mistaken in assuming we are unanimous in wanting to rid Serenity of this Ebony person?" She looked at them, her chest heaving with restrained rage.

"Of course not, dear," replied Vivian gently as she moved beside Lavinia.

"Do not try to placate me, Vivian. I am not a simpleton!"

Yolanda had been taking in the scene and did not care for the way things were going. It was time for her intervention as the "expert."

"Exorcism is performed only when sanctioned by the Vatican, Mrs. Brisbane," she explained. "As a medium, it is not my duty to expel lost spirits, but rather to guide them to the other side and their final resting place." She punctuated her statement with a tight-lipped smile.

The "Mrs. Brisbane" was all Lavinia needed to calm her down. She wanted to dislike Madame Winston, but the woman always referred to her with the respect Lavinia felt she deserved. In truth, Lavinia was a bit frightened of the medium. She had heard stories of spirits rapping and tables floating, presumably by conjurers like Yolanda Winston. She easily recalled her mother and father telling stories of the Fox sisters and Madame Blavatsky of the spiritualist movement. The raising of spirits was all too real for Lavinia, despite their assurance that there was nothing to worry about.

"Have you a suggestion, Madame Winston?"

"You seem to be a conduit for Ebony, Mrs. Brisbane. I would be inclined to suggest a séance as the means for aiding the spirit of Ebony home."

"Fine." Lavinia linked her arm through Jonathan's and started to walk.

"Wait now." Jonathan swung her around to face him. "I agree that Ebony should be at peace; however, the idea of a séance does not appeal to my better judgment." He shot a look to Vivian and Yolanda who understood immediately and continued down the lane.

Lavinia watched them disappear into the gardens. Returning her attention to Jonathan, she rested her back against the picket fence. Her smile was sweet as she reached out and grabbed hold of his tie, drawing him into her.

"Oh, Jonathan, what's wrong with a little séance if it will rid us of this pest?" Her arms around his neck, she pulled his face closer to hers and pressed her mouth to his.

Jonathan did not want to respond—was loath to—and every muscle in his jaw tightened as her kiss deepened. Yet, he knew that if she were to believe that he still wanted her, he would have to return the kiss. The only way he knew how was to believe those lips were Amanda's. The moment he did, he became lost, his lips burning into hers. Jonathan slowly broke the kiss and Lavinia stared up at him, her eyes wide and startled, her breathing belabored. Could a year change a man that much?

"I...want you back, Jonathan." She spoke breathlessly. Her hands touched his cheek and Jonathan reached up and slowly brought them back down.

Pretending Lavinia was Amanda had obviously been a mistake and was too convincing. From the look on Lavinia's face, she believed that fire within him was ignited because of her!

"We must concentrate on this Ebony issue." He took her arm and they began to walk. "I need time to think, Lavinia."

"What am I to do while you are thinking?" Lavinia whined, her body leaning into his.

"You can visit with the Cranes. Linwood and his mother would take offense if you were not to afford them the courtesy of a visit." He looked up at the cloud that suddenly darkened the sky.

"The Cranes. Of course I shall visit them." Lavinia batted her lashes and planted a light kiss on his cheek. "You do think of everything, Jonathan."

She was definitely up to something. What that was, he hadn't a clue. One thing was certain, he had to see Amanda, and it had to be this evening. The past two days and nights had been pure torture. He found it nearly impossible to ignore Amanda's presence, even for the sake of getting rid of Lavinia. Just knowing she was in the house was driving him to distraction. He could still picture her poured fully into those tight black trousers and looking positively impish in that mysterious black hat.

Thinking about the fedora brought a smile to his lips as he remembered Amanda wearing nothing but that hat! God, he could actually smell her lemony scent, his visualization so vivid it frightened him. He needed to feel her softness against him...feel her warmth embrace him. "Tonight", he had said in his note, and tonight it would be!

* * *

"How could he?" Amanda turned from the window and looked at Renee.

Renee cocked her head to one side. "I do not understand." She came closer and touched a hand to Amanda's shoulder. "Miss Amanda?"

"I'm sorry, Renee. I don't know what I'm saying lately. I guess I'm losing it."

Amanda sat down at the small table and lifted one of the domes. Lobster tails. She loved lobster, almost as much as she loved—no, she couldn't afford to expose what she felt for Jonathan; especially after seeing the obviously passion-filled kiss he shared with Lavinia. Shaking her head, she placed the dome back over the platter and looked up sadly. "I'm not hungry, Renee. Please send my apologies to Ruth."

Renee's hands flew to her hips. "Whatever it is you have lost, I will help you find it, but you must eat."

"What I've lost, Renee, is most likely gone forever."

"Then you get another one!" With the nod of her head, Renee marched confidently to the door as if her resolution solved everything.

Amanda stabbed a piece of lobster with her fork, but it never hit the sweet, hot butter. Her fingers started to shake and the utensil slipped from her hand as a wave of dizziness claimed her. She got up and left the security of her room.

CHAPTER THIRTY-TWO

"There is no reason for me to be here. There is no reason for me to be here," Amanda chanted in a litany as she walked down the long corridor that led to the third floor. The complexion of things had changed. By all indications, Jonathan and Lavinia had reconciled.

"There is no reason for me to be here," she repeated one final time as she reached the door. Her hand shot out to the doorknob and she turned. The door would not open. *Maybe it's stuck.* Both hands grasping the brass knob, Amanda turned and pushed in with the force of her body. The door swung open with a jerk, hurling her inside, her head connecting with the shiny redwood floor.

It took a moment to identify the sound; so faint it was at first. Then suddenly it increased in volume as a current of wind carried the music to her.

"*You can't always get what you want. But if you try some time, you just might find....*"

"...you get what you need," Amanda finished. *Oh, NO! The Rolling Stones!*

"Amanda!" Jonathan spied her distress in an instant and was rushing down the long hallway to her.

She turned and tried to rise to her feet. *He was coming in! He can't!*

The realization of what was happening assailed her immediately and an undeniable fear folded over Amanda like a dark canopy. On her feet now, she steadied herself and stuck out a hand in abeyance, only to be knocked against the stairs by the force of the strange wind, this time her head making contact with the cold marble steps.

Jonathan braced himself against the current and charged through the entrance where he landed against the floor with a thud. The door slammed closed and the howling wind abated instantly. Within moments, he was scrambling to his feet and at Amanda's side. Gently, he pulled her up to a sitting position.

"Amanda?"

She slumped forward like an old rag doll. In one swift motion, Jonathan swept her unconscious body up into his arms and climbed the stairs, taking them by twos. He rounded the corner and was heading for Lavinia's old bedroom when a voice stopped him.

"No one is permitted on this floor." The man turned off his radio.

Amanda's limp body flopping in his arms, Jonathan swung around and stared in confusion at the strange man.

"Is the lady all right?" the man asked while coming closer to them.

Jonathan's eyes flashed around and then back to the strange man. "She hit her head." With speed, he rushed over to the bedroom, his only concern to bring Amanda back to consciousness.

The man followed and pushed open the door for Jonathan as he shifted Amanda in his arms. The bed was in the same place, as was the vanity, but the room was not right. The windows were bare and the only item truly familiar to Jonathan was his safe.

"She needs water. Please...some cool water," Jonathan asked as he placed Amanda down on the bed and gently moved a tendril of hair from her forehead.

"Be right back. Don't you two move."

Jonathan sighed evenly and ran his fingers through his hair. She was going to be all right; just a knock on the head. He moved from the bed and over to his safe. A plaque on a stand stood beside it. *Lavinia Brisbane's safe for the precious jewels Jonathan Brisbane graced her with during their long and happy marriage.* Jonathan shook his head as if to clear his vision and will the sign away.

Amanda stirred, her mumbling bringing Jonathan to her side.

"Amanda?" he whispered, his hand clutching hers. "Where is that strange man?" he murmured, and as if in answer to his question, the man hustled into the room carrying a pitcher of water, a glass, and a small towel.

With a nod of thanks, Jonathan dipped the towel into the water and pressed it to Amanda's forehead.

"Is she gonna be all right?" the man asked.

Jonathan poured water into the glass and, as she began to come around, he brought it to Amanda's lips. "Look, whoever you are, just leave us alone, please."

"Can't do that."

"Excuse me?" Jonathan stared at the strange brown uniform and squinted to read the sign on the man's jacket: JOSH, Serenity Security.

"I said I couldn't leave you."

Jonathan put the glass down on the table beside the bed and stood to his full assuming height, dwarfing the older man.

The man inched back a bit. "I have to report this."

"To whom?" Jonathan bellowed.

"Where am I?" Amanda's eyes fluttered open. "My head."

Disregarding the guard entirely, Jonathan returned his attention to Amanda. "How do you feel?"

Amanda strained to focus in on the face of the man leaning over her. His green eyes were so concerned, his angular jaw tight with tension. Dark hair fell over his forehead in a tousle and he was smiling reassuringly.

Amanda forced a smile. She had to be dreaming. None of the doctors she knew were as handsome as this guy. Except on her favorite soap, *General Hospital*. She closed her eyes briefly, but when she opened them, he was still there.

"You're at Serenity, Miss," answered the guard. "The historical home of the Brisbane family."

Jonathan's mouth fell open and a strange feeling of loss crept over him. *Something is definitely wrong here.*

"I need to get home." Amanda attempted to raise herself up, only to fall back again against the pillows.

"You are not going anywhere," Jonathan confirmed. Didn't she realize she could never get home, not to her present time; that was certain. Or was it? Everything seemed slightly off kilter. This strangely uniformed man...Serenity...the room...Amanda.

"Thank you, Doctor, but I'll just rest a moment."

Doctor? Lord, didn't she remember who he was? "Do you know who you are?" he asked while removing the towel and refreshing it with cool water before returning it to her forehead.

"I'm Amanda Lloyd and this is Serenity."

That was a start. Jonathan turned to the man to offer some brief explanation so that he could be alone with Amanda. "Josh, is it? We will be down momentarily."

"Just make it snappy. I'm not supposed to leave you up here and this is Reenactment Day."

Jonathan walked to the barren window and stopped short, his eyes widening at the scene below. Those metal horseless carriages Amanda showed him through her camera were lining up in front of Serenity on a paved road as strangely dressed people emerged from them. Jonathan's breath quickened as he watched the scantily dressed women, unruly children, and men in extremely short trousers, all noisily converge on Serenity. Alarms rang off in his head as the realization of what he was seeing fully took hold of him. He turned to Amanda, his mouth suddenly dry, his heart pounding fiercely against his chest.

※

CHAPTER THIRTY-THREE

"I do wish Jonathan could have seen his way clear to joining us," Lavinia was saying to an astonished Linwood Crane. "I fear he is deluged with business affairs."

Linwood looked from Vivian to Madame Winston, but neither offered explanation as he escorted the women into the front parlor of his home.

"I'm surprised to see you, Lavinia." He cleared his throat and made haste over to a bartender's cart. "May I offer you a cool beverage? Mother is visiting family in Richmond. I'm sorry she could not be here."

"I trust everyone is well," Vivian inquired while sitting down beside Yolanda and accepting lemonade.

"Everyone is fine. Mother misses her sister and decided to take a holiday with her." Linwood poured himself bourbon and swallowed it in one swift gulp before quickly pouring another.

"I wonder, Linwood, if I may have a word with you in private." Lavinia smiled sweetly.

Vivian and Yolanda exchanged startled glances his way, but Linwood did not pick up on their silent message.

"Excuse us, ladies." Linwood led the way out to the back porch with Lavinia taking quick steps behind him.

He pulled a whiskey-soaked cheroot from his inside pocket and lit it.

Lavinia watched the puffy white smoke flow through the air in rings as he leaned against the stark white post of the railing. She wasted no time in getting straight to the point.

"I know it was you who detained me, Linwood." She sat down in the porch swing and rocked slowly, confidently.

He nodded, a smile curling the corner of his mouth. "You planted a spy in my house. I had every right to retaliate." He moved to where she sat and abruptly stopped the swing's motion with one hand. "What are you doing here, Lavinia?"

Lavinia leaned toward him, her white-gloved hand palming his cheek. "Poor, Linwood," she cooed softly. "You were always jealous of Jonathan." She inched closer, her lips a whisper away. "After all...you had me first."

"Somehow I doubt that."

Lavinia dropped her hand and easily smoothed it down the length of her dress. "Well, delaying me did nothing to change the facts."

"Which are?"

"That I am still married to Jonathan."

Linwood's laugh was strong and deep. "You acquired a divorce, remember? Knowing you as I do, I suspect you tore your copy up in the frivolous misconception that it makes a difference." He leaned into her, his eyes angry flames. "And robbing Jonathan's copy from my safe doesn't either."

Lavinia smiled tightly, her plump lips a thin line. "Whatever are you rambling about?"

"Never mind." Taking another puff from the cheroot, he blew several rings into her face before moving away.

"Well, dear Linwood, I can tell you with assurance that Jonathan only has eyes for me. He proved it today in the gardens."

His eyebrows raised in amused disbelief. "Not with a woman like Amanda around."

"Who?" Lavinia asked lightly.

"Ah...so, he's keeping her all to himself, is he? Pity."

Lavinia rose quickly from the swing. "Don't you be smug with me, Linwood Crane. Who is Amanda? I demand you explain yourself this minute!"

His laugh echoed across the porch. "Amanda is a beautiful, sensual, young woman I would gladly give up my own life for. However, Jonathan seems to have beaten me to her."

With a rustle of skirts, Lavinia rose confidently from the swing. She moved closely up to him and ran her fingers smoothly down the edge of his collar. With slow, determined force, she pressed her mouth to his in a long, deep kiss, for which Linwood eagerly responded and reciprocated with matched determination.

"Yes..." he murmured. "You are good...very good, but not good enough, Lavinia," he said, reluctantly breaking the kiss.

"If this woman truly exists, why have I not met her?"

Flicking the cheroot over the porch, Linwood shrugged and moved away. "I don't know. She is an honored guest at Serenity. It should be no secret."

"Honored? At Serenity? Now?"

"Yes. Amanda Lloyd is Thomas Edison's cousin."

CHAPTER THIRTY-FOUR

Lavinia kept her rage in check during the return trip to Serenity, deciding not to inquire about the woman Linwood Crane had described. Her sole intent was on locating this Amanda Lloyd and confronting her openly. When the carriage stopped in front of Serenity, Lavinia was the first one out, rushing to the front entrance and leaving Vivian and Yolanda to follow in her dusty wake.

"I do wish he hadn't mentioned Amanda," Vivian whispered to the medium.

"We can only hope that Linwood Crane did not say too much in his private conversation with Lavinia."

Vivian shook her head. "I have a morbid feeling, Yolanda."

"As do I," the woman agreed.

* * *

"I have decided to transfer my belongings to the third floor bedchamber, Alan," Lavinia announced. "Please have Renee prepare my wardrobe in that room."

"Yes...Mrs. Brisbane." Alan offered a slight bow and left to seek out Renee.

"Why do you need to change rooms?" Vivian asked as she swept into the front parlor and removed her bonnet. "Your present bedchamber is near Jonathan's," she reminded.

Helping herself to the bartender's cart, Lavinia poured bourbon and reeled around to address Vivian. "Who is Amanda Lloyd?"

Vivian turned pleading eyes to Yolanda Winston who immediately intervened. "Mrs. Brisbane, have you made your decision regarding the séance?" she asked in an effort to divert Lavinia's attention.

Lavinia smiled wickedly, one eyebrow arched in mockery. "Do you honestly think me a fool, Madame Winston?"

"Of course not."

"Then why are you asking me to participate in a farce? And why are you both avoiding my question?"

"I do not understand."

"Allow me to explain, then." Lavinia sat down in one of the large wingback chairs, her drink perched delicately in her still white-gloved hands. "Surely this relative of Mr. Edison is your Woman in Black...a flesh-and-blood woman, not a specter. A séance would only prove to further my suspicion that you are all attempting to drive me away."

Vivian sat down slowly in her chair by the fireplace and immediately reached for her fan. "I, for one, do not know what you are inferring."

"I am not inferring anything, Vivian. I am stating a fact. The woman Linwood Crane informed me of is most certainly your Woman in Black. Amanda Lloyd is this Ebony person."

Yolanda Winston's laugh was more a nervous reaction to the truth than folly.

"You find my statement humorous, Madame Winston?"

"Yes, of course. Such a monumental deception would be most difficult to execute. Surely, you can see that."

"Yes...yes," Vivian agreed. "And as to Amanda Lloyd, she was a guest here at Serenity for a few days and has returned to New York."

Lavinia twirled the amber liquid in her glass and watched the light filter through it. "I can see I will not be finding the truth I seek, and, for me, a séance is out of the question." She rose to leave, opting to take the half-filled glass along with her. At the doorway, she turned and smiled. "Enjoy your conjuring, ladies."

"What shall we do?" implored Vivian the moment Lavinia disappeared up the staircase. "And where do you think Amanda and Jonathan are right now? We must inform them of these new developments." She fanned herself furiously, her fingers tight around the stem of her glass, eyes brimming with the tears that threatened to spill onto her cheeks.

* * *

Yolanda Winston thought about this for a long moment. She'd had a feeling that something had happened at Serenity while they were at the Crane's house, and it was fast becoming an uncomfortable fact. Amanda and Jonathan's long absence confirmed her worst fear—that both had somehow found the portal that had led Amanda to this century. If that were the case—and she was sure it was—she would have to find a way to get a message to Amanda in her time.

"Dreams," she said aloud, not realizing she had done so.

"Dreams?" Vivian questioned as she put down the fan and reached into the pocket of her skirt for her handkerchief. Dabbing gently at her eyes, she settled her hands into her lap and nervously twisted her fingers around it. "Dreams?" she repeated.

Yolanda's eyes rested on the softly distressed features of Vivian Brisbane. It was time to reveal the truth to the woman, for she would need as much positive reinforcement as could be managed.

"Vivian," she began gently, "I have something I need to share with you, but I need your sworn word to keep the information to yourself. Above all, I ask that you keep an open mind."

* * *

The bedcovers were turned down in a rumpled ball at the foot of the bed, the pillows strewn about in flourishes of white satin. The aroma of stale champagne lingered heavily in the room. Lavinia shot a questioning look to Alan who simply shook his head and shrugged.

"That will be all, Alan." With the wave of her hand, Lavinia moved quickly into the room and slammed the door behind her.

Lifting the voluminous folds of her dress, she rushed over to further inspect the bed. "Crumbs!" she shrieked while patting the mattress furiously with both hands. "What else have you been doing in this bed, I wonder."

With a turn, she noticed a flash of red sticking out from the partially opened bathroom door. The flash of color and fabric appeared familiar, yet the impact of the familiarity did not lend itself to her until the garment was actually in her trembling hands. It was only then that the scream escaped her throat.

"My dress! How dare another woman wear my property!"

Taking the dress with her, Lavinia hopped onto the bed. Crunching up the layers of material, she leaned back into the pillows, the red dress clutched tightly against her chest. "I will find a way to get even with you and your harlot," she whispered fiercely to no one. "You will not win, Jonathan Brisbane." Her straining blue orbs stared straight ahead, laser sharp in their intent. "I will meet this Amanda Lloyd and I will do something about her." She clenched her teeth and smiled.

A ghost, indeed!

CHAPTER THIRTY-FIVE

Leaving Amanda to rest a bit more, Jonathan rushed down the stairs of Serenity to confirm his suspicion—he had traveled with Amanda to the future. Stopping abruptly at the bottom, he viewed with indifference the bustle of activity of the strangely clothed people. So, this is what was to become of his Serenity; nothing but a museum for tourists to trample about in. He didn't like it one bit and intended to find a way to get back to 1884 as soon as possible, if, indeed, that was possible.

"Oh, good, you're here," a woman chirped from behind him. "I've been looking all over for you."

Jonathan turned as she descended the bottom step. "You have?"

"Yes, of course. I must say, though, it's remarkable how much you resemble Jonathan Brisbane."

"Well, I assure you that is because I—"

"Yes, yes, you actors are always in character. Very commendable."

Jonathan stared at the oddly dressed woman with her long-sleeved dress, apron, and what he assumed was a maid's cap and shook his head. He was about to correct her on her attire when a young woman marched over to them.

* * *

Carrie Stern had moved through the crowd inside Serenity with quick, frustrated steps. She had already wasted an hour searching the grounds with no sign of Amanda. It was as if she had simply disappeared, but the car parked on the street indicated that Amanda should still be inside.

"I'm looking for a friend of mine. She was dressed in black and carrying a video camera."

The description drew Jonathan's attention and, while the woman, whom he assumed to be the person in authority—a docent, according to what Amanda had taught him—related that she had not seen this woman. Jonathan immediately intervened.

"I have seen her," he offered, recognizing Carrie Stern from Amanda's moving pictures.

Carrie smiled and glanced down at her watch in relief. She could still make the bus for work. "Great. I was leaving and remembered I have the house keys with me."

"I would be happy to take them to her," Jonathan offered with an eager, outstretched hand.

Leery of trusting a stranger, Carrie pulled back the hand with the keys. "Just tell me where you saw her. Where can I find her?" She glanced down once more at her watch before looking up into Jonathan's eyes and tapping her foot impatiently.

The docent had been watching their exchange with equal impatience. She had waited all day for the actor portraying Jonathan Brisbane to show up, and now that he was here, it looked like he'd be further detained. This Reenactment Day was certainly not one of her more organized ones, a fact becoming more painfully obvious as the day wore on.

"Give them to me," she said quickly. "We'll hold them for your friend in the director's office."

Jonathan watched in dismay as the docent pocketed the keys, the only obvious means of getting Amanda into her home. He was at a loss as to how to go about returning without her help and, certainly, he could not live among these people. Nor did he wish to. As soon as Amanda's recall returned—and he silently prayed it would—they would have to discuss their incredible journey and ultimately find their way back to 1884; back to Vivian and, regretfully, to Lavinia as well.

* * *

One hand gripping the banister and the other rubbing the swelling bump on her head, Amanda carefully descended the grand staircase. What had happened to her? A hazy vagueness draped over her mind like a thick veil, preventing her from catching any memory of how she even got to this historical site. Was she fond of history? Had she made such trips before? And that strangely dressed doctor...he must be part of a reenactment. Yet, there was something curiously familiar about him. It was as if those startling green eyes of his had known her intimately. *I must know him. Didn't he call me by my first name...?*

"Amanda!"

There he was, rushing up to her at the landing. Amanda stared down at his strong shoulders, remembering how his assuming frame had dwarfed that of the guard.

"Doctor!" She reached out a hand, and with his assistance, stepped firmly onto the bottom step.

"It's Jonathan,"

"Dr. Jonathan."

"No. Don't you remember?" He led her over to the side of the staircase and out of the way of the mingling tourists who were invading his home.

In an attempt to disguise his alarm, Jonathan patted her hand reassuringly. Hopefully, her memory loss was temporary; he prayed that he would prove correct in his assumption.

"I'm sorry," Amanda was saying, "but, I don't seem to recall anything before falling."

"You should be home in bed, resting," he offered.

"Home?"

A blank stare replaced the one of recognition Jonathan had hoped to find in Amanda's eyes.

"Do you remember home?" he urged. "May I escort you there?"

"Home," she repeated. "Yes, I remember where I live."

Jonathan heaved a heavy sigh, thankful for small favors. In time, she might remember him as well. She had to, else how would he be able to return to his time without her? He was sure they were in her time for a reason. He smiled reassuringly and glanced around at the plaques on the doors along the corridor. His eyes settled on the one labeled Director. Ironically, this room had once been his study. Grabbing Amanda by the shoulders, Jonathan spun her around and asked that she wait while he retrieved her keys. She did so, gratefully, without question. It was absurd to be knocking on his own study door, but this was not his time, and certainly not his door. He raised his fist and rapped several times before swinging the door open. Amanda's keys lay on a mahogany desk not unlike the one he used over one hundred years ago. He quickly grabbed them and rejoined Amanda in the hall. Once more, he took her hand and together they moved toward the entrance.

"You can't leave now! Where do you think you're going?" The head docent stopped them by the door, the Serenity brochures tucked close to her bosom.

"I am escorting Miss Lloyd to her home." Jonathan flashed her his best smile. "She has had a nasty fall..."

"Goodness!" The woman's hand flew up to her lips in alarm, the brochures falling to the floor. "We could be sued!"

Jonathan bent down and scrambled them up while tucking one into his breast pocket. "No litigation should be necessary. I will make certain Miss Lloyd arrives home safely."

"And who will play the part of Jonathan Brisbane?" the woman asked.

Amanda had been silent during the exchange. This doctor appeared to be firm in his insistence and the docent was unrelenting. For some inexplicable reason, Amanda wanted him to accompany her. He was the only truly kind face she'd seen since awakening from her accident.

"Please. I need to get home." She rubbed a hand to the rising bump on her head before snatching the keys from Jonathan's hands and automatically singling out the car key.

"Surely, you do not intend to...drive?" questioned Jonathan, horrified at the idea of being a passenger in her steel motor carriage.

"Yes, Miss Lloyd, is it wise?" put in the docent.

"No problem." Amanda smiled before resting her eyes on the gorgeous emerald pools of Dr. Jonathan. "Shall we?"

Nodding, Jonathan nervously followed Amanda out the door and officially into her century.

CHAPTER THIRTY-SIX

They rode in silence, Jonathan held tightly by the thick strap that folded around his body the moment he had sat down and shut the door of Amanda's steel motor carriage. He did not move—was afraid to move. In truth, he didn't know if he was supposed to move. Why else would one be strapped in place except to hinder movements? For several long minutes his head was spinning as fast as the wheels beneath him. Amanda's insistence that she was driving the vehicle "only thirty miles per hour" added to his fear. The fact that she was operating this vehicle in a state of partial amnesia increased his uncertainty and panic. He turned his head slowly and looked over at her, a smile playing nervously on his lips.

"You are certain no harm can come to us?"

"My, you people certainly stay in character."

"I imagine I am a consummate actor."

At the next light, Amanda faced him. "You mean you're not really a doctor? Well, you sure fooled me." The light turned green and the car resumed its movement.

"You are not alone in your assumption."

"Anyway," she continued, "you're perfectly safe as long as you keep your seat belt on. I'm a good driver." She reached over and tugged the belt, which tightened around Jonathan's body. He stiffened. "It's OK," she reassured.

"I shall trust your judgment," he replied while attempting to relax. "I pray this journey will not be an arduous one."

"I only live the next town over."

Only? Jonathan shook his head. The people in this time seemed to move so fast, and he wasn't sure he found that appealing. Nor did he care for the outlandish costumes they wore. No...he shook his head vehemently and his eyes caught movement as they passed a gathering of trees. The movement was that of a woman; he was sure of it. Her sparse attire did little to disguise that fact. Her pantalets were at least a good three inches above her knees, her shirt had no sleeves, and, as attested to by the warmth that blushed to his cheeks, the woman wore no bosom restraint.

"Men are all alike." Amanda smiled.

Jonathan pulled his eyes away from the freely bobbing breasts of the young woman who ran along the paved walk. "Excuse me?"

"Men. A pretty face turns their heads. It never fails."

Jonathan cleared his throat uncomfortably. "That was more than a pretty face. How can one help but stare, considering her attire...or lack thereof?"

Amanda laughed. "Are you ever going to get out of character?"

Jonathan leaned back into the seat. "Probably not."

Suddenly, the car lurched forward and his belt tightened against his broad chest, pinning him to his seat. He turned startled eyes on Amanda whose hand, in reflex, reached out to his chest to prevent him from falling forward.

"Sorry about that. I didn't see the stop sign and stopped just short of it."

Jonathan straightened in his seat, finally letting out the breath that had come abruptly to a halt. "I should hate to see the results had you stopped long."

Amanda stared at him, and then narrowed her eyes. *Was he for real?*

"The house is just ahead on the right."

Jonathan was relieved to see the quaint two-story structure come into view. Red brick with rustic shutters, its paved yellow path welcomed visitors in warm invitation.

"Do you live alone?"

Amanda swung the car into the driveway as far as the garage doors and pushed the car into park. She switched around in her seat and faced him. "No, I have a roommate."

"Ah, yes. I believe I had the pleasure of meeting her. Miss Stern, isn't it?"

"Carrie Stern, yes. We've been friends since college."

"College...as in a university?"

"Yes, of course."

Jonathan followed her up the drive and to the front door, his eyes closely watching her for any indication of recall as she frantically searched through her key ring.

"May I be of assistance?"

"No, really, I know which one." Amanda separated the key and, singling out the one to the front door, swung it open and Jonathan followed her inside.

"You remember your name, where you live, and you even remember how to operate your..." He searched for the word. "Automobile."

"I guess I'm making progress, then," she said over her shoulder on her way through to the kitchen. "Care for some tea?" she called while filling the kettle at the sink.

Hands behind his back, Jonathan paced the length of the living room, his eyes ever observant. This was, after all, Amanda's world—her time. The plush burgundy furniture with pale mauve and pink pillows sprinkled about was Amanda; the circular table set in the center in front of the sofa was Amanda. The vase atop it was Amanda. Leaning forward, he inhaled the intoxicating blend of the freshly cut spring flowers, forever branding him with the fragrant reminder of her. And, too, a reminder of his beloved Serenity and his blue-ribbon blossoms that centuries of Brisbanes had tended to with prizewinning loving care.

"Jonathan?" Amanda was at the doorway holding a tray bearing two cups of tea and a platter of crackers and jam—the only decent food left in the house.

"When you didn't answer I decided to offer you a cup of tea and something to eat anyway." She placed the tray on the table and sat down. "Unfortunately, I still have to go food shopping, so we are stuck with this."

Jonathan smiled at the innocent reminder of their snack on the third floor of Serenity. "Thank you." He sat beside her and took the cup she offered. "It's soft," he said, bouncing lightly. "Your furniture. It's very soft," he marveled.

Amanda nodded. "I believe furniture should be designed for comfort."

Jonathan ran a hand over the velvety cushion. "Very sensible of you."

"Thanks." Amanda leaned back, cup against her chest, and eyed him curiously.

"So...where's your next gig?"

Jonathan turned and looked at her, eyebrows knitted together. "Gig?" His mouth formed the sprout word around his teeth.

"You know...your next acting job."

"I'm afraid I don't have one." He returned his attention to his cup thinking she must believe him to be a fool, with his outdated clothing and no means of employment. If only she remembered him... remembered his wealth, his time, his neglected law practice.

"If it's all the same to you, I was going to ask if you would stay the night especially since Carrie isn't coming home."

Again, he marveled. She trusted him. Granted, he was not truly a stranger, but in her amnesiac state, he certainly was.

"I would be happy to oblige."

"Great!" Amanda set down her cup and rose abruptly. "I've got to get out of these clothes. I feel like I've been in them forever."

Jonathan could not help the smile that claimed his lips. He would have enjoyed reveling in that particular undertaking, and with a generous offer of assistance!

Darkness began to close around the house by the time Amanda returned, and with the flick of a wall switch, she set the living room ablaze with light. Jonathan shook his head in awe.

"Thomas would surely be pleased," he mumbled, half to himself.

"Thomas?"

"Edison. Thomas Edison."

"I'm sure."

She stood before him in a pale pink slip of a nightgown, her matching robe slightly open. He could not pull his eyes away from the jarring image. *And those legs! Good Lord, it was as if they had no end!*

"You talk like you knew him," she was saying.

"I have done extensive research on Edison."

"Oh? Then you've worked as an actor at Glenmont as well?" She sat down on the sofa, her nearness so threatening he loosened his tie to breathe.

"I have never been to Glenmont." His words came softly as he reeled in his emotions.

"Well, if you would like, tomorrow we can reserve tickets and visit together."

"Is that wise?" He reached a hand up and palmed the perspiration from his brow. The room was closing in on him and threatened to swallow him up.

"As long as you're staying the night, and have nowhere to go in the morning. Besides, it will be my way of repaying you for your kindness back at Serenity."

Jonathan could stand it no longer and nearly jumped from his seat. He pulled a cheroot from the inside pocket of his jacket and snipped off the end between his teeth and lit it. "Indeed, why not."

"Good. It's settled then." Amanda picked up the tray. "I'll be back in a jiffy. Once I rinse these cups I'll make up the bed in the guest room."

Jonathan puffed small circles into the air as he watched her slender form race from the kitchen and up the stairs, his eyes riveted to her sloping contours. He was aching for her now, and he wondered if she would ever remember him at all. Had he lost her completely? The ache seared right through his heart and sent a chill up and down his spine. He wanted his Amanda back, yet he was helpless to do anything but bide the time. Time. Blasted time was interfering again. Sitting down, he leaned against the soft cushions of the sofa and quietly smoked, his thoughts all absorbed on the beguiling woman on the floor above him.

This could drive me mad, he thought dismally. Foremost on his mind was the essence of time itself. Had it ceased while he was here? Or was life continuing in

1884 Serenity? If the latter was true, he wondered how Lavinia was reacting to his disappearance. He sighed heavily and slipped the cheroot in the ashtray on the table, all at once remembering the guidebook he had picked up from the floor of Serenity. An unsettling feeling swept over him as he held it in his hands and began to leaf through it. Astonishment replaced fear as he stared at the photographs. One was of himself that he found most unflattering. The others were of a confident Lavinia and a somberly defeated-looking Vivian. He read the words typed neatly beneath his name:

"With the sudden disappearance in 1884 of prominent patent barrister Jonathan Brisbane, whose most famous client was Thomas Alva Edison, Serenity lost most of its light and drive, not to mention funds for upkeep. By 1886, most of the sixty-five acres of land were sold off just to keep Serenity operating. Though his disappearance was investigated, Jonathan Brisbane was never found. It is assumed he met with foul play from an Edison detractor."

"Humph!" Jonathan tossed the guidebook onto the table, eyes afire. He had to do something. According to this book, he would never return, and that, he decided, was out of the question. "I will not let this happen!" he yelled in a booming voice. "I have my obligation to Edison...to my family!"

* * *

Amanda had been watching her curious new friend for several long minutes, duplicitous feelings invading her. On the one hand, he was a stranger, an actor who was never properly introduced to her, but who had helped her after her fall. His kindness in reaching out to a fellow human being was touching, and, she was sure, sincere. Yet, here he was yelling nonsense in her living room with a look of horror on his face that had stopped her in her tracks.

"Is everything all right?" she asked cautiously.

Her voice brought Jonathan's head up with a jerk, and the sight of her soft body folded into the sheer garment brought a smile back to his lips.

"I...have no nightclothes with me," he said, thinking quickly. "I was cursing myself for not remembering my luggage, which I'm afraid is back at Serenity."

Relieved, Amanda smiled. "No problem. Come with me," she said while leading him up to the guest room on the second floor. "I'm sure I have something that will fit you just fine."

"This was my father's." Amanda held a powder blue robe against Jonathan's chest and marveled at how quickly his eyes changed from green to deep blue. Her eyes moved down to his angular jaw, so strong and firm, before resting on his full, sensuous mouth. This was ridiculous! She hardly knew this man. Where were these steamy feelings coming from?

Jonathan looked down at the garment and grinned. "Am I to wear only this?"

"It's all I have in men's sleepwear." She smiled and quickly smoothed a hand over the already neatly made bed of the guest room.

Jonathan watched her intently. She appeared to be fidgety and suddenly quite silent. "Have you no servant to do that?" He slipped off his jacket and neatly folded it over a nearby chair.

"I can't afford one. Money doesn't grow on trees, you know." She tugged the end of the sheet and tightened a rounded corner.

"Well of course it doesn't."

"That's what it takes for hired help these days." She stepped back and admired her work before turning to him. "Do you like the robe?"

"Yes. I would like to wash up before I put it on." His eyes scanned the room.

"It's down the hall on the right," she said, reading his mind. "I'll say good night now."

"Pleasant dreams, Amanda."

CHAPTER THIRTY-SEVEN

Amanda tossed and turned in her bed, kicking off the light sheet that covered her body as rivulets of sweat dripped from her face.

"Amanda...Amanda..."

Voices called her name, echoing somewhere in the dark rafters of her mind.

"Amanda, you must return. You must right things for those you love at Serenity. And you must return with Jonathan, and above all, secure the document to take back with you. Amanda? Amanda...heed our words. Hear our plea! We invoke your spirits to return once more to your life in the year 1884."

With a sharp intake of breath, Amanda's eyes flew open and wildly scanned the inky corners of the room before she released a bloodcurdling scream.

"Jonathan!"

Jonathan had been stirring restlessly, the hum from passing motorists doing little to ease him into slumber. Leaping from the bed at the sound of Amanda's voice, he hurried down the hall to her room, his fingers flying blindly to the wall switches as he had seen Amanda do. Soon the surrounding hallway was filled with bright electric light. With a quick turn of the knob, he swung open the door. Amanda lay trembling on her bed, the sheet pulled up to her chin. Rushing to her, he gathered her tenderly into his arms and gently rocked her.

"What is it? A bad dream?"

Clutching her arms around his neck, Amanda collapsed against his chest. "Oh, Jonathan, I remember. I remember!" Her voice was soft and cracked with emotion, and she began to sob.

"Thank God. I thought I may have lost you forever."

Kissing her tear-stained face, he eased her back against the soft pillows and lay down beside her, his arms still tightly encircling her soft body as he fit himself around her like a spoon.

"I can't believe it." Amanda let out a deep sigh. "One minute we were in Serenity in 1884, and the next thing I remember is hearing music from my time and hitting my head."

"And a hard fall it was. Enough to knock you senseless."

Amanda looked up at him, her dark eyes wide and fearful. "I tried to stop you, Jonathan, but that inexplicable wind sent me reeling." She reached up a hand to the swollen lump on her head and winced.

Jonathan gently peeled back the tendrils of damp hair that stuck to her cheeks. "I feared for your life. I had no alternative but to run for you. When you woke amnesic, I could only pray that your memory loss would be temporary."

Amanda turned and rested her hand on his chest. "My poor Jonathan. This must have been an unnerving ordeal for you."

Jonathan smiled. With all she had been through, she was thinking only of his safety. He lowered his lips to hers in a sweet kiss. "Tell me about your dream."

"I heard a voice telling me I had to return with you with a document to make things right at Serenity. The voice sounded familiar...like Madame Winston, but it was too faint for me to be sure."

Jonathan shook his head in dismay. "Lavinia must be wreaking havoc, else why would you receive such a message?"

Amanda bit into her lower lip as the realization of his words embraced her. "A message...? A message! Of course...that must be it!"

"I must be missing something important here. I still do not understand."

She sat up on her knees and tugged on his arm excitedly. "Our purpose here must be to find your original divorce papers. They must still be here!" She smiled triumphantly.

"How can you be sure they still exist or that we can even return? I fear you are assuming too much." He dotted her face with tiny kisses. "Poor mother. She must be frantic at our disappearance. She is the innocent in all of this, you know."

"She knows the truth, Jonathan."

"How can you be so sure?"

"Madame Winston is also a time traveler. By now...I'm sure she has had to tell Vivian the truth in order to send a message through time. There is strength in the power of prayer, and prayer backed up by intention is even more powerful. I'm sure they had both."

Jonathan's laugh was rich and deep, and Amanda welcomed the sound of it.

"Nothing should surprise me anymore." He gazed down at her lovely face and kissed her forehead. "I love you, Amanda."

Relief flowed through her like a soft subtle breeze, and with both hands, he pulled her face to him and wrapped his lips around hers in a flaming kiss.

"You have captured my heart, sweet Amanda, and I will love you forever. But, first we need to find the way home."

CHAPTER THIRTY-EIGHT

The sun streamed through the window of the third-floor bedroom and Lavinia's eyes flew open, a curse pouring from her lips; the red dress, a sore reminder of Jonathan's betrayal. Ripping at the buttons of the dress she wore, she scrambled to the closet and pulled out a wrapper. *I'm going to find out what's going on if it's the last thing I do!*

"Why are they locked in the front parlor? Is Jonathan in there? Is that woman with him?" Lavinia shot questions at Alan like arrows at a target. The faithful servant offered only shrugs in response.

"Mrs. Brisbane does not wish to be disturbed."

"Is that so?" Lavinia crossed her arms akimbo. "Well, we'll just see about that!"

Inside the room, where their "séance" had taken place, the women were completely drained of energy, signs of fatigue clearly evident from the paleness of their faces. Yolanda took out her Rosary and began her prayers of gratitude, while Vivian poured a cool glass of water from the pitcher Alan had thoughtfully provided only moments ago. The night had been a long one, and Vivian was not confident that the message had gotten through to Amanda.

"What will we do if they do not, or cannot, return?" Vivian asked, her eyes red from the intense concentration required of her.

Yolanda looked up and noticed the deepened lines of worry on Vivian's forlorn face. "Life is never beyond hope. The Lord will right this, Vivian. The universe will see to it that the message was received. Have faith."

"Oh, please do not be cryptic with me, Yolanda. We have been through too much together on this night. You insult me...how will my faith, my hope, physically bring back my son and Amanda? It is a nice thought in theory, but I do not believe it in practice."

"Cryptic? I am only conveying to you the power of intention, and that if you have faith in what we *intended* here tonight—which was to send a message to Amanda across time—that very *faith* will carry that message to her as if on the wings of an angel." Yolanda laughed sardonically. "In my time they would call what I just told you...'New Age nonsense' but I have faith, and so should you," the medium implored. "I may not really be a psychic medium in the true sense of the word, but I am intuitive and I believe Amanda heard me. I have faith that the dream message was received." Her statement rested unfinished by the intrusion of a rapping on the door.

With a rustle of skirts, Vivian rose to unlatch the door. "I told Alan that we were not to be disturbed."

"Still calling up the dead, are we? I thought perhaps Jonathan was here." Lavinia breezed into the room uninvited, her blue wrapper trailing behind her.

"Well, he is not." Vivian glared at her, blue daggers matching those of Lavinia whose look spoke volumes.

"So, the master of Serenity has not returned? Strange, don't you think?" Lavinia turned to Alan who still stood by the partially open parlor door. "Inform

Ruth that I will not be a participant for breakfast. I have...business...in town."

Vivian's lips formed a tight line. "Off to join Linwood Crane?"

"How perceptive of you, *Mother* Vivian." Lavinia smiled sweetly to add emphasis, and was not disappointed when Vivian flinched. "In fact, I do intend to visit with Linwood. I fear he is the only person available to provide answers to my many questions regarding the...disappearance...of my dear husband." She inched backward slowly, her eyes holding Vivian's in defiance. "Perhaps we can locate Amanda Lloyd so I may get to the root of this deception."

"No one is deceiving you, Lavinia. You are more than capable of doing that all by yourself," Vivian spat.

Ignoring her, Lavinia called upon the waiting Alan. "Have Renee draw a bath; a proper bath, please."

CHAPTER THIRTY-NINE

"Your father was a tall man," Jonathan said after dressing in the gray trousers and blue shirt Amanda had found in her parents' trunk. He joined her at the kitchen table.

"Yes, he was." She poured two mugs of coffee from the brewer and sat across from him at the round table. There was a long silence before she spoke again. "I guess the next step would be to go back to Serenity and inquire about any papers the library may have pertaining to your family." She blew into the cup and took a small sip.

"Logical, but unlikely to offer results. I had the opportunity to read the guidebook again. It does not paint a pretty picture." He stretched his long legs out in front of him and rested his hands across his chest. "I disappeared in 1884, the presumed victim of foul play."

Amanda forced a smile. "That's not necessarily a bad omen, Jonathan. Clearly, it indicates that the guidebook changes history as we move through time."

Jonathan slammed his mug down on the table, his hands trembling in a rage he wished he could control. "Damn it all! This moving through time business is trying my nerves. While we sit here in your sunny kitchen spouting conjecture, Lavinia is most assuredly making mother's life a living hell!"

Amanda reached over and touched her hand to his. "We need optimism, Jonathan. Collective optimism. We will accomplish nothing with anger." Amanda surprised herself with that statement. She had heard it often in her tender years from her mother who believed true accomplishment could be wrought only through peaceful means.

"All right then," Jonathan conceded. "What have you in mind in this fast-paced world of yours?"

Amanda ignored the comment and bit into her lower lip as she thought about his question. Obviously, Jonathan was not happy in her century. If they were to be together, it would have to be in his.

"We go to Serenity." She lifted her head to the wall clock bearing the depiction of Scarlett O'Hara and Rhett Butler from the movie *Gone with the Wind*, and she shook her head. The movies knew nothing of reality. *They truly are fantasy.*

* * *

The Serenity Library was not in Serenity at all. Instead, they were directed to an old house next door. Amanda figured it to have been built around 1900. They knocked on the door and a rotund woman with wavy silver hair greeted them, and admitted them with a warm smile. Amanda had expected her to be dressed in the period of the day, but instead she wore a pair of jeans and a white "Serenity" T-shirt with blue lettering. Jonathan groaned as he strived to keep his temper in check at such blatant commercialism, deciding he disliked this century more each moment he lived in it.

"Come in. The name's Marge and I'm senior librarian here." She smiled with full white teeth as Amanda and Jonathan stepped in to the cluttered front room. "Excuse the mess. We're in the process of disposing of what the historical society feels is of little consequence. It's a big job."

Jonathan scanned the haphazardly stuffed boxes of books and papers that lined the walls and made a great effort to swallow down his anger. "Indeed."

Marge stared at him through her bifocals. "My... how very remarkable. You could pass for Jonathan Brisbane himself!"

"So, I have been told," he replied tersely.

Amanda shot him a look of reprimand. "We would like to see Jonathan Brisbane's divorce papers."

Marge frowned. "The Brisbanes didn't divorce. At least not to my knowledge."

"May we have a look around?" Amanda pressed.

Marge obliged, indicating a wall of framed documents and shadow boxes protecting the papers and articles regarding the Brisbane family. With each document, it became more obvious they would not find what they were looking for in this room. Inquiring with Marge again, they discovered there were more family papers in a storeroom on the grounds. Though logged, the society had decided they were not of much importance, and for the sake of space, would soon be discarded and shredded. A noticeable sweat formed along Jonathan's brow at the very thought, and his heart hammered against his chest as a deluge of new rage flooded through him. Amanda touched her hand to his and clasped it firmly, her words pouring forth in a rush.

"We would be pleased to take them off your hands."

Marge smiled. "Be my guest. As long as you haul them away personally, you can have them. The volunteers here are far too busy to be dealing with that pile of trash too."

Thanking Marge profusely, Amanda and Jonathan followed her down to the dark storeroom behind the house. Marge flipped the light switch in the musty room and left them to their task. Jonathan was already heaving up a dusty box and heading for Amanda's vehicle.

"I'm glad we won't have to make a second trip," Amanda announced a half hour later as they crammed the last box into the car.

He nodded. "We have a considerable burden before us."

Amanda smiled confidently. "We'll find it, Jonathan."

"I wish I shared your optimism," he said while rounding to the passenger's side and opening the car door.

"Look on the bright side."

"There is a bright side to all this?"

"Of course. You're here in person and will be able to identify most of the paperwork in these boxes. Without you, it could take months—even years—to sift through this stuff."

CHAPTER FORTY

Once the boxes were scattered around her living room, Amanda prepared a pitcher of iced tea and returned to help Jonathan in the search. He was scanning papers at an alarming rate, tossing them aside the moment they proved useless, which was usually after the first sentence.

"Most of this is worthless." He looked up from the stack in front of him, his eyes darkening along with his mood.

The sun was going down as they silently pored over the boxes, papers of insignificance being hurled to one side. Near the end of the box in front of her, Amanda touched upon a leather-bound book. She carefully reached in and removed it, silently reading the title across its face.

"Jonathan!"

"Have you found it?" Jonathan stretched from his kneeling position beside his box and hurried to her side.

Amanda sat cross-legged on the floor, her back against the couch. "I'm not sure what I've found. It looks like a journal."

"A journal?"

Amanda smoothed her fingers across the raised lettering and looked up at him. "'Vivian Brisbane: A

Journal to My Son," she read. "It's dated 1884." She looked up at him in dismay. "It makes no sense. Why would the historical society cast this aside?"

"Let me have a look."

Jonathan recognized his mother's handwriting immediately; the familiar curls of her penmanship tugging at his heart. "Perhaps it was merely misplaced." He looked into her eyes and smiled. "For sure, it will lead us somewhere. It must!"

Together, they reviewed each entry, slowly and painstakingly recalling the once vibrant woman they shared a love for.

April 30, 1884 – *My dearest Jonathan, I miss you. I wonder often in my sleepless nights how you and Amanda are faring in your world beyond time. We tried so hard to contact you—to pass along our message—in vain as it turned out.*

May 2, 1884 – *Yolanda Winston has departed Serenity this day. I pleaded with her to extend her visit. In desperation, I suppose, for without her, I am devoid of an ally, and I will miss a woman who has become my dearest confidante. A courier arrived with an envelope for you bearing a governmental seal. I assume it contains the divorce documents. What little good do they now, my only son?*

May 4, 1884 – *Hell hath no fury like a woman scorned! None of us has been spared Lavinia's constant interrogation as to your whereabouts, and I dare not offer answers. She would only laugh and accuse me of deception...or lunacy! The woman is quite out of her mind. I pray you will one day return.*

May 18, 1884 – *There has been no word from Linwood Crane in some time. I strongly believe that he blames himself for disclosing Amanda's existence to Lavinia. I took it upon myself to send word with Alan that I do not hold him accountable. Lavinia is here to stay and the documents, for what good they are, have been secured.*

Before Yolanda parted, we performed the most eccentric of ceremonies. She called it a "Time Capsule." Therein lies your document, near my precious blue-ribbon roses in the southwest gardens, buried as deep as two women stealing into the night could bury.

June 1, 1884 – *My tears stain these pages as thoughts of you torment my sleeping world, while Lavinia torments my waking one. I pray that you and Amanda are together and faring better in the future than I am in my present.*

Jonathan flipped through the remainder of the journal before looking up at Amanda; his eyes glistening with unshed tears. "The rest of the book is blank."

Amanda's tears flowed freely and she folded her arms around him. They sat that way for a long time, neither seeming to find words to declare what they were feeling. Amanda finally found the strength to break away. Lifting an arm, she wiped her tears with the back of her hand.

"It all makes sense now, Jonathan. The reason the guidebook doesn't mention your divorce is because the documents have been buried all these years."

Jonathan rose and stretched his long legs, his hands on his knees for support. He moved to the mantel of the fireplace and stood before it, fingers tapping rapidly.

"Apparently, we are doomed to remain here," he finally remarked with thinly disguised bitterness. "Meanwhile, my dear mother, once a strong and willful woman, will be ultimately reduced to insanity from loneliness and abuse."

Amanda unfolded her legs and slowly got up. "No, Jonathan, there is still hope. She and Yolanda Winston buried a time capsule. Don't you see? All we need to do is dig it up!"

He turned and stared at her as if she had lost her mind. "And how do you propose we do that? How can we be sure it's still there? Is it not a fact that most of my acreage was sold off? And is it not a fact that the historical society is not about to allow strangers to dig up the property behind Serenity? And is it not a fact that doing so without permission would be outright vandalism? Surely, there are laws even in *this* century that protect its citizens." He eyed her sternly.

Hands on hips, Amanda faced him squarely. "Facts they may be, but I am going to find that time capsule with or without you."

"And how do you propose to do that, may I ask?"

Amanda came closer to him, her voice trembling. "You once accused me of being a spy. I guess I was pretty good at it or else we wouldn't be in this fix in the first place. And as for my century, we certainly do have laws to protect our citizens. We are not barbaric simply because we are not like you!" She reeled around and with firm steps walked up the stairs. "I'm leaving tonight...with or without you."

Jonathan watched her disappear to the second floor, a string of curses quietly leaving his lips. "Well, I'm not about to allow you to go alone," he shouted up to her. "You wouldn't know where to look. I'm coming along!"

"Fine!" she called down.

"Fine!" he shouted back.

CHAPTER FORTY-ONE

They could hear the soft ripple of water as it washed over the rocks in a stream somewhere behind Serenity. Amanda—dressed in her familiar black from head to toe, including fedora—stopped abruptly at the sound and turned questioning eyes to Jonathan.

"The stream where I once sought repose," he whispered beside her. "I also fished there to relax when my law practice overwhelmed me." He leaned his arms over the white picket fence surrounding his beloved Serenity and rested them around the slats; hands locked together, eyes seeing something only Amanda could imagine.

She touched a hand to his shoulder, the inky blackness covering them like a blanket. She wanted him to paint the picture for her—to see what he saw. Now was not the time, or the century.

Jonathan turned to her and smiled. "As soon as we return I shall take you there, Amanda."

She smiled and stepped up on her toes to kiss his cheek. "Now that's what I call optimism! Come on, the sooner we get this over with the safer I'll feel." She raised a leg to climb the fence.

"Now that sounds suspiciously pessimistic." With both hands, he boosted her up from behind and a giggle escaped Amanda as she felt him pinch her there.

She darted him a scandalous look and swiftly cleared the fence.

Jonathan followed, clearing the fence effortlessly and without help. He dusted off the knees of his trousers before standing erect.

"Show-off."

He grinned and together they inched around the house to the gardens, their flashlights deliberately off. Jonathan didn't need one; he knew his grounds better than anyone. He took her hand into his as they silently crossed the darkness down the path to the rose gardens.

"Do you smell it?"

"Yes."

"Mother's roses...so sweet to the senses." He pointed to a row of plants. "Japanese quince," he remarked. "And yonder, those leafy plants are called burnet. We often use them in salads. Ruth outdoes herself in that department."

For a long moment, they stood inhaling the fresh night aroma of another time, one thy equally yearned to return to. Amanda's shoulders sagged and she pinched his arm.

"Ouch! What was that for?" Jonathan rubbed the tender spot vigorously.

"For dreaming. I hate to use a cliché, Jonathan, but wake up and smell the roses. Save the history lesson for later. This is no time to reminisce."

"Forgive me, but it's difficult not to."

She nodded and they continued along the path of roses of yellow and red, tea blooms of pink and white. He's right, Amanda thought, it's easy to dream while encircled by such a heady bouquet.

"I wish Vivian had been more specific as to where in the gardens she buried the capsule." Flashlight held low, Amanda walked fluidly through the thickets of roses, careful to avoid their prickly thorns.

"Mother was distraught, and I'm sure both she and Yolanda Winston were acting in urgency."

"God only knows how many times this ground has been dug up and tended to by the historical society," Amanda pointed out, her light flashing on newly turned soil. "Maybe I should have gone into the spy business rather than photography."

They were both in the kneeling position when Jonathan's flashlight fell to the ground, it's beam shimmering on something at the end of the garden. He rose quickly.

"Jonathan, what's the matter?" Amanda stood.

"Listen."

Amanda took great pains to prevent the pounding of her accelerated heartbeat from reaching her ears. Then she heard it too: weeping, the heart-wrenching sound of a woman weeping.

Jonathan pointed, mesmerized by the statue situated at the end of the garden, the precise area of his mother's prize-winning roses. "It was not here in my time." His voice held a tremor as he moved aggressively to the statue, the pressure within his aching heart heavy against his chest.

Amanda followed, dropping her own flashlight in the process as she stumbled up to the eerie moonlight mist that draped the sculpture. She watched as Jonathan fell to his knees, his hands clasped together in prayer. The identity of the likeness eluded Amanda until she passed like liquid through the formidable mist and to Jonathan's side. She gasped, her hands flying up to her mouth to smother her scream.

CHAPTER FORTY-TWO

"Vivian!"

Her hands moved to the artfully sculpted face of the woman she had embraced as she would her own mother. With her finger, she traced the lines of the single chiseled tear etched below Vivian's left eye. Amanda looked down at Jonathan's figure slumped over the image of his mother, his shoulders shaking as deep sobs wracked his body. She stared blankly at his neatly tailored blue jacket that seemed to turn old and gray before her eyes. Realizing what this monument was, she knelt down beside him.

"Oh, Jonathan, I..."

"Look down," he demanded softly.

Amanda rested her eyes to where his lingered. A reedy line of shallow water trickled down from the statue and formed a moat around Vivian's marble form.

He turned to her, his tortured eyes a murky green, like the turbulent high seas, as they locked to hers.

"We dig here. Where is the shovel?" He stood abruptly, a hand reaching to assist Amanda up.

"B-by the front gate," she stammered, appalled by his intent.

"Never mind. There's one in the shed." He walked to the right comer of the garden with purposeful movements.

"The shed?" she repeated, following him with quick steps.

"I keep them in the shed."

"You *kept* them in there in 1884! Jonathan, please! We can't do this." She tripped over a tree stump, Jonathan all but ignoring her once he came upon the shed and opened the door.

Taking out a shovel, he smiled grimly. "I will do the digging."

"Jonathan, you are defacing private property."

He spun around angrily, shot her a burning look, and staggered back to the statue. In her haste to catch up with him, Amanda's fedora fell from her head, her long hair a tangled dark mass of curls falling around her shoulders.

"Damn it, Jonathan, you can't dig up your mother's grave!" She was beside him now and tugging at his sleeve, her face an angry crimson. "Please listen to me!"

"No." He touched a hand to her cheek tenderly. "My mother is not buried here. There is no date of birth or death to denote that. This is merely a statue of cold marble, a monument erected in her honor." With a plunge, the shovel hit the dirt as Jonathan heaved forth a mighty mound from the moat.

"It's her grave, Jonathan!" Amanda angrily repeated.

"For the last time, no one is buried here!" His furious digging abated only for the moment, he leaned his body against the handle of the shovel to catch his breath. "If one thinks of it logically one will come to the conclusion that what we experienced here was the whisper of the wind, the result of constant watering from a gardener, and the vivid imaginings night so easily invokes." With that, he removed his jacket, loosened his shirt, and struck the shovel into the deepening hole.

Frustrated, Amanda backed off. He was losing his mind; that was it. It had to be. Her eyes never left the rippling movement of his muscles as they bore the shovel deeper in the hole, not a bead of perspiration for the effort.

"Has it occurred to you that maybe you're digging in the wrong spot?" she asked hopefully.

"No! Now hush!"

The shovel hit something and Amanda cringed. She let out a long breath, dreading the sound of the contact of the shovel once it hit its mark. She shut her eyes tightly and covered them with her hands as Jonathan brushed aside the remaining dirt in further investigation.

"Well?" Spreading her fingers, she peeked through them in fearful anticipation.

Jonathan lifted out a brown canvas sack and began to unroll it. Amanda watched as a dusty green jar came into view. "Thank you, Mother," he whispered. Fingering the remaining dirt, they could clearly see an envelope inside.

"It's OK, my darling. We're going home."

CHAPTER FORTY-THREE

The hours at Serenity were ten to four, except Sundays, which was Reenactment Day when the docents came out dressed in the garb of Jonathan's day, or so they thought. Earlier that morning, Amanda had freshened up her black ensemble and done her best to dust off the remains of Jonathan's digging from his suit. The faded marks at his knees, despite modern detergents, were there to stay.

Jonathan was relieved when he and Amanda knocked on the front door. Marge, in her jeans and tasteless Serenity T-shirt, was actually a welcome sight. At least he would not have to contend with the aggressive head docent. The last thing he wanted was to have to invent excuses regarding his "acting gig," as Amanda referred to it.

"Well, hello there!" beamed Marge, her puffy cheeks a cheery red. "How are you doing with your research?"

About to comment, Jonathan felt Amanda's hand lightly touch his shoulder. "It's a chore, but we happen to love history. You might want to say those boxes are a blessing to us."

"Well, good!" Marge clapped her hands together and ushered them inside. "It's so refreshing to see young people taking an interest in history. Too many fine old buildings have been torn down over the last few years, and it's all because of ignorance. Young and old alike just don't have the appreciation of the past, too busy to preserve it." Marge stopped at the guest registry that lay open on a mahogany desk in the foyer and picked up a pen. "The government has gotten involved now. Considering your love of history, I'm sure you'd like to sign this petition." She handed Amanda the pen.

"Petition?" It was Jonathan who posed the question, his barrister's mind attentive as he bent over to read the paragraph above the row of signatures. Impressed, he took the pen from Amanda and was about to sign his name when she slid the pen from his fingers. He nodded. He didn't live in this time. His signature could change that and could prevent them from returning to his Serenity, if that was possible at all.

"From what we've heard," Marge explained. "Some corporate people in California may be thinking about building a theme park right in the middle of some very historical battlefields."

"Why?" Jonathan looked from Marge to Amanda with the face of someone who found the whole concept preposterous.

"For money, of course." Marge pointed to the tin coin box beside the registry.

"That's why the society has been forced to increase admission to Serenity. There's still enough acreage around here for developers to want to get a hold of, and there's been talk that Serenity may be on the list for the wrecking ball."

Wrecking ball? Though he wasn't sure what it was, it sounded ominous. He looked at the sign in front of the box: *Admission $5*. Though a good deal of money in 1884, if what Amanda said about the depreciation of the dollar was true, his beloved Serenity was begging to be saved. He looked over at Amanda, the anguish in his eyes like murky water in a muddy pool.

"Two tickets, please," Amanda said quickly, desperate to try to return. She missed Serenity...Vivian...Renee. And she wanted Jonathan to show her the stream behind Serenity, to experience the solace he'd found there; to love him there.

Marge handed them each a ticket and guidebook. "You're the only visitors. Remember, the third floor is off limits."

Amanda nodded and they walked on.

"She didn't even question my choice of apparel." Jonathan's voice was a whisper as he took Amanda's hand into his and they walked up the grand staircase to the door that would lead them to the third floor, and hopefully, 1884.

Stopping just in front of it, Jonathan pulled Amanda to him as a fearful coolness flowed through his veins. "I love you, my dear sweet Amanda. We are going to marry and have lots of children." He kissed her hair, his other hand stroking her cheek. When he looked into her eyes, Amanda could see the water building behind his lids. "And we will grow old together, my darling, sitting on the porch of Serenity as we entertain our grandchildren with stories." Lifting her chin with his forefinger, Jonathan bent his head and fully kissed her mouth.

Amanda let her own tears flow freely and placed her hand on the doorknob.

Jonathan placed his hand over hers and together they turned the knob.

CHAPTER FORTY-FOUR

Amanda looked up at the long ascent before them, her hand tightly within Jonathan's as they proceeded to take the stairs. She climbed in slow motion, her feet heavy, and each lift a supreme effort that afforded her no progress. Rather than coming close to the landing, she felt it slipping away. The stairs were actually getting smaller! Alarms rang off in her head. *Something's not right.* Where was the wind? Was there a wind the first time? She couldn't remember. She was sure there was a force at work that had propelled the door to slam shut. Yet right now, she didn't remember hearing it slam. It was as if she and Jonathan just opened a door to the next floor instead of another century.

Stopping on the stairs, Jonathan took his hand off the banister and reached into the breast pocket of his jacket for Vivian's envelope. Shaking it open, he released the documents of his divorce and shook them out flat, all while still firmly holding Amanda's hand.

"Why did we stop? Something is wrong, isn't it?"

Pulling his eyes from the page, Jonathan gave her hand a tender squeeze.

"I...something told me to take the papers out of the envelope. I don't know how to explain it."

Relieved, Amanda sighed. "Intuition, Jonathan. Madame Winston doesn't corner the market on psychic awareness, you know. Everyone is psychic. The reason some more so than others is because the successful psychic listens to that intuition, and acts upon it."

Jonathan's deep laughter reverberated against the hollow stairway. Leaning his back against the wall to contain himself, he drew Amanda to him and continued to laugh.

"What's so funny?" she fumed.

"You are wonderful, you know that? I have never known a woman like you, Amanda. I'm laughing because for years I wanted to find that special part of me—the faceless, nameless woman I dreamed about, and she forever escaped me. How could I have known she would come not from across the sea, but across time itself?" His hand palming her face, he tilted his head and drew her lips to his. "It doesn't matter which century is at the top of the landing," he said, breaking the kiss, his words breathing life into her mouth. "As long as you are living it with me."

* * *

"Sneaking up to our parlor of passion, are we?"

The voice startled them. Hands still locked, they slowly turned to the source.

Lavinia stood on the landing in the red dress, hands on hips, lips strikingly painted as crimson as the flush of red on her cheeks, the anger in her eyes evident by the veined, bursting corpuscles that were once white. It was like staring at a caricature of the real person; *an angry, insane, very red* caricature. She shook her head as if she could will away the appalling vision.

"Lavinia?" Jonathan could hardly believe his eyes. Should he feel relief in knowing they were home, or terror at the hell ahead of them? He decided to be relieved. Hastily, he folded the papers in his hand and stuffed them once more into his breast pocket.

"Where have you been?" she asked, tapping her foot in impatience.

All she needs is a rolling pin, Amanda thought angrily.

"Come up, Jonathan," Lavinia curled her finger inward. "And do bring your little friend with you," she added sweetly.

Jonathan was all too familiar with that sugary voice. It was the one she used when she wished to be someone else, somewhere else. When she was Lavinia Beauregard, sixteen-year-old daughter of one of the wealthiest families of the South. The poor South, Jonathan thought bitterly. Hearing that very tone of voice had made him question her sanity on many occasions. He often wondered which woman he married, the siren or the belle?

"The belle from hell," Amanda hissed reading his thoughts, her voice low and conspiratorial.

Taken aback, Jonathan stared at her for a long moment. "Prepare yourself. This won't be very pretty."

"Neither is your wife," Amanda remarked while continuing up the stairs.

"What on earth is taking you so long?" One foot in front of her, Lavinia prepared to take the steps necessary to force them up to the third floor.

"No!" Jonathan and Amanda shouted in unison, the singular thought of Lavinia possibly running loose in the twenty-first century terrifying them both. After all, they couldn't be sure the portal was closed.

Taking the steps by twos, they rushed up to the landing as Lavinia stepped aside with the sweep of her hoops.

"Trousers?" She stared down at Amanda in reprimand. "My, my, but that will never do. Though I do recognize them. There most certainly must be an apparition fluttering around Serenity without any clothes!" She laughed an actual belly laugh.

Jonathan leaned in to smell her breath. "Brandy! My dear wife," he emphasized, "you are inebriated!"

"I am more than that, dear husband, as you shall soon discover." Lavinia wrapped her arms around Jonathan's neck and pressed her bosom against him, kissing his mouth hard and long.

Amanda felt the blood course through her veins at the display. She knew it was for her benefit and tried to hide her jealousy, but inside she felt like a thermometer about to explode. After what seemed like forever, Lavinia released him and gently trimmed away the fire-red of her lipstick from his lips with her fingernail. Wiping his mouth with the sleeve of his jacket Jonathan grabbed Amanda's hand and brushed past Lavinia.

"Why, how thoughtless of me." Lavinia put an arm around Amanda's shoulders and walked with them until she reached her bedroom door. "Lavinia Beauregard Brisbane, at your service." She curtsied and nearly lost her footing as she slammed her back into the door.

"This is Amanda Lloyd," introduced Jonathan quickly. "She is..."

"Yes, yes," Lavinia waved her hand in the air, unimpressed. "Thomas Edison's so-called cousin. I've had the pleasure of hearing all about her from Linwood Crane."

She patted Amanda's cheek.

"Is that so?" Amanda moved away from Lavinia's hand.

"Surely you are aware that Linwood is quite smitten with you, but, enough of that. If we are to have a party you must be dressed properly."

"A party?" Jonathan's eyes narrowed.

"That's right, you've been gone." Lavinia tapped her forefinger against her temple. "How silly of me to forget." She reached a hand up and patted the loose strands of her upsweep in place, lipstick smeared across her right cheek. "I thought it only proper that we present our esteemed guest to our friends." She tried another curtsy and stumbled awkwardly before regaining her footing. "However, I believe I shall take a tiny nap before the festivities."

With those words, she disappeared into the bedroom. Hearing the door latch, Jonathan pulled Amanda across the hall and into his office where he hugged her to him fiercely.

"The woman is intoxicated, and certainly acting queerly."

"She's insane," commented Amanda simply as she pushed away from him and wearily sat down in the wingback chair near the fireplace.

Jonathan began to pace the length of the room as if he hadn't heard her.

"Throughout my gratefully brief time with Lavinia I have always sensed her to be two people rather than one. At first, I believed her to be toying with me, later I called upon some physician friends of mine to offer an opinion. The diagnosis was always sadly the same." He shook his head. "I had even entertained thoughts of taking her to Dr. Freud."

"Sigmund Freud?" Amanda shook her head. "I personally don't agree with the good doctor. He's not held in such high regard in my century, some of his methods notwithstanding. "

Jonathan stopped his pacing and knelt in front of her, his arms wrapped around her waist as he laid his head into her lap. She stroked his hair lovingly.

"Amanda, the insanity is...it's frightening to behold."

She cupped his face with both her hands. "I don't pretend to understand her, Jonathan, but I agree and I hope her episodes do not become more violent."

He nodded grimly.

"I'm not a doctor, Jonathan, but in my time great strides have been made in the field of mental health beyond your Dr. Freud's expectations."

Jonathan stood abruptly. "We are not in your time and we are not returning to your time," he stated firmly. "Lavinia will have to seek the treatment offered in this century. To do otherwise would only prolong my pain."

Amanda shot up from the chair. "That's selfish, Jonathan!"

"That's survival, my lovely Amanda." He walked to his safe and bent down to tumble it open to secure the documents when he thought better of it and tucked them into his jacket pocket. "Why are you defending her?"

"I am not defending her, but her right to obtain treatment."

"What do you want me to do?" he bellowed. "Send Lavinia to the future in the hope that someone will recognize her condition and seek to aid her? That's how it will be because neither you nor I will be accompanying her, whether it is possible to do so or not!"

"But, we may be able to."

Jonathan came to Amanda in one quick stride and held her solidly by the shoulders. "You are not a doctor. Neither of us knows what is wrong with Lavinia, except that it may be of a cerebral nature."

"I may not be fond of Lavinia, but I shudder to think of anyone being locked up in the archaic loony bins of your time!"

Jonathan's eyes widened. "Loony bins? Is that with too Os or a U?" he taunted.

"Asylum, damn it!"

Running his fingers through his hair, Jonathan gritted his teeth in an attempt to control his temper. This wasn't the way it was supposed to be. They were supposed to live happily ever after, deciding their own fates rather than arguing over Lavinia's.

"Look, Amanda, I'm tired and I would very much like to see my mother and find out what's been happening around here in my absence. We can discuss this later. I think you should have the grace to recognize that my mother's opinion in this matter is significant."

Amanda watched him leave the room and sank sullenly into a chair. Together in 1884 for five minutes and already they were arguing. And Vivian! She was ashamed for allowing Lavinia's outrageous performance to cast Vivian to the back of her mind. She leaned her head back and reached up a hand to pull the smooth velvet drawstring that called to Renee. A nicely scented bath was in order. *"A bath cleanses the soul."* She could hear her mother's voice breathe over her shoulder in gentle reminder, the hair on the back of her neck rising at the verbal caress.

"In some way you're here, aren't you," she murmured. "I love you, Mom, and I really miss you and Dad." The water began to build behind her lids and soon her tears spilled over her cheeks. "A day doesn't go by that I don't think of you." She reached into her pants pocket, found a tissue, and blew her nose into it. "You'd never believe where I am." She laughed softly as a gentle breeze grazed her cheek. She smiled and sniffed. "Then you do know. You probably knew all along. But, hey, I don't know what to do; I'm new at this time travel stuff. There's no travel agent to guide me."

At that very moment, a love crept into her heart like no other in the universe and Amanda knew at once who would be guiding her. She bit her lower lip to keep the tears abated.

Amanda choked as the smile curled around her lips. "I'm still trying to picture you at Woodstock!"

"Woodstock? We have plenty in the shed, but it's much too warm for a fire."

Amanda looked up into the lovely face of sweet Renee and rushed up from the chair to hug the girl.

"I'm so happy to see you, Renee!"

Renee blushed. "I have missed you as well, Miss Amanda."

Amanda put her arm around the girl's shoulders as the two headed out of the office and down the stairs.

"What I need, Renee, is a nice hot bath in that wonderful alabaster tub near Mr. Brisbane's room." They stopped by Amanda's bedroom door. "Afterward, you will tell me all about Miss Lavinia and this party she's having."

Renee rolled her eyes and sighed. "Oui, Miss Amanda."

CHAPTER FORTY-FIVE

"My darling, I had my doubts, but you apparently got the message." Vivian swept toward Amanda and hugged her to her bosom.

"Both messages," put in an irritated Jonathan in the midst of pouring himself a drink.

"Yes, that eccentric ceremony Yolanda and I performed." She gathered Amanda's hands into her own and led her over to the sofa. "Yolanda called it a time capsule." She patted Amanda's hands and hugged her again. "It amazes me to think that you are actually from the future! The fact that Yolanda was able to convince me at all is a miracle."

"You have always been open-minded, Mother." Jonathan poured another shot of whiskey smoothly down his throat.

"This time capsule," Vivian continued in a rush. "Did it work to your advantage? I assume so; else you wouldn't be here, though I'm curious as to how it worked."

Jonathan removed the guidebook from the pocket of his trousers. "The proof lies in this book." He flipped the pages, for the first time noticing a picture of himself beside a miniature photograph of Lavinia, an unsmiling Lavinia. "Interesting..."

"Give me that." Amanda snatched the book from his hands and read aloud the paragraph beneath Jonathan's name. "Lavinia and Jonathan were divorced in 1883. Brisbane was linked for a time with a distant cousin of Thomas Alva Edison, the famed inventor."

She cast him a knowing look, her eyes smiling.

"In 1884, word was received by the Edison camp that the woman, whose signature was to dress in men's black clothing, was a spy who managed to infiltrate Serenity and gain Brisbane's trust." Amanda noticeably blanched as she went on in a voice trembling with emotion. "She was arrested and found guilty of..."

Jonathan ripped the book from her hands. "Treason!" He threw the book against the wall in a rage. "Now do you believe me when I say Freud is better equipped to handle Lavinia?" he shouted at Amanda, his eyes darkly reflecting his anger.

Deciding it was left to her to act as mediator, Vivian rose slowly. "Jonathan, calm yourself this very moment." Then she turned to Amanda. "Explain to me the importance of this book, and why anyone would accuse you of treason." She sat down again, neatly spreading her skirts, her hand slipping into Amanda's. "Jonathan," she commanded without looking at him, "pour Amanda a brandy."

"In my time, Serenity is an historical landmark. People visit during special hours."

"Like a museum?"

"I guess." Amanda looked up at Jonathan whose hand held out a goblet of brandy. She accepted it, quickly taking a sip. "The guidebook tells the story of Serenity and your family." Placing the goblet between her hands she stared, mesmerized, into the golden liquid. "Prior to my arrival here, it told of a happy marriage between Jonathan and Lavinia and that he lavished her with jewels."

"Jewels, my eye!" Jonathan folded his arms in front of him and marched to the mantel where he drummed his fingers in agitation.

Amanda ignored his outburst. "We retrieved the divorce papers in the jar you and Yolanda Winston buried and returned with them. Now the book mentions the divorce, but someone invented a story of treason to get me out of the way."

Vivian's nod was all knowing. "Lavinia. That woman is forever creating one sort of scandal or another at every turn. But, what does Dr. Freud have to do with her?"

"Jonathan believes Lavinia would benefit from the care of a doctor who deals with mental illness. Dr. Freud apparently comes highly recommended."

"And I assume you do not agree?"

Amanda shook her head and drained the remainder of the brandy as the liquid warmed away some of her fears.

"Well, dear, neither do I."

Jonathan spun around, his face a flaming red. "Mother, how can you sit there and say that when you know what you know about her?"

"What, son?" Vivian arched an eyebrow. "That since discovering the presence of Amanda, Lavinia believes herself to be a woman scorned? If you had thought yourself a cuckold husband, I'm quite sure you would be inclined to act in a similar manner. In fact, if my memory serves me, you did just that."

Amanda stifled a laugh. Vivian's words had stung sharply. Jonathan was positively livid.

"It is Lavinia's heart that ails her, not her mind, son."

Jonathan ran frustrated fingers through his dark hair. "Meaning?"

Vivian leaned comfortably back into the soft cushions of the sofa. "Lavinia is a Beauregard. Save for one sister, she lost her entire family. All her life, both real and imagined, is based only on memories. Memories before the War between the States."

"The Civil War," corrected Jonathan.

"There was nothing civil about it," came her stern admonishment.

Stillness slowly fingered itself around the room and Vivian once more leaned back, taking deep meditative breaths before speaking again. The action forced Amanda to smile. Good deep breaths were as cleansing as baths, and she recalled that particular wisdom from Madame Winston. It was easy to see that part of Yolanda's influence remained long after she'd gone. Unaccustomed to this, Jonathan respectfully took a seat in the armchair beside his mother.

"From the moment I met her I knew that time would forever stand still for Lavinia—that she would never allow anyone, least of all a Yankee, to get close to her again. I knew she longed for a past that died along with her loved ones. I knew the war would never be over for Lavinia." Vivian reached for her handkerchief and twisted it thoughtfully between her slim fingers.

"The old South, Amanda, was more a way of life than a place." She paused with a sniffle and dabbed at her eyes, at the water accumulating there. "I lost Jonathan's father in the war. He used to say the gentlemen from the South were fighting the war with arrogance for weapons. Arrogance is Lavinia's weapon too. When she is Belle Beauregard that is when she is escaping reality. The other woman—the one we know too well—is a woman without hope, a woman who wishes she too had been left to perish on some battlefield."

Jonathan leaned forward, his third whiskey in hand. "That would mean she is delusional, would it not?"

Vivian shrugged as if just coming out of a trance. "It is simply her way of coping. She married you, Jonathan, with the best of intentions, though admittedly misguided. She was desperate to secure funds to restore her beloved plantation."

"To hear you speak one would be inclined to believe you side with her." Jonathan finished the drink in one swift motion and put the glass on the table beside him.

"Think of it, Jon," his mother said facing him, her blue eyes holding his. "What if it were our Serenity in danger?"

The wrecking ball. Remembering the bleak future ahead for Serenity only proved to drive his mother's point home. He was as determined to save his homestead as Lavinia was her plantation.

The clinking sound of Amanda's glass hitting the table drew their attention. "Lavinia needs counseling. In the future, we have support groups to guide people and help them cope with their problems."

"You'll find nothing like that here," confirmed Jonathan. He picked up the guidebook and fanned the pages.

"Would a clergyman do?" offered Vivian.

"Maybe. As long as Lavinia can be talked into it."

Jonathan pulled out a cheroot, snipped off the end, and fired up the whiskey-soaked tobacco. "I can always show her the documents. That should end her game right quick."

"Or drive her over the edge. There must be some other way...Vivian, this party. Renee told me it's tonight, and that I'm the honored guest."

Vivian sighed evenly. "Yes. Poor Ruth has been running her team ragged in the kitchen."

As the two women chatted over the event to come, Jonathan once more scanned the pages of the guidebook. A page slipped from the binding to the floor. He picked it up.

"Mother, who did Lavinia invite to this party?"

As Vivian rolled off a string of names from Jonathan's circle of influence his face grew pale and a groan escaped his lips.

"...and the Morgans, Treamonts, Cartells," he finished for her.

"Why, yes, how did you know?" Vivian looked over at the page in her son's hand. "Why, that's the list! The very list!"

Jonathan handed the sheet to Amanda. "Read the very last paragraph." Amanda looked down at the page and he watched her mouth form each word. "The arrest came as a complete surprise to the prominent guests in attendance. Amanda Lloyd, spy and traitor, was taken away by government officials that very night."

CHAPTER FORTY-SIX

Renee was developing an aversion to the third floor, but Lavinia's repeated jingles from the velvet cord were not to be ignored.

"You had better go up," advised Ruth. "She's going to break that cord and probably wrap it around your pretty neck."

"Why is it always me she requests? Why must I be the object of her abuse?"

Alan stood in the doorway of the warming kitchen and stared at the impressive spread of freshly baked pies, the aroma of apple, blueberry, and cherry permeating the air in a delectable mixture.

"Is there a problem?" He walked in, hands clasped behind his back. "Speak up, Renee. We are all family here."

Renee frowned. "Miss Lavinia is ringing for me, sir."

"Then you must see to her needs as you would any other member of this household."

With a slight curtsy she rushed off, a string of quick French curses fluttering from her lips.

Alan's heart went out to the girl. It wasn't easy for Renee, and the fact that she was beautiful only made Lavinia hate her all the more, which added to her anguish. He smiled when he thought of Renee's soft curtsy in her lovely navy blue uniform with the white apron she kept so crisply starched. Renee was a loyal servant who took pride in her position. Loyalty reminded him of Ruth and he turned soft eyes of admiration on her.

"I assume your feast will be the talk of the town," he commented warmly. "No one, not even my late wife, bless her soul, could match your culinary skills."

"Your flattery doesn't dispel the bad feeling I have within me about this evening, Alan, so keep such compliments to yourself." She reached a hand up to wipe her brow before heading back to the ovens.

"I suggest, woman, that you keep your bad feelings to yourself," he called after her. "The staff is already alarmed. We don't need a mutiny on our hands. Not with *her* among us."

* * *

Where the hell is that stupid girl! Lavinia impatiently sat in front of her dressing table and stared at her freshly scrubbed face. "You look a fright!" she scolded her reflection. "We must keep our wits about us if we are to succeed with our plan."

Renee tapped lightly on the door before entering, Amanda's black outfit fresh from the iron and still draped over her arm in her haste to see to Lavinia's wishes.

"It's about time," Lavinia looked at Renee through the mirror. "Need I remind you that I do not intend to ring more than once? I expect you here on one ring, Renee. One!"

"Yes, Mrs. Brisbane."

Lavinia turned from the vanity. "I will need a bath, a proper bath, one with lavender beads, lest you forget this time. Now help me get out of this dress."

Renee dropped Amanda's dark clothing onto the bed and rushed to unhook the red dress. As it fell away from Lavinia's body, Renee felt a pinch on her arm.

"Ouch!"

"Are those what I think they are?" She arched an eyebrow in surprise and pointed to the bed, a smile curled around the corners of her mouth.

Renee looked at her in confusion.

"Never mind. Why you insist on defying me I shall never understand." Lavinia stepped out of her hooped skirt and turned.

Renee's eyes widened as Lavinia glared at her.

"You are a poor excuse for a servant, my dear." She touched a palm softly to Renee's cheek. "Such a lovely face," she whispered, then pulled back her hand and slapped Renee soundly.

Tears welling up in her eyes, Renee moved back quickly, the sensation of Lavinia's stinging palm yielding a bright, red print where hand met face.

"My bath, dear. Afterward you will freshen my red dress and assist in fashioning my hair." Slipping into a green wrapper, she followed Renee into the bathroom.

Standing behind the partially open door, Jonathan witnessed the treatment of Renee and could feel the anger rise to his throat. This had to end. He swung the door open just as Renee scurried by him, Lavinia's demands still lingering in the air. He put a finger to his lips and nudged her silently out the door. It was then that he saw Amanda's black clothing in a neat pile on the edge of the bed. Like one of Tom Edison's electric lamps, the realization seized him immediately. He cursed himself for not reaching the conclusion sooner. Grinning with full teeth, he walked to the doorway of the bathroom.

"You are a simpleton! Bring me my towel! Now!"

Reaching an arm over to the chest of drawers, Jonathan picked up a towel and threw it in the water, the bubbles splashing into Lavinia's eyes.

"Why you little..."

"You were saying?" he interrupted while tossing her another one, this one she caught deftly and hurriedly dabbed at her stinging eyes.

"I thought you were someone else."

Jonathan leaned against the doorframe, one leg crossed over the other. "Apparently so," he chuckled. "Preparing for your gala, I see."

Lavinia sat up slightly in the tub, enough so that her breasts bobbed above the water. "Care to join me, darling?" she purred softly, her hands pressing her breasts together so they lobbed enticingly to the surface.

"As you can see, I am already dressed."

Yes, Lavinia could certainly see that, for he looked particularly handsome in his charcoal evening wear, his white shirt matching his sickeningly white teeth. She hated him, and she loved him. No, she decided, she hated him and his Yankee ways, but she loved making love. Jonathan Brisbane was merely a body to fulfill her needs.

Jonathan walked straight up to the tub and lowered his face until his lips seductively grazed her ear. "You missed supper, my sweet."

"I-I ate in my room," she stammered.

"Lavinia, Lavinia," he whispered. "I promise you a dessert you will never forget."

Lavinia rested her head on the edge of the tub and closed her eyes in preparation of further seduction. Jonathan kissed her forehead. On the way out, he gathered Amanda's black garments in a heap and silently left the room.

* * *

Amanda paced up and down the length of the room. *What does one wear to their arrest?* There seemed to be no escaping the fate in store for her. With a long sigh, she sat down in the armchair near the window and peeled back the curtain. Sprawled before her in innocent splendor, Serenity was a comforting sight.

And one I'm sure not to see again after this night.

"Jonathan has been asking for you."

Amanda turned to find Vivian at the entrance to the room. "How long have you been standing there?"

"Long enough." Vivian moved softly into the room in a green gown, the graceful small train of sea-foam silk following in her wake.

"You look positively beautiful!" Amanda proclaimed.

Vivian sat gingerly on the edge of the bed, her back straight so as not to disturb the train. "Renee is responsible for my hair." She smiled, a hand reaching up to the high coiffure clustered with pink and green ostrich tips. "A bit too elevated, wouldn't you say?"

"Not at all, Vivian. You truly do look lovely." Amanda came to sit at the woman's side and gave her bejeweled hand a squeeze. "I'm going to miss you," she mumbled softly.

"You're not going anywhere!" Vivian admonished. "Not if Jonathan has his way, and I assure you he will."

Amanda shook her head. "He can't change what lies ahead for me. I have racked my brain to scrambled eggs and I haven't been able to come up with a single way to get out of this mess. How then will he?"

"Faith, my dear Amanda. The Lord will provide, as I recall Yolanda proclaiming when I had lost hope of ever seeing the two of you again. Yet, here you both are!"

"Not for long."

"Hush, now! Think positive." Vivian reached for the velvet cord and gave it a slight tug. "We must prepare you for the party."

"You can't be serious! I'm going to hide the entire evening."

"I won't hear of it."

"Vivian, I'm serious."

"As am I, my dear. As the guest of honor you must be in attendance and you will be dressed...how would they say in your time?"

"To the nines." Amanda laughed. "You always seem to cheer me, Vivian. My own mother was good for that as well."

"I love you, my dear, as much as if you were my own."

CHAPTER FORTY-SEVEN

Amanda stared at herself in the full-length mirror, her head shaking violently in disbelief at the woman who looked back at her.

"Please, Miss Amanda, stop moving about. You look lovely." Renee was pleased with her work. "Sit down so I may fix your hair."

"I want to wear it down, Renee."

"For evening? But you are the guest of honor!"

Faux pas or not, if this might be her last night in either century she would be hauled away in a hairstyle she was comfortable with.

"I'll do my own hair. I'm sure you have enough on your hands with Lavinia."

"But you will wear the combs, yes?"

"Yes."

With a curtsy, Renee prepared to leave the room. She stopped at the door. "Mr. Brisbane will not believe his eyes!" She giggled softly and closed the door behind her.

Amanda picked up the sterling silver brush and ran it through her long hair, the waves curling smoothly around her shoulders and down her back. Renee had lined up two combs of blue sapphire that Amanda used to push her hair up on the sides. Standing before the mirror once again, she marveled at her reflection. Her dress was blue velvet, cut low around the neckline and embroidered with small roses of Chantilly lace at the neck and sleeves. Richly beaded lace fell in tassels in front and behind her. A front breadth of satin hung in a drooping fashion with pleats that cut around her waist to further the illusion of an hourglass figure. She turned for a side view and frowned. The only thing she didn't like were the panels of the long square train. Sitting down was not going to be an option.

If Carrie could see me she'd split her sides laughing. The thought of Carrie quickly brought Amanda back to sobering reality. What would happen to her life in the future if she were arrested in 1884? What would happen to her roommate?

Wouldn't Carrie be frantic? Was she frantic now? Would Carrie's life be changed as well? With each question she posed to herself the past, the present, and future all appeared a bleak reminder of her predicament.

"How does a woman of such dazzling beauty manage to look so grim?" Jonathan stepped into the room and quietly closed the door.

"You look like the cat that swallowed the canary."

"The what?" He was behind her now, his arms around her waist, fingers inching up to the sides of her breasts as he pulled her against him.

"Never mind," she sighed.

Jonathan moved her around to face him, his eyes sparkling mischievously. "You fret too much, my love." His lips traced along the column of her neck in tiny, little kisses. "I love the taste of you, do you know that?" he murmured, his mouth now pressed against the swell of her breasts.

"Stop it!" She wriggled from his embrace.

He leaned back and laughed. "I promise I will not distress you further, my dear." He laughed again, louder, the richness escaping Amanda, for she did not share his humor.

"What do you find so funny?" She narrowed her eyes with suspicion at the sack he left by the door. "What's in the sack?"

Picking up her hands into his own, Jonathan kissed each finger. "My love, I would not laugh had I not good reason, I assure you."

"You're avoiding my questions."

Jonathan rubbed his hands together, his lips parting into a grin. "Madame Winston is not the only one prone to ceremony."

"You've lost me entirely, Jonathan. Care to fill me in?"

"Shall we sit?" He motioned to the bed.

"Now, *that's* funny."

"All right then, if you insist on being disagreeable..."

"Jonathan, please! My life is at stake here!" she snapped.

"*Our* lives," he corrected. "I am an honorable man and, if I must say so myself, quite insightful."

Amanda's hands were on her hips now, her pale cheeks turning a bright red. "If I could move in this gown as well as I could in my pants I would wring your neck!"

"Yes, your trousers, they are certainly the issue at hand. I shall miss them," he said as he took a seat in the armchair near the fireplace, his hand playing with the brass knob of the poker. "I shall also miss the black jacket that sequestered your beautiful breasts. But most of all," he looked up at her now, locking her dark eyes to his dancing green ones, "most of all, I shall miss your hat. I believe you left it in your time."

Amanda rolled her eyes. "OK, OK." I surrender. "Will you *please* stop teasing me?" Tears sprang to her eyes and she knew the floodgates were about to open.

Glimpsing her distress, Jonathan inwardly scolded himself for his flagrant disregard of her feelings. He hastily rose and drew her into his arms.

"My dress," she cried, and now her tears were real, falling in torrents down her cheek. "Y-you'll spoil it."

"The dress be damned." He pressed his lips to hers in a deep kiss and she responded fully, throwing her arms around his neck. Freeing a hand, he reached into his pocket and took out his handkerchief to lightly blot away her tears. "I'm sorry for toying with you. I fear I carried on a bit too long." He kissed her again, and leaving her side for the moment, lifted the sack and dropped it on the floor in front of the fireplace.

Drawing a long match from the container on the mantel, he sparked it to flame and bent down to touch it to the wood below. An immediate heat warmed the room and Amanda was about to protest—or faint—when she saw him pull her black outfit from the sack. All at once, she understood, and a smile replaced her frown as she watched him cast her twenty-first century clothing into the fire, setting it ablaze.

"Why didn't I think of that?" she asked in amazement as the tiny fragments of black smoldered to ash.

"Attribute it to my amazing legal mind," he teased, rising to open a window.

"Now, let's put it to the supreme test." He reached into the sack again and revealed the Serenity guidebook.

"Wait." Amanda touched his hand, preventing him from opening the book, her heart beating so furiously she thought it would leap from her chest. "What about Lavinia?"

Rather than answer, Jonathan opened the guidebook and scanned it with a keen eye before he was satisfied. Folding it over, he tapped a finger to the page and handed her the book. Amanda's mouth dropped open in disbelief. History had indeed changed again. What amazed her most was the detail with which the Lavinia problem had been resolved. Jonathan had managed the impossible.

CHAPTER FORTY-EIGHT

Together in the front parlor, Vivian, Jonathan, and Amanda awaited their guests, and the ultimate arrival of Lavinia who insisted on making a grand entrance only after the guests arrived. She had sent word through Renee to have Jonathan escort her down promptly at eight o'clock. Until then, she would be resting in her room on the third floor.

The three were in a jovial mood, quite prepared for a party and Vivian was actually looking forward to it now that Jonathan had resolved Amanda's problem. She was already ticking off the list for future events so pleasingly mentioned in the guidebook she held in her hands.

Alan stood by the doorway, willing himself to enter, in his hands he carried a stack of cards atop a sterling silver tray.

It was Jonathan who noticed him first. "Alan, come in."

"I thought, sir, well, I thought it my responsibility to inform you of a recent discovery." He entered slowly and placed the tray on the table among them. "Ruth found these in one of her closets in the kitchen. To say she is agitated would be highly understating her feelings."

Jonathan picked up each gold-embossed calling card and read the messages, his smile fading with each one. "My regrets, Vivian, but surely you understand." He tossed it aside. "Regret we have another engagement."

Amanda moved to his side and picked up several of the cards. "Regrets, regrets, regrets. I don't understand."

"I should have known." Jonathan turned to his mother who was shaking her head.

"Whatever was I thinking?" she scolded herself. "It never occurred to me to inquire who from the list had accepted the invitation."

"Ninety-nine percent declined, Mother, and Lavinia knew this all along."

"You mean denied it all along," opined Amanda. "Why else would she have hidden them?"

Vivian nodded in agreement. According to the responses, only eight people were attending. Those eight were either curious gossips like Frances West and Ella Crocker, or loyal friends of Jonathan's like Linwood Crane and his mother.

"Alan, inform Ruth of my personal apology, and to bear in mind that none of her preparation is for naught. Tomorrow we shall dispatch the staff to circulate the leftover food to those families in need."

Grateful for his employer's foresight, Alan left to speak with Ruth.

"Well, all dressed up with no place to go."

They both looked at Amanda. Vivian was the first to speak. "So it will be a small dinner party. Just as well under the circumstances."

Jonathan looked up from the card in his hand. "Imagine. She had the audacity to invite Tom Edison." He looked up at Amanda. "Lucky for you he declined."

* * *

Linwood Crane was the first to arrive, cutting a handsome figure in his black evening suit, his lovely mother on his arm. Jonathan asked Alan to escort Mrs. Crane to be received by Vivian and Amanda while quickly leading Linwood to his office down the hall.

"I'm sorry for the trouble I've caused you," Linwood was saying while taking a seat across from Jonathan's desk.

"Please," Jonathan raised a hand. "We've been friends for far too long, Linwood. No apology is necessary." He leaned back into his leather chair and smiled. "I did not call you in here for that purpose."

"What then?"

"Amanda and I plan to marry and I would be delighted if you would honor me as my man in attendance."

Linwood's reaction was not what Jonathan had expected. His eyes grew wide, his mood changing quickly as the nervous smile left his lips.

"You received the documents?"

"I did acquire them, yes."

Linwood's laugh was bitter and unexpected. "I never had a chance, did I?"

"Excuse me?"

"With Amanda. Surely you could see my open attraction to your lovely intended."

Jonathan's face screwed up angrily. "Are you telling me you are responsible for my missing documents?"

"No. At least not those contained in my safe. That was Lavinia's doing."

"Then what?" Jonathan straightened in his chair and pounded his fist down onto the desk. "Speak up, man!"

"I delayed the messenger." Linwood cleared his throat uncomfortably. "When you and Amanda disappeared, it was only in defeat that I finally arranged to have them delivered."

Jonathan shook his head, incredulous at his friend's confession. "But, Linwood, why?"

"Because I actually believed I had a chance with her." He leaned into his friend, his voice a whisper. "We fought side by side during the war as brothers would. Alienated my family when I rejected the Confederacy and fought for the Union. But I did so for the love of your sister. When she died, my heart died with her." He leaned back into the chair. "Amanda was your payment to me. I never dreamed that love would cultivate between you."

Jonathan was shaken, and speechless. Linwood's deception seared through his heart like a poisonous blade. The gentle tap at the door jarred them both as Amanda swung it open and gingerly stepped in.

"Linwood, it's good to see you. I've just met your mother and I must say she is a wonderful woman." She looked at Jonathan's disturbed expression. "Have I interrupted business?"

The men just stared, Linwood's face red with embarrassment. "It's good to see you, Amanda."

"You and I are not finished with this conversation, Crane."

"My congratulations on your engagement." With a light bow, Linwood left the room.

Amanda walked to Jonathan's side and tenderly adjusted the collar of his jacket.

"What was that all about?"

"Linwood betrayed us."

"How?"

Jonathan took out his pocket watch and glanced at it quickly. "We shall discuss it another time."

Amanda gritted her teeth. Something was wrong and he was keeping that something from her. "Jonathan, don't shut me out, not now—not ever!" she shouted.

He walked past her, his hand lightly touching the small of her back. "Let's get this over with."

He wasn't sure he wanted to discuss Linwood Crane's hopes of securing her for himself, wasn't sure of himself to acknowledge his friend's deceit. He had come to know Amanda as a woman who would take on any cause to bring forth harmony to those she cared about. She would want to help Linwood, and Jonathan was too hurt to consider it.

* * *

Lavinia smiled at her reflection in the full-length mirror in her third floor room. Her blond hair was held by one comb and cascading over to one side.

"You certainly look lovely," came a voice from behind her. "Red is certainly your color, my dear."

Lavinia stared at Jonathan through the mirror. "Do I? Does your flattery mean that you still love me?"

"Of course," he declared gently.

She whirled around quickly. "The black clothes are gone, you know. I should care, but I don't." She looked up at him through hazy blue eyes. "Your *friend's* black clothing has simply disappeared," she whimpered. "And I did so want to shatter her dreams of owning you, Jonathan. She does not deserve Serenity or the Brisbane money."

Though she tried to avert his gaze, Jonathan raised her chin up and looked deeply into her disturbed eyes, obviously clouded over by laudanum, a drug she had been known to take when distressed.

"I have something for you."

"You do? Oh, Jonathan, I thought you would wait for dessert, as you promised. All our guests should be in attendance, don't you agree?"

"No, my dear. This present is one you should wear to greet our guests," he explained gently, aware she was certainly not with him in this world, but clearly confined to her own—one that pained him to believe even existed—a world of insanity.

"What have you behind your back?" She was beaming hopefully. "Please, Jonathan, I cannot bear to wait another moment!"

He handed her a red rose and pinned it to her dress. She bent her head to inhale its fragrance, delighted by his offering.

"Shall we go?"

"If we must," she whined. "Though, it would be wonderful to remain in this room instead."

Lavinia turned to her reflection once more and saw her sixteen-year-old self: Lavinia Beauregard, whose beauty was unsurpassed. She turned and faced him, placing her hand atop his outstretched arm, her manner confident, her demeanor that of a woman lost somewhere in a time and place long gone. Together, they descended the first set of stairs. At the top of the grand staircase, Lavinia paused and looked at the brightly dressed people below. She grinned widely and continued down the steps, slipping slightly as the laudanum began to overtake her. With Jonathan's strength to guide her, Lavinia Beauregard did not give a second thought to the startled and saddened faces staring up at her. She was the belle of the ball, and those she did not recognize, she assured herself, would be introduced to her.

Gently aided by Jonathan, she touched down to the bottom step and he escorted her over to the doctors, deceivingly dressed in evening dress. Dr. Morris, the man Jonathan had summoned, smiled warmly and reached an arm out to her.

"Why thank you. Have we met, sir?"

Morris looked to Jonathan who simply shrugged. "No, my dear. But I am an old friend of your father's," he explained quickly. "I've come to take you home."

Lavinia was glowing now. "Father has summoned me? Goodness, we must make haste!" She turned to Jonathan. "Surely you're able to entertain our guests, Jonathan. My father needs me."

Jonathan bowed and kissed her hand. "Of course, my dear."

Vivian cast a disparaging look to Frances West. "More grist for your gossip mill, Frances," she whispered in disdain.

Tucked into the shadows of the corner of the grand hallway, Amanda watched closely, tears glistening in her eyes, her heart lending itself out to the broken woman being led away. She hoped and prayed that Lavinia would get the help she so desperately needed.

CHAPTER FORTY-NINE

Dinner was a solemn one, over after the engagement toast. The guests were happy for Amanda and Jonathan, but forever branded with the wretched picture of Lavinia being tenderly taken away. Jonathan had made a point of avoiding Linwood's futile attempts to converse as he kept a watchful eye on any attention he might pay Amanda.

The evening ended early and once Vivian retired, Amanda returned to her room to sort out her thoughts. Nagging at her was the realization she would never see her friend Carrie Stern again, or know how her disappearance affected her friend and roommate's life. Surely, it had to. One didn't just vanish and be forgotten. *Or did they?* With each question there seemed to be more left unanswered.

Amanda changed clothes and donned the blue wrapper laid out on the bed. She settled into the armchair by the window, her thoughts soon wandering from Carrie to Linwood Crane. What on earth had transpired between the two men to cause Jonathan to become so angry? She had hoped to have a moment alone with him, but as the night wore on it was obvious that wasn't going to happen. With a heavy sigh, she drew back the drapes and stared up at the full moon, grateful for the breeze that lent itself gracefully through the room.

Jonathan had been wonderful tonight, his sympathetic treatment of Lavinia commendable under the circumstances. Where was he now?

The tap on her door answered her question as Jonathan came into the room carrying a sliver tray with a bottle and two glasses.

"Ah, good, you're still awake." He flashed her a smile and closed the door with a kick of a bare foot. He was wearing nothing more than a pair of night bottoms and an open shirt. Placing the tray down on the table near her chair, he popped open the bottle. "Champagne my darling, to celebrate." He poured the bubbling liquid into two fluted glasses and handed her one.

"I don't feel much like celebrating." But she took the glass anyway.

Leaving his own glass on the tray, Jonathan sat down on the bed. It was time for them to have a discussion regarding Linwood. Yet, all he wanted was to hold her, to feel her warmth against him. Logic told him such delight would have to wait. He stared at her for a long time...waiting.

"Linwood was quiet this evening. In fact, he hardly spoke a word to me all evening."

There it was. He shook his head. "Linwood's deception is inexcusable." Jonathan said softly.

"What deception?" she asked. "You have yet to share that with me." She looked into his eyes then and saw his pain. "Jonathan, you must tell me."

"Must I? I imagine so." He got up and paced around the bedroom, hands clasped tightly around his back. "Linwood detained the messenger. Linwood Crane, my darling Amanda, is in love with you." He stopped his pace in front of her and looked down into her dark eyes. "Do you understand what I'm saying?"

"I sensed Linwood was interested in me from the very first, but he is not in love with me. He doesn't even know me." She met his steady gaze. "Though for certain, Linwood Crane is a man who needs the love of a good woman."

Jonathan cocked an eyebrow in surprise and laughed deeply. "And here I thought that by telling you of Linwood's feelings, you would want to rush into his arms."

She smiled. "Not very confident, are you?" Only then did she take a sip of champagne.

"Linwood Crane was once engaged to my sister."

"Susan?" Now it was Amanda's turn to be surprised.

Jonathan nodded. "Then came the war. Despite his family's ire, he joined the Union to please Susan."

"And when he returned?"

"Susan had died." Jonathan felt his heart ache at the memory. Dear sweet Susan, so good and kind and...

"I'm sorry." Amanda put the glass down and stood before him, her hands gently tracing the contours of his chest. Then she bent her head and lightly kissed him there.

Jonathan pulled her face up to meet his, taking her lips to his own in a possessive kiss. "I love you so much, my darling, that it pains me."

"The feeling is mutual."

"Then why are we discussing the lost love of others? Isn't it time we concentrated on us?" His arms encircled her waist; he tightened his grasp. "I need you, my love… I ache for you." In one swift motion, he lifted her up and placed her on the bed.

They lay quietly together for a long time, his kisses feathering lightly down her neck. Amanda snuggled closely to him.

"I have something for you," he murmured into her ear. Moving a hand into a pocket, he withdrew a small pouch and handed it to her.

Amanda gently pulled the drawstring and turned the pouch over into the palm of her hand. Out sprinkled a heart-shaped ruby ring encircled within a cluster of diamonds.

"Jonathan!" The tightness in her throat closed off further speech.

"It was my grandmother's ring," he explained while slipping it on her finger. "Would it be a proper engagement ring in your time?"

"Of course," she said, finally finding her voice. "And this is my time," she confirmed.

She could no longer hold back the tears and let them fall. Jonathan pulled her closer, tighter.

"Women. I will never understand them." He began to kiss away her tears, the salty taste branded to his lips. "Why are you crying?" he finally asked.

"I was thinking about Carrie," she sniffed.

"Carrie?" He shook his head. "You mean your friend in the future?"

She nodded, thinking it funny that he should speak as if the future was merely in another state. "I'm so happy and she must be so worried. In fact, she probably has the cops out looking for me."

"Cops?"

"Authorities."

Jonathan hugged her tightly. "I'm sure she'll be fine."

Amanda moved away from him and sat up in the bed. "Jonathan, I didn't even leave her a note! No explanation! At least Vivian had Madame Winston to enlighten her when we disappeared. Carrie was the only family I had in my time."

"Carrie's fate is her own," he whispered softly.

"But, Jonathan, what if my fate has a direct influence on hers? Have you thought of that?" she challenged.

No answer came to Jonathan, for he was fully aware of the tricks fate could play. Fate was an unpredictable adversary. He knew no words would reassure Amanda that her friend was all right.

"Wouldn't it be interesting if Carrie and Linwood met? Though I'm not sure she's his type…"

"Amanda!" he groaned in annoyance. "I cannot believe you are even contemplating such a thought. Do you intend to attempt to be a matchmaker across time?" His eyes widened at the thought.

Amanda had to agree that the very idea was absurd. Defeated for the moment, she smiled and began to nibble affectionately on his ear.

"I'm losing this battle, aren't I?" Jonathan leaned over on his side, his arm propped up on the pillow. "Whether the portal is open or not," he added.

"It's closed for us."

"Meaning?"

"Maybe it's open for Linwood…or for Carrie." She smoothed a hand down his rugged cheek.

"No," he said simply, his free hand clutching hers at the wrist.

"Well, have you any suggestions of your own?"

"Let me think on it," Jonathan said. "At least afford me that much. Tonight, I only wish to hold you in my arms." Bending his head, he captured her lips to his and drew her to him.

The heat from his body flowed over to hers as the kisses deepened. "You know," she whispered wistfully. "I always promised Carrie that she would be by my side the day I married."

Jonathan looked down into her beautiful face and shook his head. "You ask a great deal from fate, my love. We should be thanking the Lord that we are together at all." He noted her darkly saddened expression and sighed. "There may be something we can do after all," he offered suddenly, desperate to please her. "It would appease you, and whether your friend Carrie is meant to be here or not, at least she would be aware of what happened to you."

"I don't understand."

Jonathan smiled. "Come with me. Until I explain, neither of us will get any sleep tonight."

CHAPTER FIFTY

"Damn it, Amanda, where the hell are you?"
Carrie Stern sat in the dimly lit kitchen, the early morning sun streaming through the window above the sink. She drained the remaining coffee from her cup—her second pot since returning home. Nothing had made sense since she first walked in the door twenty-four hours ago. Boxes of historical significance relating to the Brisbane house were strewn about the living room. Amanda's clothes still hung neatly in her closet, but there was no note of explanation held under any of the refrigerator magnets to indicate where she had gone. Most of all, the stale remains of the cigar in the ashtray disturbed Carrie most. She stared at the phone, willing it to ring. When it did, she jumped.
"Hello?"
"May I speak to Amanda Lloyd?"
"She's not home. Who's calling?"
"My name is Marge Kincaid. I'm affiliated with Serenity."
"The Brisbane house?"
"Yes. It appears Miss Lloyd was visiting and left her camera here."
Carrie's concern grew with this information. It wasn't like Amanda to leave her equipment behind.

"Would you please tell her I called?" Marge continued.

"My name is Carrie Stern. I'm her roommate. I'll come pick it up for her."

"We open at ten thirty."

Carrie looked up at the kitchen clock. "I'd like to come right over, if it's all right with you," she inquired impatiently.

Marge hesitated for only a moment. "I'll be here."

Carrie showered quickly, pulled on a pair of jeans, and threw on a T-shirt.

Without a car, she would have to take a bus and from the feel of the humidity it was going to be a scorcher. She gathered her hair up into a ponytail and headed for the bus stop. An hour later, she found herself in front of Serenity, the sight of Amanda's car on the corner doing little to still her fears. Rounding to the driver's side, she peered in. The gas tank was half empty, and if she wasn't mistaken, when she last saw Amanda there was almost a full tank. Before knocking on the front door, she hopped over the fence, deciding first to investigate around back. What she hoped to find, she hadn't a clue.

"Women disappear every day," she told herself. "Oh, Amanda, don't become an unsolved mystery on me! Please!"

As her eyes combed the grounds, she did not feel the same sense of wonder as on her previous visit. Everything appeared as dark as her mood as she allowed that negativity to embrace her. Then she saw it. Amanda's fedora lay on the ground at the far end of the garden. Panic set in as she ran to pick it up.

"Something is terribly wrong here," she said to herself, while dusting it off.

"Miss Stern?"

Carrie whirled around, the hat clutched tightly between her white-knuckled fingers.

"My friend's hat," she explained in a desperate effort to hold back the tears she was sure would follow.

Marge walked over to her and put a comforting hand on Carrie's shoulder.

"Come inside, dear. We can discuss this over a cool glass of iced tea."

Carrie's throat closed up and she nodded as Marge led her into the house.

"Something has happened to my friend, I just know it," Carrie finally said when Marge poured the tea. She looked around in confusion. *This was a museum, wasn't it?* It didn't seem right to be sitting in this archaic kitchen having tea. "I'm not usually an alarmist," she went on. "But, you see, my friend's car is still here and I found her hat in the gardens." She swallowed hard to push back the lump in her throat. "And she would never, ever leave her equipment behind."

Marge sat down across from her. "Are you sure you are not jumping to conclusions, my dear? I'm sure your friend is fine."

Carrie still wasn't convinced. "I thought this place was a museum."

"It is. But I sneak in a snack now and then."

Carrie nodded.

"You've been here before?"

"Yes, but I never took the tour inside."

"Then you must see..."

"The camera," Carrie interrupted. "I want Amanda's camera."

Marge heaved a heavy sigh. "I assure you it's tucked securely away in our office safe." She pushed herself up from the table. Carrie followed Marge from the kitchen to the grand hallway and waited patiently for her to return. Two portraits hung side by side across the parlor. Carrie stood staring, and then shook her head.

"I know it's my imagination, but I seem to be seeing Amanda everywhere," she commented when Marge finally returned and handed her the video camera.

"A relative," she replied as she led Carrie hastily to the door. "I'm sure you'll find your friend soon. Perhaps she's merely on another photographic journey."

"Without her camera? I doubt it. But, thank you anyway."

Marge smiled and watched Carrie hurry down the front walk to Amanda's car before she closed the door.

Dipping into her purse for Amanda's spare car keys, Carrie unlocked the door and hopped in. Tossing the camera and fedora onto the seat beside her, she took a deep breath before inserting the key into the ignition. Nothing made sense. Where was the rest of Amanda's equipment? Where was Amanda? She pulled the camera onto her lap, switched it on, and pressed the rewind button, thoughts of foul play terrorizing her. Maybe, just maybe, something Amanda had filmed would provide her with a clue. Carrie jumped as the recorder clicked to a stop. She bent her head and zeroed in on the small square screen on front of her, and then hit the play button.

"Ugh!" The groan escaped her lips at the immediate sight of herself, her finger automatically fast forwarding to the next frame.

Serenity with its sparkling chandeliers, immense fireplaces, and priceless tapestries came easily into view. Amanda had apparently swept through two floors before the picture juggled and the segment ended. Carrie remembered that moment. It was when she caught Amanda off guard with a tap on the shoulder to tell her she was leaving early for work. It was the last time they saw each other.

Private: Visitors not allowed beyond this point. The words drew Carrie into the scene once again, a smile claiming her lips at her friend's boldness as she followed along as Amanda took the stairs to the prohibited floor.

Jonathan Brisbane, Private. The room Amanda had filmed was a library, her professionalism as a photographer evident in the scrutiny of her camera's eye. Each movement pulled Carrie further into the room and she felt as if she were with Amanda as she scanned the rich leather-bound books and over to the framed photographs before moving to what appeared to be a journal. A journal, Carrie discovered, relating details of the writer's experience with the magic of Thomas Edison's electric light.

Carrie blew out a puff of air, "OK, so what does this prove?"

"Who are you, sir? And what are you doing in this room?"

Carrie's eyes widened at the deep resonant voice demanding an answer of Amanda, and she found herself mesmerized as the camera focused in on what surely had to be one very delicious-looking docent. Her surprise matched that of Amanda's as the man's hands shot up in the air in surrender. Gripped by the drama unfolding before her, Carrie found she could not look away as the man accused Amanda of being a spy, insisting the camera was a weapon. The next frame was a slow scan of the man's body, before settling on his angry face.

The screen went black and Carrie's face paled, her heart thumping rapidly with fear.

"The man is crazy!" She shouted to no one. She shook the camera in a vain effort to bring further visualization. She fast-forwarded again. Nothing. Clutching the camera to her chest, she began to cry. She had been right. Amanda was in trouble—might still be.

Carrie scrambled out of the car and ran back to the house. She pounded her fists on the door. When no one answered, she turned the knob. The door easily opened.

"Marge! Marge!" she called as she searched each room on the first floor.

No reply came as Carrie continued her search, taking the stairs to the second floor by twos, her call to Marge now a steady scream.

"Marge!" Carrie stopped abruptly when she reached the door leading to the third floor. She opened it without hesitation. Marge had to be up there, and if she was, then she might be part of this man's plans to hurt Amanda. No, she decided, Marge Kincaid didn't seem to be that kind of person. Then, again, she had watched enough television news to know those were the ones to watch out for.

A slow rush of wind smacked her face, propelling her forward. The camera slung over her shoulder, Carrie reached out a hand to the banister to prevent herself from tripping, and continued up the stairs to the third floor. Her feet felt like lead, each step a struggle. Finally, after what felt like hours, Carrie reached the top. The curious wind that had slowly spiraled her up subsided and she breathed a long sigh, legs aching, and eyes stinging.

"Marge!" she yelled once more.

"In here," came a faint reply.

Relieved at finding the woman, Carrie opened the door to Jonathan Brisbane's office and...screamed.

CHAPTER FIFTY-ONE

"Where the hell have you been?" Carrie screamed as she rushed up to Amanda and hugged her solidly before pushing her at arm's length. "And what are you doing dressed like that?" she continued, her hands still firmly grasping Amanda's shoulders.

"I..."

"Never mind," Carrie rushed on. "You gave me quite a scare. I mean, I come home and there's no note, boxes are all over the living room..." she arched an eyebrow, her eyes narrowing. "And unless you've taken up smoking, someone else's cigar was in the ashtray." Carrie sat down on one of the soft leather chairs. "You certainly don't owe me an explanation to that last one, but you had me so worried! Then I got a call from Marge."

"Marge?" Amanda finally managed, but the name fell on deaf ears.

"Marge Kincaid found your camera. And that's another thing." Carrie pointed an accusing finger. "Since when do you leave your camera equipment behind?"

"Stop!" Amanda threw her hands up in exasperation. "For heaven's sake, Carrie, take a breath!" Then came her laughter, full and hard.

"Well, I was worried about you," Carrie defended with a sheepish smile as she leaned back and finally drew out a long, needed breath.

Amanda sat down in the chair behind Jonathan's desk, her long blue skirt fanning around her in a flourish. "Carrie, we have to talk."

"I thought that's what we were doing."

"No, you were talking. Now it's my turn." Amanda took a deep breath of her own and blew it out fully as her eyes rested on the questioning ones of her dear friend.

This isn't going to be easy. She'll think I went off the deep end. Amanda's eyes fell on the nervous fingers that twiddled in Carrie's lap. Suspicious by nature, Carrie Stern would not be easily convinced of the circumstances. Time travel was something she only watched on television or at the movies, her favorite movie being *Somewhere in Time*, and she watched it more for the actor, Christopher Reeve. Time travel was pure fiction.

"I'm all ears."

"Not here." Amanda led Carrie by the hand to Lavinia's old bedroom across the hall and closed the door.

* * *

While Amanda was explaining the facts of life to Carrie upstairs, Linwood Crane waited patiently down in the front parlor for Jonathan to receive him. After their falling out the evening before, he was positive their friendship dangled by a dangerously thin thread. He knew Jonathan well enough to realize that betrayal in any form was unacceptable. And by all accounts, Jonathan Brisbane felt betrayed.

"Linwood." Jonathan stood in the doorway in a crisp gray business suit. Alan was behind him carrying a loaded silver tray. "I trust you can use a strong cup of coffee." He stepped back for Alan who brushed past him and placed the tray on the table. He poured two cups from the sterling silver pot.

Jonathan thanked him and, with a slight bow, Alan left the room.

"Good morning, Jonathan," returned Linwood once they were alone. "I must say I'm surprised at your cordial greeting, all things considered."

Jonathan pulled two cheroots from his breast pocket and extended one to Linwood.

"Thank you."

There was a long silence as they smoked while Jonathan paced the length of the parlor in search of the appropriate words to convey.

"I shall get straight to the point." Jonathan stopped pacing and took to the armchair opposite Linwood. Leaning forward, he rested one hand on his knee, the other still gripping the cigar. "Admittedly, I was gravely disappointed in you. The very idea that you would delay a messenger to my home, regardless of the circumstances, is deplorable; and in light of the circumstances, almost unforgivable."

"Almost?" Linwood blew a full circle of smoke into the air.

"Yes. I do not believe a friendship that spans the years of ours is without fault. Friendships go through many a detour and we are supposed to learn from them." He cleared his throat and straightened. "I think Amanda was one such detour for us. Having been unaware of my true intentions for her, your reaction was understandable."

"You were certainly not very gracious to Amanda, at least not in my presence." Linwood smiled, a sense of relief washing over him.

"Yes, well, all that has changed now and Amanda has agreed to become my wife."

"I was certainly smitten with her. She must think me a fool."

Jonathan laughed and finally relaxed against the soft cushions of the chair. "On the contrary. She thinks you a charming man in need of a good woman."

Linwood joined in the laughter. "You are one lucky man to have found her. My congratulations."

"Which brings me to a request. Would you do me the honor of being my second at our wedding?"

"Second?" Linwood asked, not sure of Jonathan's meaning. Then he brightened. "As long as we are not dealing with swords I would be honored to be your attendant. Shall we toast to your good fortune?"

Jonathan made haste for the liquor cabinet and poured two bourbons.

"Have you set the date yet?" Linwood asked before making his toast.

Jonathan frowned. "Not yet. There is another matter of a personal nature which Amanda must attend to."

"Well, here's to a bright future for you both."

"Thank you, Linwood." Jonathan touched his glass to his friend's. "To friendship, as well. For without it, we have neither love nor happiness."

CHAPTER FIFTY-TWO

"Have you lost your mind? You honestly expect me to believe this?" Carrie Stern's mouth screwed up in a cynical smile. "Time travel? Oh, Amanda, now you've really got me worried." She got up from the chair, her head shaking back and forth. "This Jonathan character has obviously brainwashed you to believe you're living in another century, and his band of pranksters are all in on it. Really, Amanda, you surprise me." Carrie's eye narrowed. "This guy, Jonathan, the one in the video, where is he?"

"Why?"

"Because he's responsible for you losing your mind! He's enlisted you in the docent brigade, right down to the clothes!"

"Well, Carrie, you've joined up too."

"What the hell are you talking about?"

"Look out the window, go ahead."

"I guess I should humor you. They say one should be gentle with people who are loony-toons."

"What do you see?" Amanda pressed, her tone a gentle demand.

Hands on her hips, Carrie stared out the window. "Trees." She turned. "I see trees."

"What else?" Amanda joined her.

"A lawn...the gardens."

"To the right," Amanda pointed. "In the distance."

Carrie squinted. "I see a carriage, which is not proof."

"Where's the street, Carrie? Where are the cars?"

Amanda knew she had Carrie on that last one as the room was on the side of the house that faced the busy street. The same one she and Carrie had parked on the Sunday they had come for reenactment day.

Carrie's face blanched as the information began to sink in. With lightning speed, Amanda slid a chair over before Carrie could hit the floor. Carrie Stern, skeptic, landed into it with a thud.

"It just can't be!" she rebelled, her eyes still riveted on the window. When she turned, her hands were trembling, and she reached out to Amanda and clutched her sleeve. "It's true?"

Amanda gently pried Carrie's white-knuckled fingers away and took both hands into her own. "It's true," she replied softly. "I love you, and obviously the door through this time was left open because of that." She moved to the pitcher of water on the night table and poured a glassful. "Drink this. You'll feel a lot better."

Carrie obliged and took a sip. Though color was returning to her cheeks, she was still feeling weak. "I believe you...yet, I don't. I know I'm not making any sense." She sipped the cool water again, drinking slowly until she finished it all.

Looking down into the glass, she noticed dark sediment at the bottom. "From the looks of this water they haven't heard of purification, have they?" She smiled. "Eighteen hundred and eighty-four, ha?"

Amanda nodded.

"Can I go home anytime I want?"

"Do you want to?"

"I don't know. It depends on what kind of life I'd be living here." Carrie's eye scanned Amanda and she wrinkled her freckled nose. "And, I'm not sure I'd be happy wearing those clothes," she pointed out. "I hate dresses, and you don't exactly look comfortable."

"You get used to it after a while."

"So, what kind of life is there in 1884 for a woman like me?"

"Well, waiting tables is out of the question."

"What then?"

Amanda knew there weren't a whole lot of options for women except the ominous task of running the staff and home. Without a man by her side, Carrie might be one unhappy camper.

"We'll have to think on it."

"I don't suppose there's a chance I'll ever get to see television again?"

"Not in this century."

"Well, I'll miss my soaps. I don't know if I want to give up *General Hospital* just yet, the story line is just heating up!" She laughed herself into a cough before composing herself, and then looked up at Amanda, who was not amused. "OK. I imagine...hey! Wait a minute! What a gold mine!"

"What?"

"Knowing the future. I could become the greatest psychic in the world! I'm surprised you didn't think of it. Just think of the money I could make!"

"Or the lives you could ruin." Amanda's thoughts drifted instantly to Yolanda, a sensitive woman who actually managed to help people without interfering with history. Carrie Stern's attempt would be a fiasco. "Forget the future while you're living in the past," Amanda advised.

"Easy for you to say."

They fell into silence for what seemed like an abnormally long time.

"Tell me, Amanda, do all men around here look like Jonathan?" Carrie asked to change the subject.

Amanda smiled. "Well, I'm quite prejudiced, but there is someone I think you might hit it off with." She winked. "A friend of Jonathan's."

"Oh, no you don't!"

Amanda anticipated Carrie's reaction. Her friend was never confident about her looks, leaning more toward tomboy than girl. "Why not? This is a whole new century for you. No one even knows you yet!"

"Look at me! I'm a Plain Jane! Mousy hair, mousy face, freckles, and a body that's straight down the line—no curves. Facts are facts. When the Lord was deciding over me he got a little mixed up."

"You don't give yourself enough credit," Amanda reprimanded. "With a little assistance you'll fit right into this time." She walked over and pulled the servant's cord. "I'll have Renee draw you a hot bath."

"They have running water?"

"And an alabaster tub." Amanda opened the closet and pulled out a green wrapper. "Now, take off your clothes and put this on."

Carrie quickly slipped off her jeans and shirt as Amanda helped her on with the wrapper.

"They call this a wrapper in 1884, not a robe." She tightened the belt around Carrie's slim waist. "You know, Carrie, if you had come inside on reenactment day instead of high-tailing it out where the food was in the gardens, you'd be more prepared."

"Oh, sure, like I knew I'd be traveling back in time. Besides, I HATE history."

"Get used to it, Carrie. You're about to live it."

The soft knock on the door drew their attention and Renee slipped in with a smile, her navy blue uniform and crisp white apron a welcome sight to Amanda.

"Renee! I'd like you to meet Caroline Stern, a very good friend of mine. She'll be staying at Serenity for a while." She ushered Renee up to Carrie.

"Caroline?" whispered Carrie through the side of her mouth. "The only one who ever got away with that was my grandmother."

Amanda poked her in the ribs.

"Please to make your acquaintance, Miss Caroline." Renee curtsied with a smile.

Amanda noted the inquiring look on Renee's young face, but chose to ignore it. She had tossed Carrie's twenty-first-century clothes far back in the closet, and with Carrie's eventual decision she would either burn them or return them.

"Hello." Carrie at once decided she liked this young woman.

"Would you prepare a bath for my friend?" Amanda asked. "She's had a tiring journey."

Carrie shot a wide-eyed look to Amanda who merely smiled.

"Perhaps some lavender beads?" Renee offered.

Amanda nodded. "Work your magic, Renee."

"May I ask where Miss Caroline's clothes are? Lottie will need to freshen them up."

Carrie grinned and turned toward Amanda, arms folded across her chest. "Yes, Amanda, where are my clothes?"

"Her trunk hasn't arrived yet," Amanda explained. Curtsying once more, Renee left the room.

"Whoo!" Carrie flew back on the bed. "My first actual encounter!" She sat up on her elbows and shook her head. "I can't believe this is all real, you know?"

"I know, but I promise you, it is." Amanda headed for the door, skirts swishing.

"And I've got to learn to speak like that."

"You will."

When Amanda opened the door, Carrie jumped off the bed in alarm. "Where are you going? You're not going to leave me! Please!"

"I'm going to find Jonathan so I can tell him you're here. Don't worry. You're in capable hands with Renee. Enjoy the pampering."

CHAPTER FIFTY-THREE

Flush with excitement, Amanda lifted her skirts and with quick steps hurried down to the second-floor landing, closing the door behind her.

"My first order of business as mistress of Serenity will be to have that door removed."

"What was that, dear?" Vivian had just come out of her room, fresh from her afternoon nap.

"Oh, nothing. Just mumbling to myself." She kissed Vivian's cheek and they walked down the stairs to the first floor together. "Have you seen Jonathan?"

"If he's not in the house, chances are good you will find him by the stream."

"I have news for him and for you as well," Amanda said as they reached the bottom step.

"From the way your face lights up, I imagine it's good news."

Amanda leaned in, her voice a whisper as she cupped a hand to Vivian's ear.

"We have another time traveler at Serenity. My friend, Caroline Stern."

Vivian's mouth dropped open. "Goodness! The traffic between centuries this past month has been quite congested."

"You don't mind, do you?" Amanda bit nervously into her bottom lip. "I mean I know it's presumptuous of me."

"Nonsense, Amanda." Vivian patted Amanda's hand. "You keep my blood circulating. I haven't had this much excitement in my life since before the war!"

"Well, good!"

"When will I have the pleasure of making her acquaintance? I assume she's one of the reasons for your search for Jonathan."

"Yes. Even if Carrie decides not to stay, at least she'll be here for the wedding."

"Wedding?" Vivian's smile brightened as she followed Amanda to the front door. "Thank God, my prayers have been answered!" She looked up to heaven before looking back at Amanda. "But there is so much to do! Have you two set a date? I must know as soon as possible, else how can we prepare Serenity?" she rushed on. "Ruth needs to know, and Alan...Renee, of course... why, the entire staff!"

Amanda threw back her head and laughed loudly. "We haven't set the date, but I will make sure that there will be time for preparation."

"Well, you have my blessings, dear." Vivian gathered Amanda to her bosom and hugged her tightly. When she released her, her eyes were wet. "Now, off with you before I lose complete control and make a fool of myself." She sniffed while pulling out her handkerchief.

Reaching over to the coat stand, Amanda grabbed her shawl and kissed Vivian again before dashing out the door. The moment she hit the air she took a deep breath and smiled.

Spring. She loved this time of year. Everything was so colorful and alive! And this one was particularly intoxicating, as the lush green foliage of Serenity's gardens danced in gentle movement against the cool breeze. A mixture of scents flowed across the path to her as she slowed her pace. She continued along to the end of the gardens and Jonathan's favorite place: the stream he had longed to show her when they were in her time.

Jonathan seized the bridle of his horse and slowed to a trot. It had been a good ride, one that cleared his head and awakened his senses. Seeing Amanda waiting by the stream only added to the peace of mind this spot afforded him. When she turned at the sound of his approach, Jonathan's smile broadened, and he eased the horse to the water to dismount.

"Jonathan!" Amanda's heart was pumping furiously at the sight of him astride his black stallion, the afternoon sun glimmering against his equally black riding outfit. "I have so much to tell you!"

"Do tell, then, my love." He was by her side in three long strides, gathering her into his arms before stealing a deep, blazing kiss on her lips—a kiss that left them both breathless. Removing his overcoat, he spread it on the ground and eased her down onto it.

"I love you," Amanda sighed.

"Ah, but I love you more." He touched a hand to her free-flowing hair and brushed it over her shoulder. "I see you have found my haven. You approve?"

"It's perfect."

"Perfect for a wedding?" He arched an eyebrow in question.

"Oh, Jonathan, really? Here?"

"Why not?" He leaned back and rested one arm over his head; the other played softly along Amanda's back. "You will be happy to know that Linwood and I have set aside our differences for the sake of our friendship. He expressed his desire to bear witness to our marriage."

Amanda looked down at him and smiled. "That's wonderful!" She threw herself over him and began kissing his handsome face. "Just wonderful."

"I only wish your friend Carrie could be with you," he said as he eased her down beside him.

"But she is!"

"What?"

"At this moment Carrie is bathing and Renee is seeing to her wardrobe. That's why I rushed out to look for you."

Jonathan shook his head and laughed. "Amazing! Utterly amazing! How did she react? Surely she must have had a difficult time believing you?"

"Oh, she was predictable," Amanda returned. "But at least she had me to lend her support."

"Unlike you. Sorry, darling."

"Now we can actually set a date." She reached up and kissed his cheek.

"Has Carrie decided to stay with us?"

"She's not sure. I'm hoping to ease her transition and convince her that she belongs here."

"Then, as I see it, we must plan to marry while she's still here." Jonathan rose slightly and rested his head on his hand. "So, when, my love? When will you marry me?"

Amanda traced her tongue over her lips. "What's today's date?"

"May the second," he replied, mesmerized by the moistness of her lips, his eyes riveted to them like moths to a flame.

"May tenth!" she announced. "Though I've always dreamed of being a June bride, I don't think we should wait much longer."

Jonathan's laughter echoed through the trees. "Oh, my Lord, mother will be in a real snit! That's hardly enough time to prepare Serenity for a wedding."

"We'll just have to work faster, that's all."

"Then May the tenth it is, my love." He sealed the date with a kiss.

CHAPTER FIFTY-FOUR

Leaving Jonathan to tend to his stallion, Amanda returned to the house for an update on Carrie. She met Renee on the second floor.

"Mrs. Brisbane instructed me to provide Miss Caroline with a room that adjoins yours on this floor, Miss Amanda."

"Thank you, Renee."

Opening Carrie's bedroom door, Amada's mood lifted further at the sight of her friend in one of the freshly starched dresses that once belonged to Susan.

"Well, don't you look like the proper Victorian lady," she teased.

Carrie turned from the full-length mirror and groaned. "I managed to talk Renee out of that damned restraint she wanted me to wear."

"Corset."

"Whatever." She turned again and faced the mirror. "I've got to admit, I never thought I could look this good in a dress!"

"Lovely is the word for it." Amanda closed the door behind her and came to Carrie's side to adjust the fluffy flounces of the mauve-colored gown. "Susan's dress looks much better on you than on me."

"I actually look like I have boobs in this getup."

"It's an illusion."

"Very funny."

"We've got to do something with your hair." Amanda began to fuss with two ivory combs, before opting for a twist at the nape of the neck. "There. How's that?"

"Great handiwork, Amanda. I'd never know it was me."

"Now who's being funny?"

"So, when do I meet the family?" Carrie asked, turning to Amanda once again. "Soon. Jonathan is tending to his horse in the stables and Vivian will meet us in the front parlor for tea."

"Oh, I don't know about this." Carrie sat gingerly on the edge of the bed. "I mean, I may look like I fit in, but looks are deceiving. And I have one killer of a headache. What I wouldn't do for an Advil right now."

Amanda smiled. "You're nervous, and that's understandable. As for Advil, you're in luck. I happened to have brought some with me to this time."

"I should have known!"

Amanda made haste for her room next door, returning quickly with two of the precious pills. Pouring a glass of water from the pitcher in Carrie's room, she handed her the glass and watched her friend gratefully pop the pills into her mouth.

"What did they do in this time for headaches?" she asked suddenly.

"You don't want to know. In fact, I'm not sure myself. But with a little research, I'll be informed enough for the both of us."

Carrie placed the glass on the tray beside the bed. "I guess I'm as ready as I'll ever be."

* * *

While waiting for Vivian and Jonathan to join them, Amanda tried to keep Carrie calm, for she could see her friend's agitation on her pale face.

"Pinch your cheeks," she instructed as they sat side by side on one of the loveseats in the room. "You're as white as milk."

Carrie drew in a deep breath and exhaled. "I'm just so nervous!"

"There's no need to be," Amanda reassured her. "Vivian and Jonathan are flesh-and-blood people just like you and me."

"Ha! For one thing, they are filthy rich. For another, we're not in our own time. I'm going to mess up, I just know it."

"Will you stop fretting?"

"Fretting? Is that a word?"

The light knock on the door drew their attention and Alan came in carrying a tray with Vivian's best china and a sterling silver teapot.

"Good afternoon," he greeted warmly, as he set the tray down in front of them.

"Good afternoon, Alan," responded Amanda. "I'd like you to meet my close friend, Caroline Stern."

Alan straightened and nodded to Carrie. "I am most pleased to make your acquaintance."

"Same here," Carrie cleared her throat. "Pleased to meet you," she corrected, her eyes darting to Amanda who was obviously suppressing a giggle.

"The pleasure is all mine, I assure you, Miss Caroline."

Alan served the tea as the women waited for Jonathan and Vivian to join them.

"I look ridiculous," Carrie whispered.

"Nonsense."

Alan straightened. "If I may, Miss Amanda?"

"Yes, Alan, what is it?"

He turned to Carrie. "For whatever my opinion is worth, Miss Caroline, you look quite appealing." He bowed slightly and smiled his approval.

"You're a man, Alan; it's worth a lot. Thanks."

"You are quite welcome."

Once Alan had gone, Amanda let out a full laugh. "You're doing it, Carrie."

"What?" she asked, easily smoothing the skirt of her gown.

"Blushing."

"I am not!"

"Yes, you are. And you'll do it often; trust me. In this time period chivalry is alive and well." Picking her cup up from the saucer, Amanda took a sip.

Carrie observed the delicate mannerisms of her friend with respectful awe. "Boy, have I got a lot to learn. You talk differently, act differently...you seem to fit right in."

"And so will you."

The parlor door swung open and Vivian Brisbane breezed in with a smile.

"Jonathan will be joining us shortly." She smiled at the sight of Carrie in Susan's dress. "And you must be Caroline Stern." She extended her hand, which Carrie took into her own.

"C-Carrie," she stammered. "My friends call me Carrie."

"Then Carrie it is. Welcome to Serenity."

Amanda watched their exchange with little surprise. If anyone could make Carrie feel as if Serenity was home, it was Vivian Brisbane. The woman exuded warmth and hospitality.

"We'll do as much as possible to ease your transition, dear," Vivian was saying while pouring a cup of tea for herself. "Serenity is your home for as long as you wish, and I do hope is isn't presumptuous of me to hope you will decide to remain."

"Mrs. Brisbane..."

"Vivian."

"Vivian. The whole idea is hard to accept as being real."

"Yet, we're here," put in Amanda. "There's no denying it."

"A ruse, it's not," admitted Carrie. "Tell me, who else knows the truth?"

"Madame Winston," replied Vivian. "She is another time traveler."

Carrie's eyes widened in surprise and she looked to each woman for further explanation.

"Yolanda Winston is a famous spiritualist medium," explained Vivian. "Married a wealthy Englishman. She has some connection with Amanda's mother, from what I understand."

"Yes," Amanda nodded and placed her cup down. "But her story is one I'll go into with you at another time, Carrie. Aside from Yolanda and Jonathan, no one else knows."

"Good afternoon, ladies." Jonathan stood in the doorway looking fresh and handsome in a crisply tailored light brown suit, his long hair combed straight back and still damp.

Eager to introduce him to Carrie, Amanda got up quickly and came to his side. "This is my friend..."

"We've met." He smiled out of the corners of his mouth.

"The man with the keys," Carrie acknowledged. "I should have let you keep them."

"You were protecting Amanda." He raised her hand and planted a kiss there before turning to his mother. "No tea for me. I'd enjoy a brandy about now."

Ignoring the slow shake of his mother's head, he poured a small amount and returned to sit in the armchair beside the fire Alan had so thoughtfully lit.

They sat for several hours talking of the future, which Vivian and Jonathan were eager to hear about. There seemed to be no end to the questions they shot at Amanda and Carrie. Gratefully, the sound of a carriage stopping in front of the house halted their probing.

"Ah, that must be Linwood." Jonathan excused himself and opened the parlor doors to greet his friend. "Linwood, it's good to see you." They shook hands and Linwood quickly passed his hat and gloves to Alan.

"My, my, whenever I return to Serenity there is always an additional beauty on the premises. He walked into the parlor and headed straight for Vivian. "Good afternoon, Mrs. B."

"Good to see you, Linwood!"

Linwood grinned sheepishly as he approached Amanda. "You are looking especially wonderful today, Amanda." He waited for her smile of acknowledgement and turned to Carrie. "And who have we here?"

Jonathan stepped forward. "Allow me to present Caroline Stern, a dear friend of Amanda's."

"Carrie," corrected Vivian. "That's what her friends call her."

Linwood lifted Carrie's hand and, turning it over, pressed his lips to her palm. "Far be it for me to be excluded from such an intimate circle." He raised his eyes to hers and smiled.

Amanda grinned and Jonathan rolled his eyes. From the pink that crawled slowly up Carrie's cheeks, the flattery was welcomed. Jonathan rang for Alan who obviously was waiting for his signal. He entered the room within moments and set down the bottle of champagne.

Jonathan nodded his thanks and while Alan stoked the fire, Jonathan popped the cork from the bottle.

"Now that we have our chosen attendants with us, Amanda and I have set the date for our wedding," he announced.

"The suspense is killing me," whispered Carrie.

"Yes, Jonathan, please don't keep us in the dark," responded Linwood who had now occupied the space between Vivian's armchair and Carrie's side of the loveseat—a move that did not escape Amanda.

"We want to have the ceremony by the stream beyond the gardens. Amanda particularly loves this time of year, so we have decided on the tenth of May."

"The tenth of May!" shrieked Vivian. "Granted, I very much want the two of you to be married, but the tenth of May is hardly enough time to prepare Serenity for such an event. There is the guest list, the gowns, food, flowers, decorations."

"I realize it's short notice, Vivian, but we can all pitch in," Amanda reasoned hopefully.

Jonathan handed out the glasses of champagne and Linwood Crane rose quickly. "To Amanda and Jonathan. May you have a long and loving life together, and may the Lord grace you with the patter of many little feet!"

CHAPTER FIFTY-FIVE

Vivian had the entire staff alerted in short order. In his ever-dependable manner, Alan cracked the imaginary whip to speed progress. Parlor maids and chambermaids dusted, polished, and waxed. Lottie and her band of dedicated seamstresses set the sewing machines humming, and Lottie personally assigned herself to Amanda's gown. While Ruth planned the menu, Alan assisted Vivian with procuring an engraver to design the invitations and to oversee the flower and seating arrangements. Within forty-eight hours, burgundy-and-black liveried footmen successfully dispatched the invitations, all except for two: Yolanda Winston and Thomas Edison. Jonathan personally rode into town to wire them. Though Amanda had balked at the Edison invitation, Jonathan insisted he be invited.

One detail remained unattended and it was a detail only Amanda could take care of. With Carrie in town helping to choose a gift on behalf of Linwood, Amanda seized the opportunity and sought out Alan for a heart-to-heart.

"You wanted to see me, Miss Amanda?"

Amanda stopped her incessant pacing in the parlor and smiled. "Yes, Alan. Please come in." She motioned for him to sit.

With the tremendous amount of responsibility in his charge, Alan was tired. He welcomed the opportunity to rest a moment. "Is there something I can assist you with?"

Wringing her hands nervously, Amanda sat across from him. "As a matter of fact, there is." She tried to still her hands by clasping them together into her lap. "My parents are not with me any longer," she began.

"I'm sorry to hear that."

"Yes...well, I would be pleased if you would do me the honor of standing in for my father and giving me to Jonathan at the ceremony." There, she said it, and it wasn't so hard after all.

"Would it not be more appropriate to bestow that honor on your cousin?"

"My cousin?"

"Mr. Edison, of course."

Amanda groaned inwardly. "Appropriate, but not prudent. Jonathan has relayed to me that my cousin is inundated with work. We do not expect him until the eleventh hour, if he is able to attend at all." Amanda paused, ashamed at having to resort to deceit.

Rising slowly, Alan confidently pulled at the hem of his vest. "Then it would certainly be an honor of rare distinction to escort you down the aisle, Miss Amanda."

Relieved, Amanda shot up from the chair, threw her arms around Alan, and planted a big kiss on his cheek. "Oh, thank you! Thank you so much!"

Alan's face turned a bright crimson at her display of affection. "You are most welcome," he answered stiffly while trying to regain his composure. "And may I say that I never did believe you to be a spy." With those words, Alan smiled. "If that will be all..."

"Yes, Alan, and once again, thank you."

* * *

The waves of excited activity that buzzed through Serenity afforded little opportunity for Amanda to spend time with Carrie, let alone Jonathan. Between fittings, Carrie was spending much of her time taking in the century on the arm of Linwood Crane. Amanda sought the quiet of her room for a reprieve, engrossed in thoughts of Carrie. She needed to know what her friend was thinking and she silently hoped Carrie would decide to stay in 1884. She jumped as the door swung open and Carrie charged into the room, clumsily tripping on the hem of her dress.

"Damn!"

"Is that any way for a lady to speak? Shame on you," Amanda teased.

"Easy for you to joke; you've got a handle on this." Carrie lifted the torn hem and wearily plopped into the chair nearest the fireplace. "This will be the third dress in three days that Lottie will have to mend. It's getting embarrassing."

"Three dresses in three days?" Amanda laughed as she knelt down to examine the torn lace. "Know what I think the problem is?"

"What?"

"You need your own wardrobe." Amanda stood up, her hands on her hips. "I wouldn't suggest burdening Lottie with the task on this one, not with her fingers and assistants working around the clock for the wedding."

"I hate dresses, nineteenth century most of all. Besides," she looked up, "where would I get the money?"

"Have you decided, then?" Amanda asked hopefully. "To stay, I mean."

When Carrie didn't answer immediately, Amanda shook her head. "I'm going to need a drink for this, aren't I?" Carrie nodded. Amanda picked up the brandy bottle from the tray on the small bedside table and poured two glasses. She handed one to Carrie.

Carrie downed the liquor in one swift gulp before leaning back in the chair. "I'm sorry, I really am, but I'm not very comfortable in this time."

"And I thought you and Linwood were getting along so well," Amanda commented as if he were reason enough for her friend to stay.

"Linwood is one hot guy and we get along fine. But, honestly, Amanda, I miss the twenty-first century too much to give it up."

Amanda frowned and bit nervously into her lower lip to hold back her tears. "So after the wedding you plan to go back?"

"Yup."

"I can't change your mind?"

"Nope."

The dam broke and Amanda's tears flowed freely, Carrie's own resolve was soon lost in the pools that crept up behind her own lids.

"I'm going to have the door to the third floor removed after the wedding."

Amanda wiped her tears on the sleeve of her dress. "We'll...we'll never see each other again," she sobbed.

Carrie reached out a hand to Amanda's and swallowed the lump that lodged in her throat. "Hey, someone's got to take care of business for you in the future," she replied lightly. "There's your house, the furniture... *explanations* as to your disappearance," she emphasized.

"I'll miss you."

"Of course you will. And the same goes for me. At least I won't be in the dark about you. I'll have the advantage of knowing the truth."

Resigning herself to Carrie's reasoning, Amanda nodded. "Do you ever intend to visit Serenity again? On a tour, I mean."

"How could I not?" She got up and sat beside Amanda on the settee and gathered her into her arms in a fierce hug. "I'm going to miss you, Amanda Lloyd. If I had a sister, she would be you."

CHAPTER FIFTY-SIX

The snow fell gently at first, then a fury of flurries descended. Amanda's heart sank as she watched the delivery carriages head for the main house. It didn't take a genius to know there would be no outdoor wedding.

"Snow in May? It's too soon!" she cried, as Renee stoked the fire in her room.

"Please do not fret, Miss Amanda. Nature is not reliable."

"Well, it is in my time," Amanda mumbled.

Renee cocked her head to one side in query. When Amanda didn't answer, she went on with the task of making the bed. "Have something to eat. It will make you feel better."

Amada hugged her wrapper to her and sat down angrily in the chair beside the table. She ignored the muffins and picked up the coffee instead. With a gentle tap at the door, Vivian glided into the room in a long dark green dress. Amanda smiled. Vivian was always a welcome visitor.

"Oh, dear, do I detect an acerbic attitude?" Vivian questioned with a shake of her head as she moved toward Amanda and took the seat opposite her.

"It's snowing," Amanda pouted. "Tomorrow is our wedding day and it's snowing!"

"Yes, dear, it's snowing. The Lord has decided to surround you and Jonathan in a blanket of white diamonds. Snow is as much His gift as the sun, and He has done so before your wedding day so you will not be out in this weather."

"I hadn't thought of it that way,"

"Come with me to the window, dear."

Amanda took Vivian's outstretched hand and allowed her to lead her to the window. Vivian placed an arm around Amanda's waist and together they watched the tiny flakes as they landed like sparkling glitter everywhere they looked. It was certainly a pretty sight.

"The Lord is a wonderful artist. He is painting a beautiful canvas, don't you think?"

"Picture postcard perfect," Amanda admitted. She turned to Vivian and kissed her cheek. "You always know how to cheer me up. I'm so very grateful to have you in my life."

"As I am to have you, Amanda. And, may I add that there is a very nervous groom pacing the floor downstairs."

Amanda laughed. "Jonathan is nervous?"

Vivian nodded. "He too was angry to see the snow. However, I had a word with him as well. He's impatient to see you, but I asked him to wait until after our visit."

"Have you seen Carrie today?"

"She's having her final fitting."

Amanda moved from the window, her mood once again darkening. She waited until Renee closed the door behind her. "Carrie has decided to return after the wedding."

Vivian sat down near the fire and poured herself a cup of coffee. "And you hoped she would stay, of course."

"Yes," Amanda accepted a refill and took a slow sip. "I thought, oh, I know this will sound ridiculous."

"What, that she and Linwood might become an item?"

Amanda's eyes widened. "You are one intuitive lady, Vivian. Just like my mother was—is—whatever."

Vivian stirred a sugar cube in her cup and smiled. "I had high hopes for them myself, my dear. Be thankful that she will be your attendant in the century you have chosen to embrace."

"You're right, as always. But I will miss her terribly."

"Jonathan wants one last visit with you before the ceremony," Vivian said, changing the subject. "I informed him that after midnight he must not see his bride until she is walking down the aisle."

"Bad luck? Do you believe in that?"

"I believe in tradition, my dear Amanda. The groom should not see the bride on the day of the wedding until they meet in front of the minister."

"And what did Jonathan have to say to that?"

Vivian rose. "He'll do as his mother asks." She smoothed a hand down the skirt of her dress. "Now I must be going. There is still much to do."

"Then I should be helping." Amanda placed her cup down onto its saucer. "Nonsense. I will be delegating authority over the staff. All you need to do is rest up for your wedding." She walked to the door.

"But I'm not tired! Surely there is something I can do."

Vivian turned and smiled. Reaching into the pocket of her long skirt, she pulled out a small square package and handed it to Amanda. "You can read."

"Read?" Amanda took the gift and unwrapped it. Turning it over in her hands, she passed a hand over the red quilted cover. "It's beautiful," she said, her fingers fluffing up the gold gilded lace at the border. "Thank you."

"You're quite welcome, my dear. Every bride should carry a Bible."

"Did you?"

"Of course." Vivian opened the door. "And it has afforded me much comfort, particularly during the war."

"Such a small book doesn't seem sufficient," Amanda mused.

Vivian smiled. "It depends on what you read into it, Amanda."

She managed two pages of the Bible before the interruptions began. First, Lottie had Renee impose upon her private time with alterations for the wedding gown. Then Carrie had paid a visit to make sure Amanda wasn't depressed because of the snow. The next visitor was a nervous Alan who wanted reassurance on his part of the ceremony. And just prior to the evening meal, Renee returned to inform her that supper would be a light one, and due to the activity in Ruth's kitchen, a late one. When Jonathan finally knocked on the door it was one interruption too many and Amanda's voice rose high in agitation.

"Now what!"

"My, my, seems the bride is out of sorts. Shall I wait until tomorrow?" he said, laughing.

"You do and I'll never speak to you again!" she shrieked, tossing a pillow, which he deftly caught with one hand.

"Not a good way to start a marriage," he commented as he closed the door behind him and in two strides was at the bed, gathering her into his arms.

"It certainly took you long enough to visit," Amanda protested, her arms wrapped tightly around his neck as she drew him to her on the bed.

"The transition from outdoor extravaganza to indoor needed my attention, my love." He kissed the tip of her nose. "But after tomorrow I will never be far from you, I promise." He rolled over onto his side, Amanda still in his protective grasp. "I have a present for you."

"You do?"

"I was going to wait until after the ceremony, but like a child prior to Christmas morn, I find it impossible." With struggling fingers, he dug into the pocket of his trousers with his free hand. "Besides, mother is adamant about us not seeing each other after midnight." He handed her a small velvet box.

"What is it?" she asked.

"The only way to find out is to open it."

With excited fingers, Amanda flipped the box open. Inside was an ivory cameo pin on a chocolate brown background.

"Jonathan, it's absolutely perfect. I'll wear it tomorrow."

"It has been in the Brisbane family for years. Each bride wore it on her wedding day. In fact, it's the profile of my great-great grandmother and was designed by her husband, an artist of considerable talent."

Amanda gently traced a finger along the woman's features. "How sweet. He must have loved her very much."

"Undeniably." He lowered his lips to hers, his voice a whisper. "Almost as much as I do you." He kissed her then, softly, yet passionately, and they lay together tenderly entwined as the snow continue to fall.

CHAPTER FIFTY–SEVEN

The noise on the floor below broke the light sleep Amanda was in and she thrust open her eyes with a start as Carrie burst into her room through the adjoining door, the cord of her pink wrapper trailing behind her.

"Boy, am I glad you're awake!" She ran to the door. "Quick, throw something on before they get here!"

"Who? Before who gets here?" Amanda's feet flew to the floor and she pushed them into her slippers while struggling into the white wrapper Renee had laid out the night before. "Carrie, answer me!" she screamed. "What the hell is going on?"

Carrie swung the door open and Amanda rushed behind her to peer down the hall. Four burgundy-and-black-suited liveried footmen made slow steps up the stairs and were now approaching the second floor, a long square object atop their strong shoulders.

"I wonder what it is," Carrie said excitedly. "Can't tell a damn thing with that cloth draped over it."

Amanda was relieved to find a sleep-weary Alan behind them. She looked at him in confusion, but he merely smiled.

"I had hoped not to awaken you, Miss Amanda. Impossible task considering the size of this," he commented as the men entered her room and carefully placed the object down at the foot of the bed.

"What is it?" she asked as the group left the room.

"A gift from Madame Winston. From what I understand, its journey from England has been an arduous one."

"Oh, presents!" Carrie gushed, clapping her hands.

"If that will be all..."

Amanda thanked Alan and turned to Carrie, whose curiosity was about to get the better of her as she began to peel away the bottom of the cloth.

"Don't you dare!" Amanda admonished with a slap to Carrie's hand.

"Come on, the suspense is killing me!"

The two fell to their knees as Amanda stripped away the cloth.

"It's a chest." Amanda eyed the craftsmanship in amazement. Made of cherry wood, the box was huge, easily surpassing the top of the mattress. The cover was embroidered in lovely tea roses that sparkled in ruby redness; and lush green leaves, each leaf encrusted with what could only be emeralds! She cast a look to Carrie whose mouth had fallen open, frozen in a comical gesture of incredulity. "This is certainly a Kodak moment," Amanda joked. "It's the first time I've ever seen you speechless."

Carrie simply shook her head. "I've...I've never seen anything like it." She passed a hand over the jewels. "Are they real?"

"I imagine so."

Carrie leaned in for a closer look. "Hey, what's that?" she pointed to a small white circle in the lower left corner, and then traced a finger around it. "Diamonds?"

"Probably." Amanda took a closer look and immediately recognized Yolanda's signature.

Carrie leaned in over Amanda's shoulder. "You know, that looks awfully familiar." She peered even closer. "If I didn't know better I'd say that's a peace sign," she said with suspicion. "But that couldn't be." She turned to Amanda for further explanation. "Or could it?"

"That's exactly what it is." Amanda laughed. "Remember I told you Madame Winston was the only other person who knew the truth?"

Carrie nodded, her eyes reverting to the peace sign for another dazzling look. "You also promised to explain." Carrie sat back on her knees, "Now is as good a time as any."

Tucking the wrapper around her legs Amanda crossed them and leaned an elbow on the chest. "Yolanda Winston is a time traveler, too...from 1969. She knew my mother and father." Amanda paused. "They went to Woodstock together."

"Wait a minute now. You're telling me your parents were hippies?" With a nod, Amanda smiled.

"And this woman too?"

"That's right."

Now Carrie was laughing. "I guess anything is possible! So let's see what's inside."

Amada opened the lid. Except for a large envelope and a knitted blue flowered shawl, the chest was empty. Carrie gave her a sidelong glance. "I thought there'd be more."

Amanda broke the seal of the envelope and found two smaller envelopes inside. She opened the envelope marked "One" as Carrie leaned over her shoulder. For Carrie's benefit, she read aloud.

"Dear Amanda: So you have made your decision and decided to stay. Somehow, I knew you would. I know that you wish Kendall and Willy Boy could be with you..."

"Willie Boy?" interrupted Carrie.

"...on your wedding day," Amanda continued. "If it is of some solace to you, they are with you through me. The shawl is the one your mother crocheted for me, the same one I wore on the day I came to this time. Some fashions are timeless. Wear it with my blessings. As to the second envelope, when you open it you will understand. I fondly look forward to your wedding. With much love and affection, Yolanda."

With shaking fingers, Amanda opened the second envelope. Out slipped a Polaroid of her mother at Woodstock. Behind her stood her father who was embracing Kendall, his hands wrapped around her, tightly clasping her to him. Clutching the photo to her bosom, the tears came down in torrents.

Carrie leaned in and hugged her, both of them crying when the knock on the door brought them back to reality. Vivian breezed in, accompanied by Renee who was carrying a tray of muffins, juice, and coffee.

"Good morning! I see Yolanda's gift arrived safely." Vivian smoothed a hand over the shimmering embroidered cover before handing Amanda her handkerchief.

"Beautiful."

Amanda looked up, vainly blinking back further tears. "You knew?" she asked as she dabbed at her swollen eyes and passed the hanky over to Carrie.

"Yolanda and I have become very close. Now come, both of you. Have something to eat. Not too much," she admonished. "You need to fit into your gowns."

Renee poked at the fire, adding more kindling to the logs, which served to warm the damp room considerably.

"Good luck today, Miss Amanda," she said on her way out. "I will return to help you prepare."

The three women sat in comfortable silence at the round serving table near the fire. Carrie spoke first, her eyes riveted on the scene outside the window.

"The snow stopped."

"Traveling should not be difficult as long as it doesn't freeze up," commented Vivian.

Cup in hand, Amada rose and walked to the window, her hands tightening around the shawl, her eyes dreamily holding onto the vision of pure white snow that blanketed the streets, the sun gleaming across it in an illusion of tiny white crystals.

"In my time the streets would be covered by the exhaust of automobiles," she said slowly, turning around as the reality of the thought broke the spell. "I'd love to take a morning walk in the white wonderland."

"You'll do no such thing! Why you'll catch your death!" scolded Vivian.

Carrie caught Amanda's "look." She said, "I kind of like the idea."

"Don't encourage such behavior, Carrie. You are supposed to be her friend."

"It's her wedding day, and because I'm her friend I'd like to take that walk with her," Carrie replied. "It's so pure and untouched right now. I may not be passing this way again."

Vivian sighed loudly. "Oh, all right, then, go for your walk. But do be back soon...and dress warmly."

* * *

An hour later, Amanda and Carrie were lying back in the snow, arms swishing as they made "angels' wings." From his window, Jonathan watched the two in amusement, the very idea of their frivolity causing him to laugh out loud.

CHAPTER FIFTY-EIGHT

There was something very familiar about Serenity this day. It was almost as if this was as the house looked when Amanda filmed it the day of her visit. Softly moving servants gracefully carried trays of Russian caviar and bottles of champagne. The scent of Ruth's exceptional culinary skills drifted throughout the first floor, the succulent infusion of aroma permeating the air in invitation.

Flowers were everywhere: roses, carnations, orchids, gardenias, and mimosa. Ivy twirled around the banister of the grand staircase shimmering against the limestone, a long red velvet carpet draped down each step from the second floor to the bottom. Gilded cases and baskets were filled with roses of pink, white, and dark crimson.

The house was ablaze with lights, not Edison's but the amber glow of candlelight, and the long dining table was draped with a white damask cloth with gold service and sparkling crystal and china set to perfection. The priceless tapestries were fully illuminated by the glowing crystal chandeliers that dazzled against the polished marble floors. Great logs glowed fiery red in the fireplaces of every room. In the grand ballroom, both fireplaces were lit and a divan was placed on a raised platform for Vivian, Yolanda, and Thomas Edison to watch the festivities as honored guests.

* * *

"My God!" shrieked Carrie in a shakily shrill voice as the two sat nervously in Amanda's room awaiting their gowns. "These people know how to throw a party!" She sat down on the bed beside Amanda. "I thought this house was outrageous before, but now..."

At the sound of bells jingling down the wintery street, they rushed to the window. Guests were arriving in snow-brushed carriages driven by coachmen wrapped in furs, the lanterns on either side casting an amber path along the way. The liveried footmen descended to help their charges alight from the carriages, and then they led the way to the front door and presented their invitations.

The furs and coats did not disguise the lovely array of dresses from Worth, Doucet, and Rouff or the gentlemen's crisp black tuxedos and top hats. Amanda turned to Carrie and smiled before returning her gaze to the window. There was one guest she was eager to see, but who had yet to arrive, causing her anxiety to reach new heights of excitement. Then she saw him, alone and refusing assistance offered him as he stepped down from the carriage. Her heart raced in anticipation of seeing his face; as if on cue, he slowly raised his head and looked directly up to her at the window.

Thomas Edison smiled and lightly touched the brim of his hat in acknowledgment.

"I can't believe he's actually here!" Amanda turned to Carrie who nearly sprinted to the door to usher in

Renee and Margaret, whose arms with were loaded down with heavy satiny material.

"Who?" Carrie returned to the window just as Amanda released the drapery.

"Thomas Edison, that's who." She drew Carrie aside and whispered in her ear. "Is the minicam in the safe like I asked? I told Jonathan myself. He told me he would take care of it. Why is it so important?"

"I thought it would be nice to film the wedding..."

"NO!"

* * *

Renee cleared her throat loudly. "Miss Amanda?"

Amanda and Carrie turned in unison. "We'll be right with you, Renee. Why don't you and Margaret ready Miss Caroline's clothing in the next room?"

"*Oui*, Miss Amanda." Renee opened the door adjoining Amanda's with Margaret trailing satin and lace behind her.

Carrie pulled Amanda by the collar of her wrapper. "OK, fess up. Why can't we film your wedding? I'd love to take it home as a keepsake."

"Because Thomas Edison can't see it, that's why. We can't interfere with history, Carrie. The man is only just now working on such a project."

"Well, that stinks! There must be some way I can film the festivities without him knowing." She bit into her lower lip. It wouldn't do to upset Amanda on her wedding day.

"No, and that's the end of it."

"OK." Carrie smiled.

"Carrie, I'm serious. I know that look of yours. Don't you dare betray me on this. Promise?"

"I promise." Carrie conceded. "I love you, Amanda." With a strong hug, the two women prepared for what would be the wedding of the century.

☙❧

CHAPTER FIFTY-NINE

Standing at the edge of the red carpet, Carrie tossed a look back at a nervous Amanda and Alan as they stood just around the bend ready to descend after Carrie touched the last step. In a royal blue satin gown with a crystal-beaded front, and blue velvet wide-brimmed hat, Carrie took the first step. In her hands, she carried a basket of white rose petals and, with each stair, she tossed them down, watching them flutter lightly around her. When she reached the bottom, she took the arm of Linwood Crane. They stood off to the side and in front of the guests who had gathered in the grand hallway for the ceremony.

Jonathan kept wetting his lips nervously, the suspense of seeing Amanda almost unbearable, his eyes glued to the top of the staircase. When she came into view on the arm of Alan, he felt his very breath leave him and his throat close up. Tightness formed in his chest, and had he not known better, he would have thought he was having a heart attack. She couldn't be real. This vision has to be a lovely dream, he thought. His eyes held fast on hers and he did not divert his gaze for a moment.

Amanda looked down at Jonathan from the top of the stairs, the crowd around him a blur. She saw only his handsome face, the flashing green eyes, the crisp black tuxedo, and the single white gardenia in his lapel. With ease, she concentrated on Jonathan and gripped Alan's arm fiercely as they proceeded down. Tiers of Brussels lace cascaded over satin, the long sleeves billowing out, silver shimmering from her shoulders and draping her in stardust. At her throat, was the cameo. Fortunately, both Renee and Margaret were carrying the immense court train of embroidered seed pearls; otherwise, Amanda might have easily tripped on the wobbly legs beneath the billows of satin. In her hands she carried a bouquet of white orchids, and with it, the Bible Vivian had given her. Tucked inside it was the picture of her parents.

"She looks like an angel," whispered Jonathan.

* * *

With all the pomp and circumstance, the ceremony itself took less than one hour with Amanda and Jonathan speaking in whispered voices, their eyes locked. When it came time for Jonathan to kiss the bride, he drew her to him as he would a piece of china, delicately and softly. His kiss, however, betrayed every feeling of desire in its deep, long expression. The guests applauded and followed the happy couple down the corridor to the grand ballroom where the orchestra strung together a lovers' melody as Jonathan took his wife into his arms and waltzed her tenderly around the room. In a daze, the newlyweds were ushered around to those in attendance. Amanda's reunion with Yolanda Winston was tearful, the remainder of the introductions quickly becoming a blur of excitement.

"Darling," Jonathan's deep voice whispered in her ear as he drew her away from Madame Winston. "I would very much like you to greet another honored guest."

Amanda turned to the gentleman on Jonathan's right and her cheeks flushed with embarrassment.

"May I kiss the bride?" Thomas Edison swept up her hand and planted a kiss there. "We are all quite good looking in this family, aren't we?" He winked.

Amanda stared at the youthful, yet rumpled inventor, and for several moments could not form any speech.

"We are thinkers, aren't we, Amanda?" he continued. "Our actions speak louder than our words." He laughed then, jovially and loudly, drawing the attention of several guests.

"I... I..." Amanda could only stutter. "I'm..."

"Overwhelmed," put in Jonathan. "It's been quite some time since she has seen her dear cousin."

Vivian watched the exchange in amusement, silently championing Tom Edison and Jonathan for their fun with Amanda. But the fun had gone on long enough and she quickly came to Amanda's rescue.

"Mr. Edison, why not join me on the platform. There are some people I would like you to meet."

Edison nodded, but did not leave until he brushed his lips against Amanda's upturned palm and slapped Jonathan on the back.

Coming out of her daze, Amanda pressed her lips to Jonathan's and...bit him soundly.

"That hurt!"

"You deserved it!" she whispered sweetly. "Some joke."

"Well, love, it's a good thing our esteemed Mr. Edison is a man of humor. He was more than happy to indulge in a little prank." He put an arm around her waist and began to lead her into another dance. "You don't hate me for it, do you?"

"I should, you know. That was mean."

"But very effective...and funny. You should have seen the look on your face."

He threw back his head and laughed.

Linwood Crane waltzed by with Carrie who managed to toss a word to Amanda.

"That was certainly a Kodak moment if I ever saw one!"

They were gone before Amanda could respond and she wondered how Carrie would explain it to Linwood. It didn't matter. She was in the arms of her husband, dancing in the grand ballroom of beautiful Serenity, and for the first time in years, she was truly happy.

EPILOGUE

"Well, that's the last of the boxes, honey." Trevor Peyton leaned over his wife's shoulder and kissed her cheek. "What have you got there?"

Miranda looked up from the page in her hands. "Great-Grandmother's Bible."

She closed the book with a snap and placed it in the open chest. "I found it in here. So much history," she mused. "And this chest is worth a small fortune!"

"I wonder what other goodies are in here." Trevor reached down and picked up a framed photograph of Amanda and Jonathan. "Now I know where you got your looks," he said with a long whistle.

Miranda stared at the bride in the photo and pointed to the cameo. "Remember that?"

Trevor nodded. "You wore it on our wedding day."

"I wonder if Mom realizes this stuff is here."

"Why don't you call and ask her?"

Miranda held her protruding tummy with one hand and accepted Trevor's assistance with the other as she rose from the floor. "Maybe later. She's got enough on her mind with her own move."

"Hey, here's a dandy group." Trevor picked up another framed photograph. "Looks like the bridal party. Any idea who these people are?"

Miranda took it from him and smiled. Before she could answer, the doorbell chimed.

"I'll get it, honey."

Trevor marched with quick steps to the front door. Miranda, wobbled behind, the photograph still in her hands. "May I help you?"

"Is Marge in? I realize I should have come during visiting hours, but I didn't think..."

"Visiting hours?" Trevor's eyebrows knitted together and he shook his head. "Serenity is a private residence, Miss."

"Stern. Carrie Stern."

Miranda pushed Trevor aside. "Let the woman in, for heaven's sake. It's cold outside."

Trevor obliged with an apology and opened the door for Carrie who, for the first time, got a good look at the woman called Miranda. The resemblance was remarkable, but how?

"Do I know you?" asked Carrie.

"I don't think so," replied Miranda. "And like my husband said, this is a private residence. As to your request to see Marge, I'm afraid you're too late. My grandmother passed away in 1974."

The blood drained from Carrie's face as the wheels of recognition began to twirl. Concerned, the young couple led Carrie into the front parlor and sat her down.

"I'll get a glass of water," offered Trevor.

Miranda nodded and Trevor was back quickly. They watched Carrie slowly sip the water.

"Thank you. I'm sorry. I remember a Marge, and you look so familiar." She put the half-empty glass on the table, and for the first time, noticed the chest.

"Marjorie Brisbane Kincaid was my grandmother." She looked at the picture in her hands and up to

Carrie. "You know, you do look familiar. But how can that be?"

Miranda sat down beside her and Carrie realized the connection the young woman was making, deciding at once to use it to her advantage.

"I guess I should fess up, then."

"Fess up?" Trevor sat beside his wife on the arm of the sofa.

Carrie reached over. "May I?" She looked down at the photograph of Amanda's wedding and pointed to herself. "My great-grandmother and namesake, Caroline. I've long wanted to visit Serenity—to see the actual rooms. I've heard so much about the wedding of Amanda and Jonathan Brisbane."

"Me too." Miranda smiled. "I was named after Amanda and Marjorie. My mother says I look a lot like my great-grandmother." Miranda rubbed her stomach at the baby's kick. "I guess about as much as you do yours."

Carrie nodded. "When are you due?" she asked, her eyes riveted to Miranda's protruding belly.

"Very soon. That's one of the reasons Serenity isn't open to the public. The family wanted this place to remain a private residence. Lord knows, there's certainly enough money for its upkeep. Amanda and Jonathan made certain of that."

"I've been arguing over how this place could be open to the public on a reservation basis and still maintain its privacy. There's so much history here."

Miranda nodded. "But, I can't oversee it all with the baby coming, and Trevor works around the clock."

Carrie saw the window of opportunity immediately. "I know I'm a stranger to you, but, well, I'd like to help. Especially since my own...ancestor was Amanda's maid of honor."

Trevor and Miranda looked at each other, amazed that a solution should present itself so effortlessly.

"Would you like to see the house?" offered Trevor.

"Go ahead. I'll make some tea." Miranda waddled off to the kitchen.

Carrie saw Serenity once again; every room, fireplace, window, and door, except the one leading to the third floor. That door was gone. She turned to Trevor. "There was a door here. Any idea when they took it away?"

Trevor touched a hand to the painted hinges that remained. "Miranda's mother told us it was taken down around 1954, the year Amanda Lloyd Brisbane died. As a matter of fact, Amanda had written it into her will."

Carrie smiled. *She waited all those years in the hope that I might still come back; she never gave up on me.*

THE END